BONGO

Books by Arnold E. Grisman

BONGO

EARLY TO RISE

BONGO

ARNOLD E. GRISMAN

HARPER & BROTHERS • PUBLISHERS • NEW YORK

BONGO

Copyright © 1961 by Arnold Ellis Grisman

Printed in the United States of America

FIRST EDITION

M-K

Library of Congress catalog card number: 61-6204

BONGO

BONGO

CHAPTER ONE

"MY NAME IS WEST," he said and hesitated.

Bongo West? He looked down and shuffled his feet. Shyly. It has long been agreed among white hunters that the bongo is the shyest of beasts.

He watched his feet and listened for the sound of his heart, recognized the rise of his pulse, felt the familiar warmth of his face. He was Bongo—the shyest of beasts.

A white hunter on the corner of West End Avenue and Eighty-first Street gave the name to him when he was twelve. Bongo he was and Bongo he remained through junior high school, high school, the College of the City of New York and sixty-three missions as tail gunner on a B-17.

Now he cleared his throat and said firmly, "Nicholas.

Nicholas West. My father sent me." At the last moment he lowered his voice, still not sure how much of a recommendation this was.

The big man behind the desk moved his pale eyes slowly across Nicholas. Once to the right. Once to the left. Then down to the desk where one finger scratched a monogram in the dust.

Nicholas watched the pearl in the big man's tie. It was large and egg-shaped and age had turned it yellow. "You went to school together," Nick reminded him. Keep the voice even, he told himself. Breathe deep.

Eddie Mack's eyes came up from the desk. They were empty.

"You were neighbors on Second Avenue," explained Nick, but the eyes stayed empty. Nick's right hand found lint in the bottom of a pocket and separated it carefully from the long seam. "On the third floor. Once he fell out of the window and broke three clotheslines. He dragged one leg for a year. They called him the Gimp."

"Ah." Eddie Mack nodded his head slowly and carefully as though shaking up old memories. "Jake West. You're Jake West's boy." It seemed to make a great deal of difference to him. "We went through the eighth grade together," he said and a smile spread out from the thick lips. "Sit down," he invited, then noticed that he himself had the only chair. He shrugged his shoulders. "This isn't my regular office. We're just using the place for auditions."

Somewhere beyond the scarred plaster walls a piano had been playing, and suddenly a dozen feet picked up its beat.

Eddie Mack looked Nick over again. "You're a lot taller than your old man," he said.

Nick returned his hands to the pockets of the new tweed jacket and stooped bonily. He moved his tongue with care. Demosthenes, he thought. He didn't want to stutter. "Six th-

three, I'm a th-throwback," he said. "My grandpa was pretty tall. Especially for those days."

Once Eddie Mack's face had been handsome. Now it was spoiled by deep lines that looked as though they'd been worked into the flesh by special exercises. His hair was thin but still black and carefully brushed. He wore a black cashmere jacket, gray slacks and brown suède shoes. His tie was a thick red silk on which green monkeys swung from yellow branches. In the cuffs of his shirt he wore links made of heavy gold nuggets. A button on the sleeve of the jacket was broken in half.

"So you want to be an actor?" said Eddie Mack, losing his good humor as suddenly as he had found it. He looked over his tie for spots, then studied his nails. What he saw depressed him still further and he climbed out from behind his desk. One of his legs had fallen asleep. He stamped it on the floor. "Throw a rock," he said, pointing to the window that faced Broadway. "All you'd hit is actors without jobs. It's the only profession in the world where unemployment is normal." He saw Nick's look and paused. "I've got a responsibility to your father," he said.

Beyond the walls the feet stopped. Then the piano. The only sound was the shifting of the planks under Eddie Mack's shoes.

Nick moved his eyes over the green walls until they found a crack that grew like a flower in the plaster. "I've just been to dramatic school," he said finally. "Madame Poirier's School of Drama. Maybe you know Madame Poirier?"

Eddie Mack came away from the window slowly, still filled with the sense of his responsibility. He raised one hand and pointed the forefinger. "Listen to me," he said. "Your grand-children will thank me." The idea pleased him. "Your children's children. Go home. Get a steady job. Someday you'll think of this moment with gratitude." It seemed that a tear might be forming in the corner of Eddie Mack's eye. He touched it with

3

his finger. "Straight from the shoulder. I wish somebody had talked to me this way when I was your age."

Why did they always give it to you straight from the shoulder? Nick asked himself bitterly. "R-really?" he asked, hoping the word was sufficiently filled with scorn and knowing at the last minute that it wasn't.

The big man hesitated. For a little longer his face held its dedicated look. Then the dedication was gone with the speed of a cardsharp's shuffle. Wisssht. "No," he said, turning honest without a quiver, and sat down again behind the desk, a new man with a new face. "I never heard of Madame Poirier. It wouldn't make any difference if I had."

Eddie Mack took a cigar from his desk and bit into it. Squinting slightly, he fired a pellet of tobacco between his lips. "All right," he said. "If you've made up your mind, you've made up your mind. But that doesn't mean I have anything for you." Leaning back, he put his feet up on the desk. "Even if you were an experienced actor."

"Nine months with Madame Poirier," pointed out Nick.

Eddie Mack stopped him with the same episcopal gesture he had used before. "Do you sing?" he asked.

"Some," said Nick.

"Operetta?"

Nick shook his head.

Eddie Mack fingered the cigar like a fat brown clarinet. "That's what I'm producing," he said softly. "Operetta by the sea. Sigmund Romberg under the summer sun. Victor Herbert on the golden shore of Secost, New Jersey. *Blossom Time*, *The Student Prince, Naughty Marietta*. The cream of the musical drama. With a cast of hundreds."

"Does everybody sing?" asked Nick.

"No," admitted Eddie Mack. "But you don't dance either." He shook his head with polite regret.

Eddie Mack sat. Nick rose bonily in front of the desk, tall,

4

skinny and solitary as a watchtower in enemy country. The silence between them was thick enough to lean on. Then something stirred in the back of Eddie Mack's eyes. It was an idea. A good idea? wondered Eddie Mack, wrinkling his brow. Yes, he decided with a shake of the head. For a moment he admired it. For another moment he studied it. He found a flaw.

A sigh traveled up from Eddie Mack's chest. The cigar wobbled regretfully in his lips. He separated himself from the whole business.

But Eddie Mack had a deep-rooted respect for his own ideas. He picked this one up, he dusted it off. He draped it on Nick for size.

"You think you could be funny?" asked Eddie Mack.

"I don't know," said Nick.

"You look like you could be funny." Eddie Mack nodded. He was pleased. When he looked this way, he gave you the feeling that he was very fond of you.

"Once I *thought* I was pretty funny," conceded Nick doubtfully. Oh, yes, he'd worn the cap and bells for two full semesters. . . . Bongo West, Clown Prince of Mrs. Mann's study period . . . Joe Miller of the Junior Class. That was the year Bongo came up to the campfire and sat down. Next year he was back in the bushes again. "I'm not sure how much that counts," he said in all fairness and remembered something else. "I was Bottom the Weaver in high school. Madame Poirier didn't take up the Art of Laughter until the second term."

"I've got a sixth sense about these things," said Eddie Mack, using the cigar like a baton to mark the rhythm of his words. "It's my biggest asset. And I have a feeling about you."

Nick bent his head and watched his feet. He shifted the feet, put his hands in his pockets. You're just too damned suspicious, he assured himself. You wish for something and wish

5

for it and when you get it you start wondering what's wrong with it. "Well," he said, "actually I always had in mind playing serious parts."

"Serious parts?" Eddie Mack was so deeply moved that he bit too far into his cigar and ruined it. "Look at all the things there are to make a man sad," he urged. "Stubbing a toe, peeling onions, losing a girl, reading the daily papers. Without looking, even a lucky man finds a thousand things in a lifetime to make him cry. But how many things to make him laugh?"

"Well, sure," said Nick. "But there's a lot more to it than that."

"Fine, fine," intoned Eddie Mack in a special bass that he kept for closing deals. He stood up quickly and came around the desk, sowing ashes in the air as he came. He swung the arm with the dead cigar over Nick's shoulder. "It's a wonderful spot for you, boy," he said, squeezing the shoulder.

Nick shifted uneasily beneath that fond, muscular arm, feeling the weight of Eddie Mack's good will even more heavily. Was all this out of love for his father? he wondered. In all honesty, he had to admit that his father was one of those people whom it is easier not to love.

"Have you ever seen Fisty Fuller work?" demanded Eddie Mack, his smile showing clearly how pleased he was to be able to do a favor for the son of an old friend.

Nick blamed himself again for having so little trust. It was one of the bitter habits that had soured his childhood. He shook his head.

"A great comic," said Eddie Mack confidently. "He's done everything from burlesque to that French thing a couple of years ago." Eddie tried to remember the name of the French thing, even snapping his fingers to make the memory come, but it evaded him. He looked to Nick for help.

Nick shook his head again.

"Never mind," said Eddie Mack. "He'll tell you about it. You'll be working with him all summer."

The door swung open. A head poked into the room. A pair of fierce eyes in an innocent, rosy-cheeked face. A long slender body flowed after the head around the doorjamb.

When both head and body were inside, Nick saw the most beautifully dressed man he had ever met. He wore a canary-yellow linen sport jacket, dove-gray silk pants, a pink sport shirt open at the throat. "We're waiting for you to start looking at the dancers," the man said.

In the narrow frame of the doorjamb and door edge Nick saw the dancers. Girls. Dozens of girls in practice clothes. From a distance at least they were all pretty. Dozens of pretty girls.

"You see Prager in the morning," said Eddie Mack, who was already in full stride toward the door, carrying Nick with him. "He's our company manager. He'll straighten you out on all the details." Turning Nick with a hand on his elbow, he faced the man in the yellow coat. "This is Nick West," he said. "Nick, Tony George, our dance director."

The dance director bowed slightly.

"Nick's going to work with Fisty Fuller," explained Eddie.

One of Tony George's slender eyebrows arched gracefully. "Ah, the human sacrifice has been selected," he said.

"Shut up," answered Eddie Mack calmly. And he pushed Nick through the doorway.

CHAPTER TWO

AS NICK opened the front door, he heard hamburgers sizzling in the kitchen. Smoke floated through the living room.

"Pop, you're burning the meat," he called.

A frying pan clanged like a ceremonial gong and his father came to the kitchen door. "Thanks for the information," said the old man, digging skinny thumbs into the pocket of his knitted vest. "Maybe you could issue bulletins regularly like the Weather Bureau."

He'd been burning supper for twenty-three years now, but he'd never gotten used to the idea. Each night's burning had the bitterness of the first, reminding him again of the wife he had lost. "You're late," said the old man, turning to go back

8

into the kitchen. His spine was as stiff and straight and narrow as the letter *I*.

It was a spine to defy misfortune with, and the old man did —daily. Since his wife's death, disaster had become a habit with him. Nothing was too small for Jake West to suffer it. Hooks reached out to tear his pants. Every mop for blocks around had been emptied on his head. His apples were always wormy, his butter turned. Hidden events in strange-sounding places reached across oceans to spoil a business he had started in good faith on Sixty-eighth Street. Important clients married women who could not bear the sight of him.

"I went to see Eddie Mack," said Nick, following his father into the kitchen.

"Yah." Mr. West bent to scrape the hamburger away from the frying pan. For a moment his face held the keen, lost-in-itself look of the technician at work. But even then there was the promise of the next scowl. "So?" he said, and the scowl came right behind.

"I got the job."

Mr. West studied his hamburgers for a little longer. Putting out the flame under them, he turned to face his son. He tried to laugh, but he wasn't a laughing man and he gave up the attempt in the middle. "That Eddie Mack," he said, shaking his head. "So now you're an actor?"

Nick nodded, his face growing warm with the memory. He felt the pulse jump in his wrist. Could he really feel that? he wondered. Perhaps he was getting high blood pressure. He slipped his left thumb over his right wrist before he remembered you couldn't tell anything that way.

"Ach!" cried Mr. West, sweeping one hand down in an angry chop. His eyes glittered, his lips trembled.

What did he want? wondered Nick. His father was the one who had sent him to Eddie Mack in the first place.

9

Perhaps the old man was thinking of that, too, for he made an effort, shook his head, stopped the words that were already on their way. Instead he said stiffly, "I forgot the vegetables. You want vegetables? Open a can. Open two cans."

"Not for me."

"Carrots and peas!" Mr. West raised the crooked finger of authority. "So long as you eat under this roof, you'll eat a balanced diet." Suddenly he was full of conviction; he had found something he believed in. "By God," he said.

Nick opened carrots and peas. He got ketchup from the refrigerator, two-day-old bread from the cabinet and jam from the shelf above the sink. When he put these things on the kitchen table, it shifted its weight slowly from one leg to another.

This was the way they had lived for twenty-three years—like an army about to march and too tired to make itself comfortable.

"There's coffee left from breakfast," said Mr. West. "You want some, put a light under it. Personally, I'm going to have tea." He wiped his lips with a handkerchief. "Personally," he repeated and listened to the sound of the word. "Personally, maybe I'm crazy." But there was no real question in his mind. "I still say the army should never have taken you," he said.

"Why not?"

"You take a boy." Mr. West reached into the air to take a boy. "You put him in the rear end of an airplane." Mr. West put him in. "He rides backward across the world, shooting a gun." Mr. West shot. "Before he's learned to shave, he gets used to seeing things from the wrong end." Mr. West lifted his shoulders high. "I don't know," he said. "You think I understand you? I don't understand you."

Nick filled the kettle with water and put it back on the stove. "What's there to understand?" he asked, turning on the gas. "I'm about as deep as a scrambled egg."

"Go," said Mr. West, "make jokes about it."

The bitterness on the old man's face reached out and touched his son. Taking two cups from the sink, Nick brought them to the table. "Look," he said, "maybe I grew up in the army. That's all. People grow up every day, it's nothing unusual." He could have left it there, but he thought he saw a question in his father's eyes, and, not knowing quite what it was, he felt he had to answer it. Nick laughed apologetically. "When they put me in that B-17," he said, "I never thought I'd make it."

"You enlisted," the old man pointed out.

"Sure." Nick was happy to agree. "But I worried even while I was signing the paper. All my life I've been worrying. I worried because it was dark at night and the floors creaked. I worried they'd use up all the coal and oil and then what would we do. I worried because it was Sunday night. I worried people wouldn't like me. I worried I'd never stop growing. I worried because I didn't have a tuxedo and what would I do if somebody invited me to a formal dance. I worried because I didn't know how to dance."

"You never asked me," said Mr. West. "You could have had dancing lessons."

Nick shrugged his shoulders. "If you're a worrier, you worry. I even worried because I worried so much."

The teapot whistled sadly and Nick dropped a tea bag into his father's cup. "Once I figured that anybody sweated as much as I did was a freak. Then I went in the air corps and everybody was in a sweat. All of a sudden it was like belonging to a club."

"Pass the sugar," said Mr. West. "Please."

"It was like Columbus discovering America," said Nick.

Mr. West grunted. The tea was hot and it took all of his attention to drink it without burning himself. When he was done, he got up and started to clear the table.

"Don't bother," said Nick. "I'll do it."

The old man stood in back of the chair, holding the cup and saucer in his hand, the saucer shaking slightly, his head nodding. "An actor," he said fiercely and made an effort to control himself that set the cup dancing harder than ever. "All right," he said, putting the cup down.

Nick watched his father uneasily. The old man was hiding something. What? He'd never hidden anything before in his whole life. Normally his feelings shone on his face like goldfish in a bowl.

"I got to see Mr. Kubek that owns the hardware store," said Mr. West, and the mere fact that he bothered to explain was strange in itself. "Kubek's putting in a new department, he should increase his insurance."

J. West and Son, Insurance Brokers. Nick tried it for sound and didn't like it. But it was what the old man had always wanted. It was hard to understand exactly why, for he himself had never made money at it. He was so unlucky that people were afraid of him.

"Take it easy," said Nick, knowing immediately that this was a mistake. People who took it easy never got anywhere— the old man had said it often. He was ready to say it again, but at the last moment he stopped himself.

"Nyah," he said instead and went into the living room to get his jacket.

Nick heard him pacing around the living room. Then Jake came back to the kitchen door, his face swollen with whatever it was that he was hiding. He was silent for one minute, two minutes. Finally he burst out, "From the time that Eddie Mack was a kid his whole ambition in life was to lay in bed late and sleep with actresses." Bending toward his son, the old man lowered his voice. "How many men you know wear silk underwear?" he asked confidentially. He straightened his back. "Silkworms by the millions slave to keep Eddie Mack in

12

shorts," he said with a curious pride. "Two hundred dollars apiece he pays for his suits." He caught himself in error and made a correction. "He *buys* two-hundred-dollar suits. *Sometimes* he pays for them. Eddie Mack needs silk and cashmere like the rest of us need air. Other people eat caviar at weddings. Eddie Mack eats it for breakfast. He changes women as often as he changes his shirt." Suddenly the old man's Adam's apple danced in his skinny throat. Raising the forefinger of his right hand, he pointed it at Nick like a pistol. "In his whole life, Eddie Mack never worried about anything. As far as he's concerned, it's *funiculi funicula* all day long."

Mr. West thought this over and found it unsatisfactory. "All his life Eddie Mack's been the kind of guy when he drinks, somebody else gets the hang-over." This was a little nearer but still not it. Mr. West looked around the room, trying to discover some final charge which would wind up all the rest. "When he was thirteen years old, he punched his Latin teacher in the nose," he said and quickly realized that he had missed the point once more. "He's a liar, a cheat and a thief," the old man cried. "His mother died of shame. His own brother doesn't talk to him."

Mr. West's breath came fast and hard as though he had driven himself into some last desperate corner. "I was brought up to respect honest work. By the sweat of their brows, it says in the Bible. With Eddie Mack and his kind, work's like a sickness they've been inoculated against." He stopped and looked at his son more closely. "All right," he said, "don't listen to me. Listen to Eddie Mack."

The old man stared—head on a slant, eyebrows bristling, his nose sharpening itself on the air, while Nick continued to struggle with the unmanageable fact that his father had sent him to Eddie Mack in the first place.

This was his father, thought Nick in surprise. Jake the Knife, all edges and points, a bag of tacks, an angry blade.

Why it was simple, he thought, perceiving in his arms and legs and nose just how simple it was. Even as the old man went out into the hall and slammed the front door, Nick felt his whole body sharpen in duplication of his father. This was what it was, the trick, the secret knack, all you needed to know to be Jake West.

CHAPTER THREE

The Student Prince was scattered all over the Avon Rehearsal Studios.

The chorus of thirty-seven trained voices had a two-story room with big pale-milky walls. The *corps de ballet* turned and sweated and jumped in a smaller, darker room, which was square at one side and rounded at the other and seemed to have been designed for some extraordinarily specific purpose now forgotten. In the smallest room of all the principal players walked through their lines under the personal guidance of Benny Wallace, the director.

For two days Fisty Fuller was on the telephone. Waiting for him to leave it, Nick wandered lonely as a cloud, shy as a bongo, lost as a tourist along the streets of Old Heidelberg, where a skinny prince in a seersucker suit plighted his troth to a blonde princess in a sun-back dress. The princess was three inches taller than the prince and had thick legs, but she was very pretty. Twice she smiled at Nick.

Otherwise the company ignored him.

The Student Corps marched, the beer mugs shook. "Drink, drink, drink" was the order of the day.

Eddie Mack had disappeared, but hairless, harried Herbert Prager, the company manager, was everywhere, making his rounds at a breathless trot. Once he stopped.

"You got a match?" he asked, fumbling through his pockets and pointing at the deformed cigarette that dangled from his lips.

Nick lit it for him, quickly lit another for himself. "You know," he said, the words coming out before he'd had a chance to examine them, "I don't even know who I'm supposed to be."

"Oh." Prager began a smile, but stopped in the middle. "Oh, my God," he said. He took one hand from his sloping stomach and the other from his pocket and put them together in front of him. "You're Hubert," he said. "Lutz's valet. Fuller's Lutz. Lutz is the prince's valet." He shook his head carefully as though it might begin to ache at any minute. "I'll get you your sides. Why don't you go see Fuller?"

"I try," said Nick. "I try all the time."

And he tried again on the day that Prager brought the sides. This time Fisty Fuller looked up from the telephone, shook his head, changed his mind and pushed the phone aside. Wrapped in good British tweed, broad of shoulder and forehead, with a round, hard belly and round, hard eyes, he had the substantial air of a man whose broker and bookie were never more than a hello away. "You got any brains you'll put your money in uncut diamonds," he said, pointing a blunt finger at Nick. Then he folded up the finger and put the hand in his pocket. On the broad, swollen skull tight curls struggled to stand up beneath a glistening coat of Vaseline. "That piece of information cost me seventy-five grand," he said, "and I'm passing it on to you free. Remember where you heard it."

Nick smiled. It was a smile he had worked on all his life until it meant practically nothing—neither amusement nor apology nor anything else you could put into words. "I've learned my part," he said, holding it out in its blue paper binding.

Fisty Fuller reached across the desk to touch the sleeve of Nick's tan rayon jacket. "Where'd you get the suit?"

Nick told him.

Fuller shook his head. "You want to go first class, dress first class."

He got up, nodded his head sharply and began an abbreviated goose step past Nick, down the corridor. He walked seriously. He talked seriously. He was one of the most completely serious men Nick had ever met, and yet you were always searching him for concealed jokes.

Nick hurried after him down the corridor.

"We might as well get started," said Fuller when Nick reached his shoulder. "The market's quiet." And he led the way into a small room with mirrors on two sides. Catching sight of himself in one of the mirrors, he stopped to adjust his tie and press down a feather of hair that had risen over his left ear. Solemnly he bent closer to the mirror to study the smooth-shaven skin over his cheekbone.

Nick automatically leaned forward too, and staring into the mirror, saw for the first time what Eddie Mack must have seen from the beginning. Short and fat. Tall and skinny. He and Fisty Fuller were a pair.

"Lemme," said Fuller, reaching for the blue-bound lines in Nick's hand. He flipped the pages with his thumb. "Nyuh," he said. "Jokes like that they can send back to Shubert." Fisty rolled the pages and tossed them at Nick. "You know what a bit is?" he asked and didn't wait for an answer. "Like the Lemon Bit," he said. "Or Flugel Street. You tell a burleycue comic the Lemon Bit, and he knows what you mean. They're all these different bits like that, everybody knows them, you tell a guy the name and he can do it with you, winging it all the way. Nobody has to have lines on paper." He rubbed the bowl of his pipe along his nose, then polished it in his palm. "In the old days no comic ever trusted lines on paper."

Fisty Fuller shrugged his shoulders. "Larceny," he said, starting to fill his pipe. When he had it filled, he lit it and sent a small island of smoke against the nearest mirror. "Maybe the Gazeeka Box." He sent a second island to die against the mirror. "This box that looks like a phone booth. When I say the magic word, beautiful girls . . . Nah," he said, "nah. That won't do."

Grabbing the pipe by its bowl, Fisty swung it like a club. "Where we going to get the girls for the box?" he asked. "They'd never spare us any girls."

"There are lots of girls," pointed out Nick, quickly partisan.

Fisty Fuller smiled cynically. "You don't know El Cheapo and Company. Rather let the girls rot than give them to us." He looked over his shoulder. "Mark my words," he said, "even if they gave us the girls, they wouldn't give us the box. If they gave us the box, they wouldn't give us the monkey."

Lighting a cigarette, Nick leaned against the mirror. When he was nine, feeling the blood run royal in his veins, he had decided that he must be the second son of a king—a princeling mislaid. For some reason he thought about that now, and the memory made him uneasy.

"Look," said Fisty Fuller, "you want your pay, see; you ain't been paid in sixteen months, you're driving me crazy for the money. Finally I break down, I say sure, sure, and to prove what a good guy I am I'll give you a chance to double it." He stopped to suck on his pipe and discovered that it was dead.

"There's this little game with the three shells," he said. "I explain how it works. You figure this is it, sucker's heaven. Got the picture?"

"The hand is quicker than the eye," said Nick.

"Ahhh," said Fisty Fuller, shedding a benignity so obviously fraudulent that it had the same effect on Nick as a cold shower, awakening him to possibilities he could not even anticipate.

CHAPTER FOUR

THE SUN LINGERED on West End Avenue, but upstairs in the apartment it was already night.

Opening the front door into darkness, Nick turned on the living-room lights and looked for his father, who sometimes spent hours in the dark, cursing life or plotting new ways around it. There was no sign of the old man.

Nick lit a cigarette from the stub of the one he had just finished. Noticing that his hand was still shaking a little, he assured himself that he was too young to shake, but the knowledge made no difference to his hands. Who would ever laugh at Fisty Fuller's shell game? he wondered, nibbling morosely on the end of the cigarette.

The front door opened and Jake West came through the

small hall into the living room. "You got stock in the Consolidated Edison?" he asked, starting to turn off the lights. Halfway around he stopped and drifted toward the nearest chair. "I'm not arguing," he said. "You made your bed. Sleep in it." He moved his right arm in a horizontal sweep that might have served to smooth a sheet. He nodded. He scowled. He scratched his head savagely. "No argument," he said, making it clear that he was brave as a wolf, sharp as a fox, beyond either intimidation or trickery. Then he marched to his bedroom on angry feet, the tendons of his neck standing out like harp strings above the blue collar.

A half hour later he came back with a thoughtful, sliding step and walked about the room pondering heavily. Suddenly his lips turned in a smile that seemed to hurt them. "I'm going to Florida," he said.

Nick shook his head. The old man had never gone on a vacation before. "In the summer?" he asked. "It must be hot."

"Not for the summer. Forever," said the old man. The word excited him and he slapped his hand on the table to underline it. "I'm closing up the apartment, selling the furniture."

Nick felt his heart roll in his chest, his legs tremble, his throat go dry—a set of symptoms so familiar that he knew them privately as West's disease—but he said nothing.

"Unless you want something." The old man waved his hand. "Maybe you'd like to take your bed?"

Nick shook his head.

"A chest? Bookcases? The library table?"

"What would I do with furniture?"

"A picture?" offered the old man. "Maybe the big ship with the sails in the living room. You always liked that. Your mother liked it too."

Nick hesitated. "There's only one thing."

"Take your choice."

"That's not what I meant. I mean it was sudden."

"Sudden?" said Mr. West, smiling sardonically. He winked confidentially at the ceiling. "Now he tells me sudden."

This, it turned out, could neither be answered nor continued, and they sat together in silence staring at separate walls. After a while Mr. West got up. Taking an old envelope from his pocket, he circled the room, mumbling, touching and making notes on the back of the envelope. When he had completed his inventory in the living room, he went through the rest of the apartment.

Presently he came back, still carrying the envelope, and read the list to Nick, stopping after each item to offer it. The giant sideboard with the bowed legs and the swollen, flower-grown belly. The long broad couch with its tapestry knights and fraying chargers—a deep-pillowed couch that sank you through feathery distances to meet a knife-edged spring. The rug like a worn blue sea. The fat and friendly armchairs. The frail bench for which his mother had made a needlepoint seat. The tall and formal secretary with its stiff-jointed diplomat's grace.

After each item Nick shook his head slowly. In all that strange, strained, silent household only the furniture had kept him company through his childhood. The sideboard was his uncle. The couch was his grandmother. He and the armchairs were cousins. Nick raised his hands and then carefully put them down again. His relatives were being sold into slavery.

"Solid oak," said Jake West, rapping the sideboard with his knuckles.

Nick looked and sighed.

"Take it," urged Jake West fiercely, needing neither furniture nor family. He was the man for the long march and the light knapsack, Jake West, happy Spartan, who'd learned early to do without aunts, uncles and amenities.

His luck had been bad from the beginning: Jake was the ugly duckling who turned out not to be a swan. He'd been born into an unhappy family which, even before he could

22

talk, was blaming him for its unhappiness.

His father was a tubercular tailor who no longer had the energy for major expenditures of affection. His mother was a plump, ambitious matriarch; in the course of a lifetime she had set herself a hundred goals and missed every one. This pair had already raised five children and buried three when Jake put in a belated appearance. Brothers blamed him because they hadn't gone to college, sisters because they couldn't find husbands. Even his mother, who was fond of him, had trouble keeping the note of grievance from her voice.

Jake grew up skinny, dirty and tough, dressed in hand-me-downs that had been preserved only by oversight. He neither gave nor took affection easily and wherever he went people found it simple not to love him. If a gang formed on a street corner, he automatically became its victim. In a debate, his side was certain to be unpopular. He spent his childhood bruised, burdened, bullied and unconquered. It hardly mattered that he was a Jew; even anti-Semites hated him for himself alone.

To hell with them.

To hell with everything and everybody.

He was a rock.

When he entered his teens, he became the main support of his parents. His father was sick, his brothers were barely able to take care of themselves, his sisters were tragically married or desperately unmarried.

At eleven Jake wrapped fish, ran errands, swept stores, watched baby carriages, pressed suits, carried water for horses. He earned a living through sheer obstinacy, and he was happier than he had ever been.

When he was twelve, his father died. The next year his mother was dead too. On the latter occasion something became apparent that everybody had overlooked for years. Jake was still a small boy. He cried—he hadn't done that publicly since he was five. With arms like broomsticks and fists the size of doorknobs, he tried to fight the men who were lowering his mother into her grave and managed to knock one of them off his feet.

After his mother's funeral the family elders spoke of sending Jake to an orphan asylum or placing him with one of his siblings, but he chose instead to disappear by taking a job as a bellhop in another section of the city.

Here, between his thirteenth and his fifteenth years, he learned a good deal about some of the more commercial aspects of love and he saved eight hundred and fifty dollars. The knowledge made him cautious, but the money made him reckless. On the advice of a politician's mistress he decided to buy land that was temporarily under water. En route to invest in this damp chimera, he was held up by a masked man pointing a gun—an irony from which he never really recovered.

By this time fifteen-year-old Jake knew exactly where he stood in the universe: he was the Rockefeller of hard luck, the Maecenas of misfortune. Although at first the thought depressed him, in the end it became the source of his pride.

He left the hotel to become office boy for an insurance broker named Crawford on Broome Street, where he remained for the next twelve years, rising to the position of bookkeeper-salesman. These were the twelve quiet years, devoid of notable misfortune, but Jake continued to think of himself as a basically unlucky man until something occurred that was to shake this conviction as nothing else ever had before or ever would again.

On a rather cold day in August a new girl came to work in the office. Her name was Estelle Berger. She was fairly tall but so thin you automatically thought of her as small and dangerously delicate. Quite pretty in an almost childish way, she smiled with a warmth which, in the beginning, embarrassed

Jake. He found himself falling in love not so much against his will as against his understanding, for, not believing in love, he had no word to explain the way he felt. Even when he finally proposed to Estelle, he manufactured a dozen substitute reasons to interpret that act to himself.

Marriage was a greater change for him than it is for most men: suddenly he found himself not only with a wife but with a family, for the Bergers were a mutually devoted clan whose joint affections frequently boiled over into feasts and festivities of all sorts. They celebrated birthdays, anniversaries, engagements and weddings with outbursts of merrymaking which were the true centers of their lives.

In the end their example proved so infectious that Jake presently found himself in touch with the brothers and sisters he hadn't seen in more than ten years.

He was beginning to think of himself as a miraculously changed man when his wife died while giving birth to their only child. This time Jake was too old to fight the gravediggers. There was no one to fight but himself.

For four weeks he stayed in the apartment with his infant son while the battle continued. When he finally came out, he looked ten years older and had lost his job, but he knew once again who he was. Jake the Unlucky. He broke with the Bergers because they had been party to the years of self-deceit during which he forgot his identity. He cut himself off from his own family because that was the natural order of things.

Nick grew up in silence, surrounded by the stillness of relatives who never came, talking to the furniture and listening to clocks. Occasionally his father spoke. Eat spinach. Wash your neck. Avoid drafts.

When Nick was six, Jake bought him a bicycle; when he was seven, a bugle. Chow calls and invitations to charge rang boldly through the damp, dark air of the apartment. If the neighbors protested, Jake dealt with them summarily. He wanted his son to grow up to the tune of martial music.

Between his seventh and fourteenth birthdays Nick survived a thousand cold showers and three sets of boxing gloves without developing either his will or his muscles, but Jake was only vaguely aware that he wasn't succeeding, for his disciplinary projects changed so frequently and erratically it was impossible to keep track of the failures.

As a result, Nick was able to lead an underground existence of which his father was completely unaware. He spent a good part of his childhood in a pleasant darkness inhabited by Ann Sheridan, Rita Hayworth, Ingrid Bergman, Hedy Lamarr and Greta Garbo—on the shores of Africa, in the golden cities of the East, across the Western plains, in drawing room, submarine and stagecoach. Nick West, with nerves of steel and cold, slitty eyes. Although Jake never found out about the nerves, he noticed the eyes. "You're going blind," he said. "Like a bat in the dark. I'll buy you a football."

For a whole week Nick had to carry the football with him when he left the house in the afternoons, but his father was too busy with more serious troubles to remember it for long.

"The die is cast," said Nick to the couch on the afternoon he lost the football in the dark at the newest Ann Sheridan picture. He fenced wildly with the spindly-legged secretary and put a permanent wound in its dark veneer. Around five-thirty he began to smuggle aristocrats out of the living room into the kitchen.

As the years passed, aristocrats by the thousands flowed into the kitchen and the secretary suffered wound on wound. The rug was a sea, the chairs were men of war, the couch was his grandmother, the chairs were cousins again; history shifted, changed and tumbled. This was the private domain of N. West, son of kings, cousin of emperors, master of a hundred cunning arts; it flourished in all its secret glory until the night the old man announced he was breaking up the household.

At that moment, examining his father in astonishment, Nick was suddenly embarrassed by the knowledge that he was too old to feel so orphaned.

"Take a chair," urged Jake West.

"No," said Nick. "Thank you."

The old man finished the inventory and stuffed the envelope back in the pocket from which he had taken it. "Look," he said, "while I had obligations I stuck it out. Now you're grown up; you've chosen your own road."

"Sure," said Nick.

They shook hands. When they separated their hands, neither of them knew what to do next.

"I think I'll get to bed," said Nick.

Jake turned aside and picked up a china dog. "I got work to do yet," he said, shaking his head at the dog.

After Nick had gotten into bed, he heard his father moving about for a long time. The old man seemed to be shifting furniture from one side of the room to the other, and the last thing Nick heard before falling asleep was the sound of wood hitting wood. Thump, thump, thump. Abruptly he was back at Madame Poirier's School of the Drama, where, in the finest French tradition, every performance started with a triple stroke of Madame's snakewood cane.

The G.I. Bill had opened the world to him. He could have become a dentist, a doctor, a high-speed lathe operator, but he chose Madame Poirier instead. Although he had made up his mind in twenty minutes on a hot morning in September, the decision had roots that ran back to the long, dark afternoons with Ann Sheridan and their dramatic aftermaths in the living room. Oh, the roots were many and long, including even the fact that he had been six foot three on his twelfth birthday, known to friend and foe as the Human Xylophone. All of his life he'd accumulated nicknames like lint—as though there were some widely felt necessity to explain and package him in a phrase. Bongo.

Nick put his head under the pillow. Ostrich, he thought. Then he fell asleep and for the first time in a long time dreamed about his mother, whom he remembered only as a photograph in a brown leather frame.

The next morning when Nick got up he found his father asleep in the red armchair in the living room. The old man opened his eyes and almost instantly his mind flooded with the bitterness of its last memory before sleeping. Jonah, he said to himself, recalling once more how it had been during the war when he had spent each day in the conviction that the son of such an unlucky father was bound to be shot out of the sky, not at some indefinite date in the future but before sundown.

"You gotta be tough," he shouted, feeling the impossibility of ever explaining to his son what he meant. He leaned toward Nick with one hand held out. "Nobody expected your mother to die," he said with apparent irrelevance. "Even the doctor was surprised." He hesitated, brooding about this event which he still discussed as though it had happened yesterday. "But *I* should have known. I've brought bad luck to everything I ever loved."

Nick sat down in the other armchair. His father had never spoken to him this nakedly before. The movement seemed to startle the old man. He shook his head and stood up.

"Get away from me," he said. "Here you can catch trouble like a disease. Maybe some of Eddie Mack's luck'll rub off on you."

And that was the nearest he ever got to an explanation of what he had done.

CHAPTER FIVE

ALTHOUGH it was nearly six o'clock when the train un-
loaded Eddie Mack's troupe in Secost, New Jersey, the sun
was still high and hot, the sky was a burning blue.

As Nick dropped to the platform, bag in hand, he felt the
vagrant sand grit between his shoes and the concrete. He
smelled the sea-blown air carefully, for the Secost air was
famous; then he went quickly out into the town, where he
walked along a broad street with wide green lawns and wooden
houses. The sidewalks tilted. The houses sprawled. The landscape was rich in columns and gables and deep, shadowy
porches, but the trees were rare and huddled against themselves as though suffering from the sun, which spilled its heat

furiously over the town. It was an old street in an old town and there wasn't even a dog in motion.

Continuing toward the sea through rows of whitewashed clam shells, Nick passed out of the region of private homes into the business district. Here were the small hotels, four or five stories high and made of wood or plaster. The big hotels, ocean-front palaces which had made Secost famous, rose in the distance, filling the sky with red brick and white marble.

The Weston House, to which Nick had been assigned, was small—square and white and unadorned. When people looked for ways to praise it, they said it was clean.

Nick's room held an iron bed, a wooden bureau, a desk, a skinny chair, a washbasin, two towels and a cake of soap. A brown stripe was painted on the wall a little more than half-way up like the Plimsoll mark on a ship.

Closing the door, Nick emptied his bag into the bureau very quickly and very seriously. Then he opened the door again and looked out.

A pair of dark orange suitcases had been abandoned in the neighboring doorway. Inside the door a matching toilet case sat bottom up on the bed. And in front of the bureau, staring into the mirror, stood a girl in a lilac dress. A tall girl, big and strong and as peaceful as some marble Venus lost two thousand years, one arm bent forever to touch her face, eyes straight ahead and watching.

She watched, Nick watched. The sun filled the room with a steady glow.

Suddenly the girl began to sing and the room grew smaller, for the voice was as big and rich as the body it came out of. When it stopped, the room went back to normal, the girl still standing in front of the mirror, but with her head tilted slightly, reviewing the sound in her mind just as she had reviewed her face. Then she turned and saw Nick.

30

"Uh," he said, "uh, uh. I wondered if the sun was still shining. It's hard to tell in the hall."

The girl began a smile and forgot it in the middle. "The voice is a little tired," she confided. "On the train Walter Kennedy said hot milk does wonders."

Walter Kennedy was the Student Prince. Nick recognized the girl as a member of the chorus.

"We haven't met," he said. "My name is Nicholas West."

Once more she smiled the half-finished smile. "Do you know where I could get some hot milk?" she asked.

He shrugged. "Downstairs, I suppose." His eyes followed hers to the luggage in the doorway. "Would you like me to move the bags?"

"I had to carry them up myself," she said, more in amazement than complaint. "This is the funniest hotel I've ever been in." She looked him over carefully. "I'm not used to cheap things," she said. The lipstick was red as blood against her ivory skin. Her eyes were violet, the lashes long and black. The skin of her eyelids was iridescent—mermaid flesh. Her large pale arms shone in the sunlight. She smelled of frankincense and myrrh. "Perhaps you *had* better move the bags," she conceded.

When Nick had shifted them to the far side of the bed, he came back to the door. "It occurs to me there isn't a kitchen in the hotel. For the hot milk," he said.

She rolled her lower lip thoughtfully beneath perfectly matched teeth, chewed on it a bit as she thought and reached a decision. "There must be some place," she said, coming out to join him. Together they went down the hall, down in the elevator, into the lobby. In the center of the lobby some doubt rose to tamper with her tranquility. "I've never been in a hotel before where there wasn't a kitchen," she said uneasily, putting out her hand as though by accident.

When the fingers touched his arm, the gesture suddenly assumed another significance, indefinable but exciting. She was one of those people with a flair for a kind of instant intimacy. You never again know them so well as you do the first time, but that once can be, through its very unexpectedness, memorable forever. On Nick West, the recent orphan, the effect was overwhelming.

"Never mind," he said, enclosing a world of solicitude and tenderness in the phrase. Taking her gently by the elbow, he guided her out into the life of the town.

At the corner they remembered to introduce themselves more thoroughly. Her name was Andrea Marston and she was the daughter of a Kansas City automobile dealer.

They wandered along the boardwalk between the quiet sea and the open-fronted stalls, where custard turned and dolls stood still. They passed the submarine sandwiches, the furniture auction, the Pokerino, the seafood snackery, the taffy twisters, the sixty-second portrait sketcher, the home of the world's largest frankfurter, the genuine lace from Belgium, the genuine linen from Ireland, the Seaside Sun Shoppe (world's largest selection of ocean notions) and the genuine gypsy fortunetellers.

"My father was a racing driver," said Andrea. "He flew for the Lafayette Escadrille. My mother was a society belle. I was born six months after they were married."

This sequence of revelations gave Nick a breath-taking sense of accomplishment; never before had he gotten to know a girl so well so soon. He insisted on paying for the hot milk, regretting only that it was not champagne.

Andrea finished the milk, sighed and looked at the water, glanced up at the sun and sighed again. "I've got to wash my hair," she said, raising one long-fingered hand to touch her head. In that moment with hand upraised and the sun glowing along her pale face and the pout turning to dark mystery on her lips, she was a goddess once more, marble cold and stately. "My mother claims that my hair is one of my most remarkable features," she said thoughtfully.

Walking back the way they had come, through the bright, quiet streets, they soon reached the hotel. A certain coolness had already succeeded the false intimacy of their first contact, but Nick hardly noticed it. In a single week he had become an actor and separated from his father. And now he had fallen in love.

CHAPTER SIX

THE TOWN OF SECOST was about to celebrate its two hundred and fiftieth year with a pageant during the third week in July.

Like a great many things in Secost, the pageant was a Bowman family project; Miss Felicity Bowman, as president of the Historical Society, sponsored it, and Mr. Henry Bowman, as president of the Hotel Owners Association, underwrote it. These two presidencies defined the position of the Bowmans with considerable exactness. They were the only representatives among the hotel owners of the old settlers, who by and large had lost control of their town while still retaining a certain uneasy social supremacy.

Ordinarily the Bowmans and their pageant would have been of little interest to Eddie Mack, for he had a strong prejudice against amateur theatricals of all sorts, but this one kept cropping up with a persistence that would have made a less sanguine man wary. It was, in fact, the excuse most frequently offered by the hotel owners for not keeping their pre-season commitments to support Eddie Mack's Broadway musicals.

Monday, they said. Call me Friday. Next week. Tomorrow. Check me as soon as the pageant is over. And Eddie Mack stalked the corridors of the Secost Theater like a seedy lion, smoking Romeo y Julieta cigars and enjoying dreams of triumph. With the whole summer ahead, there still were infinite opportunities for the exercise of an optimism unshaken by five successive years of complete failure.

Onstage Benny Wallace stood in the familiar glare of the footlights and gave off an air of absolute confidence, which was his greatest asset as a director. His pale blue jacket and gray flannel slacks were as crisp as newly made money. His face was as neat as a pie crust. He had the look of a man who was well cared for, well scrubbed, dusted, polished, ironed, fed —a triumph of domestic economy. And indeed he was an exceedingly domestic man who had been a good and faithful husband to six wives in a row.

Benny waited until the silence turned a little painful before he started. "Some of you know me," he said. "You don't have to listen. For the rest this is all new, so I'll explain. In the next three months we're going to do sixteen shows. Rehearse one during the day, put on another at night. You'll never have as much time again as you've had with *The Student Prince*. From now on we fight the clock all the way."

He glanced at his watch, looked into the pit. "Let's go," he said. "From the top. Gimme the overture."

The orchestra gave it to him and Benny started to put the pieces of *The Student Prince* together on the vast stage where Bernhardt had once appeared in *L'Aiglon* and honorable chairmen called conventions to order every winter.

It took all morning to move the prince from the royal castle to Heidelberg, for you couldn't make a step or complete a gesture without an interruption from Benny, who verified the smallest item against a blueprint in his head. Over the years he had learned *The Student Prince* down to the last swing of a beer glass, the final stamp of foot and swirl of curl, and he allowed no deviation.

This presented no great problem for most of the cast. Long-time residents on the banks of the River Neckar, they had played their roles in company after company, season after season, from coast to coast. They knew *The Student Prince*. And they knew Benny Wallace. They read his mind, they interpreted his grunts, they translated the way in which he leaned against a table.

Not so the prince. Although he had never been a prince before, he didn't want to learn from Benny. A very skinny, very vain young man with a pleasant voice and serious intentions, he was determined to pour all of his resources into the role even if the effort made his face pale and his manner cranky.

Very quickly this clash between the immovable prince and the irresistible Benny became a matter of principle from which neither could retreat, and then there was nothing too small to become an issue. Meanwhile Dr. Engel yawned, Princess Margaret smiled, Von Mark shed disapproval through a monocle, Kathie looked as though she might cry, Gretchen was bored, Toni sneered. The duchess retreated behind a flat, where she calmed herself with the help of a flask.

The chorus, recruited largely from music students on the first rung of what they hoped was a ladder, went to pieces altogether. Intimidated by the size of the stage and unnerved by constant interruptions, they sang in a giant whisper which barely rolled to the far side of the orchestra pit before it stopped dead.

On the podium Charlie Miller, the musical director, coaxed,

cursed and broke two batons, but he succeeded only in depressing them further.

It took such spreading confusion to save Lutz and Hubert from public disgrace—of this Nick was sure. For Fisty Fuller wandered the streets of Old Heidelberg with a permanent glaze over his eyeballs. In the grip of a giant inertia he seemed unable to choose between the elephantine humor of the original script and the various substitutes he had been proposing, and as a result he spoke only in patches of disconnected dialogue. Occasionally he made some vague reference to his shotgun act, or the cigar bit, or maybe even the whiskers business, but his attention shifted before he could explain what he meant.

Every once in a while Nick took out his part and looked for something funny in it, but there was no cheer to be borrowed from Lutz, the pompous bully, and his bumpkin assistant, Hubert. So Nick mumbled along, happy he was not being watched, hoping that in some way not immediately apparent this was all a blessing in disguise.

Bongo West, shyest of beasts.

Was it funny enough that he was tall and skinny, while Fisty was short and fat? After a lifetime passed in terror of being laughed at, there suddenly dawned on Nick the terror of not being laughed at.

At three-forty-five P.M. Frederic York—chairman of the board of Lovalee Cosmetics, director of two banks and a shipping line, fight fancier, horse lover, thirty-second-degree Mason and Eddie Mack's backer—swept into town with a small retinue.

CHAPTER SEVEN

WHEN NICK GOT BACK to the hotel, he found a letter from his father written on the stationery of a discarded corporation.

Son Nick [it said under the carefully x'ed-out title], by the time you read this I will be on the train for Miami, Florida. Beware of everything. Restaurant food is dangerous, eat mainly chicken. Chew carefully, it might have broken glass. Do not swim after eating. Cover the seat in a public toilet. Gargle aspirin for a cold and wear a hat at all times. Never fight a burglar. Watch out for Eddie Mack. Your father, JAKE WEST

P.S. I enclose $10 in money order. Cash at Post Office or hotel desk. Do not cash until ready to spend.

Nick folded the letter five times and buried it in his wallet, having lost his bed, his chest, the bookcases, the library table, the ship with sails in the living room, the rug like a worn blue sea. He didn't even have an address.

That night he waited for Andrea to come back to her room, but although he stayed awake late into the night she never came.

Nick woke up at five o'clock in perfect darkness to await the apocalyptic dawn. Until five-fifteen there was darkness. At five-fifteen the sun appeared with a roar of light. By getting up then Nick could spend almost four hours at the beach before rehearsals started.

When he arrived at the water's edge, he found Andrea there ahead of him, and he stopped beside one of the steel poles that supported the boardwalk to watch her.

She was running along the sand at the point where it had been pressed smooth by recent waves. She ran a hundred, two hundred, three hundred yards, until she met a pile-up of rock put there to break the force of the waves. Then she turned and came back, running all the way, crossing in front of Nick three more times before she stopped and removed a yellow dressmaker's tape she had been wearing as a belt.

As Nick approached, Andrea started to measure her right thigh, shifting the tape carefully in search of the greatest circumference.

"Good morning," said Nick.

She nodded.

He stretched out his arms, lifted himself on his toes and inhaled deeply. "The early morning," he said enthusiastically.

Andrea shifted the tape to the other leg. "You can have it." Withdrawing the tape, she rewound it on her waist and slapped the firm flesh of her thighs. "If it weren't for these, you'd never find me awake at this crazy time." She turned and stared across the sea, dark purple in the distance, apple green as it lurched into foam on the beach. "I've got to watch myself. Oh, how I've got to watch myself!" One large yet elegant foot kicked a furrow in the sand. "That's the kind of heritage I've got. Why I have an Uncle Harry weighs over three hundred pounds." She shuddered. It was the first time Nick had ever seen anybody shudder on such a scale, and he watched in admiration as Andrea's great body performed the movement with a peculiar majesty—from the first princely upheaval that rocked the whole torso to the secondary quivers that danced in the deep, rich flesh of her bosom. "I study myself inch by inch," she said. "At the first sign of trouble!" She snapped her fingers. "Running for the thighs. Push-ups for the shoulders. Jumping for the calves. Torso twisting for the stomach." Like many specialists Andrea was shamelessly simple-minded when talking about anything but her subject, and so you were doubly impressed by her erudition in her field. She discussed her body with a scholar's passion. "Each part has its own exercise," she said as though she had just discovered this pleasant fact.

Nick felt the sunlight slide off the water into his eyes. "You going to run again?" he asked.

"No. You can't overdo or you wind up looking like a shot-putter."

She sank easily to her haunches in the sand, swinging her long, dark hair behind her. "Now I can rest a little," she said. "Ten minutes. I don't want to get a real burn. Mother says it isn't ladylike to be brown. Not that I ever agree with Mother about anything."

What an easy girl to get along with, thought Nick, crouching beside her. The trouble with most people was that you never really knew what was going on in their heads, but in Andrea's case it was all quite clear.

Once more he enjoyed the sensation of intimacy that he had felt so sharply at their first meeting, and, startled by his own

40

unsuspected flair for managing beautiful young women, he examined Andrea with a lover's partiality.

Suddenly a question floated up from the bottom of his mind. "Where were you last night?" he asked.

"What?" She poured sand through her fingers; then she heard the question. "Is it really any of your business?" she said reasonably enough. Andrea wasn't offended, for she considered her activities a legitimate subject of interest to everybody; nevertheless, a certain note of mockery came into her voice. "Wouldn't you like to know?" she asked.

It occurred to Nick that quite possibly he wouldn't, and he stood up quickly, feeling that he had been betrayed by his own ignorance of women. "I didn't mean it the way it sounded," he said with dignity.

Each night Nick looked for Andrea and each night she was away from her room. Although he lived next door to her, he was probably the last person in the company to discover that she was spending the nights with Eddie Mack. The bitterness of this discovery seemed to sharpen his eyes; he realized that while he was finding the way to the beach, they had been forming up two-by-two all around him—Eddie Mack and Andrea, Charlie Miller and Danielle, the list went on and on.

In his loneliness he took out the letter from his father and read it again, but Jake West was no help. Love was not his subject.

CHAPTER EIGHT

AT EIGHT-THIRTY on opening night Nick West looked
through a special peephole into the auditorium of the Secost
Theater.

It was, he decided immediately, a mistake.

There were people everywhere—in the seats, in the rows,
in the aisles. People talking, smiling, sitting, walking. People
singly, in pairs, in troops and tribes. Young and old, white-
haired, gray-haired, black- and red-haired, blond, bald, even
one tall pale woman whose short-cropped curls were lollypop
orange.

Disaster sat in four thousand seats. Who would ever make
these people cry? Who would ever make them laugh? Certainly not those sad mumblers, Fuller and West. The fear that

had been sitting quietly in Nick's stomach jumped into his throat. He moved his lips, cleared his throat, turned away from the peephole, sure now that he had lost his voice.

Around him people were heading toward their places for the opening scene. He whispered experimentally and felt his throat go dry until it started to crack. Keep cool, he advised himself, and raised his fingers to see if they were shaking. Steady as a rock, cool as a cucumber. He looked down at his knees in the purple breeches. They seemed unusually distant and somewhat stiff, but otherwise all was well. He licked his lips. Except for stomach and throat, he was absolute master of his body. Then he noticed his heart. It was going up like a balloon. If it pushed against his ribs any harder, it would break them.

Eddie Mack came by, having just left Benny Wallace on the far side of the stage. A week of passing through the Secost streets had blistered the end of his nose and made bright red scallops over his cheekbones. Anxiety or lack of sleep had blackened the eye sockets. He scowled as he walked through this landscape of canvas, wood, rope and actors, filled with his own terrors.

He went by Nick without seeming to notice him, then stopped and came back. "Get Mrs. Crory to pin those pants in place," he said.

Nick nodded. "I can't talk," he said.

Eddie Mack's scowl went a little deeper and his right hand patted Nick's shoulder—a quick one-two. The left hand went into a pocket of the white jacket, where it found a miniature whiskey bottle. "Mother Mack's elixir," he said, "the actor's friend."

He took a second look and drew out a second bottle. "Drink it slow," he recommended, starting to leave. "Avoid surprises."

Cutting the seal of the first bottle with his fingernail, Nick loosened the metal cap but looked for a more private corner

43

before drinking. All about him the Student Corps prepared to march. At the rear of the stage the garden of the inn was in flower. Everywhere he turned he saw a blur of people, canvas, rope.

Finally he reached a small plaster alcove, the size and shape of a telephone booth, and here he drank his first bottle. Going down it was hot and smoky, filled with promises of courage, but once down it produced no result at all.

Unexpectedly Nick thought of his father, who would not have approved. Jake West's tolerance was only for the ceremonial drink; he didn't believe in drinking when you needed it.

Nick cut the second seal with his thumbnail, emptied an additional ounce down his throat, gagged and stopped, afraid the whiskey might be having more effect than he suspected.

Mike Roberts, the stage manager, went by chanting, "Places, places, everybody."

Then the orchestra was playing the overture, the curtain rose. Adrenalin on the rise throughout his body, sweat tickling his ribs, Nick watched the prologue, unable to believe that he was going to be out there himself in a couple of minutes.

He was not aware of the moment when he left the darkness of the wings for the paralyzing light of the inn garden, but suddenly he was there.

Fisty's hair stood up on the back of his head like a wire ruff. His nose was as big and red as a tomato. He seemed to have grown bigger and stronger. He walked as though he could walk through walls.

At some point Nick made his first speech, then he spoke again. When he spoke the third time, he felt a sting on the side of his head and realized that Fisty Fuller had hit him. He opened his mouth to complain, but closed it again, remembering that the script had given him no complaints to make. He clenched his fist, unclenched it, started to move out of range and stopped.

He stared at Fisty Fuller. Lutz stared back—royal valet, blusterer, coward, bully, plump demon.

Hey, muttered Nick internally. Bang, Lutz hit him on the other side of the head. Then once in the chest, once in the stomach, a shove on the right shoulder that turned him and a kick that moved him forward. Lutz swung his walking stick like a club, but missed Nick's head.

There was a distant swelling sharp wild hooting cawing sound which Nick could not place. All at once he realized that it came from the audience. They won't stand for it, Nick thought grimly. If Fisty keeps it up, they'll rush the stage. He enjoyed the pleasant picture of their revenge for a little longer before he understood that they were laughing.

In the middle of a final spasm of laughter, the beating stopped as suddenly as it had begun. Lutz moved on, following the affairs of his master, the prince, and Nick was alone in a corner of the garden. When Fuller left the stage, Nick followed.

In the long hall that led to Fisty's dressing room, they met. "I'm sore all over," Nick complained.

"Really?" said Fisty. He thought for a moment, interest fat and honest on his face. "You got to watch yourself in the sun," he said at last. "The sun here is guaranteed to raise welts on a suitcase."

"I never burn," said Nick indignantly.

"Don't say that." Fisty shook his head in gentle rebuke. "You got skin just like the rest of us."

Looking straight into Fuller's face, Nick began to question his own memory. Perhaps he was exaggerating because he was excited, he thought, even as he tried to rub the soreness out of his side.

Then the act was over and the audience, which had been playful and only partly committed throughout, clapped good-naturedly, setting off two or three erratic volleys of applause

45

in sheer delight at their own capacity for making noise.

During the second act they began to value their own independence less and the play more. When Dr. Engel sang, they were moved and they sat quietly, watching the stage, feeling the music inside them. They were pleased by the prince, who had finally surrendered to Benny Wallace. They stirred to the clink of the beer steins and the swing of marching students, they were filled with a pleasant nostalgia for a past that was not their own.

The good feeling went across the footlights into the audience and it came rolling back like a warm, golden wave more delicious than any beer ever brewed, inspiring the dancers, bracing the principal singers, exciting the chorus who, unexpectedly finding their courage, sang out with a boldness that excited them further. In the pit Charlie Miller, small and neatly wonderful, danced and strutted like one of Napoleon's marshals. His tightly curled black hair shook like Jello, his eyes shone, he skewered invisible hosts with his baton.

By the third act the audience was completely under control. They laughed at Nick's punctual beatings, they sighed, they listened, they played their part as well as anyone could ask; when the act was done, they applauded in a fury of delight.

The fourth act was the last, the final chance to captivate the people in the seats, and Fisty started to beat Nick with a virtuosity that made his previous performances seem mild and uninventive. He hit Nick with his fists, with his umbrella, with his open hand. He stuck his fingers in Nick's eyes, kicked him in the shins, deftly caught him in the ribs with a wandering elbow. He tripped him, slapped him, kneed him, cuffed him, pushed him, pulled him, swung him, rocked him. He did these things with a casual fury, with a negligent ease, with a look of cunning indifference—happy artisan of assault, cheerful master of battery.

Nick rocked, tripped and twisted, a tower of bone and skin

being attacked at its base by a plump private demon. Not knowing what else to do, he clung grimly to his lines, throwing them at Fisty Fuller as though they were rocks.

And the audience laughed, chuckled, hooted and howled, delighted with the finger in the eye, pleased with the rabbit punch, enchanted by the stabbing umbrella—driving Fisty Fuller on to new displays of virtuosity as he strained to wring the last drop of appreciation from them.

But at last the affairs of the kingdom pushed Lutz and Hubert aside. The prince had his princess, the innkeeper's daughter her memories. The Student Corps gave their steins a final swing.

When the curtain fell, the audience took charge, clapping and stamping their feet on the hollow floor. They were delighted with their own exuberance, carried away by their own generosity. Time and again they sent the curtain flying upward, while the cast danced out, singly, in pairs, in greedy platoons.

There was enough applause for the greediest, and the new ones, who had never truly tasted it before, got drunk on the sound; even Nick, not really believing it was for him, felt the drunkenness.

Coming on with Fuller and going off at his heels, he said, laughing in confusion, "I didn't know you hit so much."

Fuller thought for a moment. "Why did you think they call me Fisty?" he asked reasonably.

Then at last the audience tired, broke ranks and came apart. The curtain fell for the last time. The house lights went up.

When the audience was gone, the curtain rose and the cast stood onstage in front of the empty seats. They didn't know yet why Mike Roberts had called them back, but the good feeling was still too strong for them to worry.

After a little while three waiters began to carry in champagne and beer, soda pop and sandwiches. Not very much champagne really and domestic at that, but it popped when you pulled the corks.

Eddie Mack made a speech, telling them how good they were, how happy he was, and he looked happy, his big face young behind the lines which age had made upon it. He promised them that this was a night in the theater he would remember all his life; then he mentioned some of the other nights he remembered, names tumbling out one after the other from Maude Adams to Florenz Ziegfeld—the Barrymores, the Drews, Minnie Maddern Fiske, Duse, Bernhardt, George M. Cohan. Eddie Mack was drunk, thought Nick, they were all drunk, on applause and champagne bubbles. Wriggling his shoulders to find out where he was still sore, he knew that he himself was a little drunk and he of all of them had the least reason.

Nick inhaled deeply, getting the theater smell, although not as strongly as in the morning, for the heat of lights and people seemed to take some of its sharpness away. What made the smell? Mold, old rope, old canvas, old wood, old leather. Ancient dust. "It's a great night," said Nick to Bernie Bannister, who stood beside him.

Bernie was Eddie Mack's press agent, a tall, cynical man who had lost his hair when he was nineteen and had regarded the world with suspicion ever since. "Yeah," he said, "sure." He licked his lips and scowled as if he found the taste unpleasant. He looked out gloomily over the great bowl of empty seats. "You just witnessed a historic moment."

"Oh?" said Nick.

"The most thoroughly papered house on record." Bernie stood straight and the movement made him more than ever like some strange fishing bird. His head shone in the light as though it had been recently waxed. "The mayor alone had five hundred cousins in on the cuff." He glared at the empty seats. "Bastards!"

"At least they liked it," said Nick.

"They're town people. They like anything that's free." He lowered his voice. "In Secost town people live on visitors. That's nature, like sharks eat flounders. If they ever got the idea we were trying to live on them . . ." Bernie drew a bony forefinger across his throat.

"Weren't there any summer people out there?" asked Nick.

"Fifty. A hundred." Bannister looked around the stage disdainfully. "When the actors outnumber the paying customers, you're in trouble."

Meanwhile, Eddie Mack continued to warm the air with his memories, telling them how on his twelfth birthday he had met Enrico Caruso in a saloon. That tough yet blissful face was filled with belief, the bloodshot eyes were convinced, there was no deceit in the man unless he was deceiving himself.

"Don't get me wrong," said Bernie Bannister, a little frightened now by his own fierceness. "It's not like New York, you go back and read the newspapers and you know where you stand. The summer's young. Wait'll the hotels start selling tickets." The thought stirred him. "Wait'll it starts to rain!" he cried. "They'll come pouring in here like Noah's ark on the day of the flood."

Eddie Mack raised his glass to toast the summer season. Frederic York raised his glass. York's tall sales manager and fat advertising manager raised their glasses. All over the stage those who had been able to get hold of champagne raised it, while the rest of the cast toasted in beer or pop or bitter coffee. "Pray for rain," muttered Bernie Bannister, sucking at a beer can. "Rain makes the tall corn grow."

For ten minutes the cast had held a rough semicircle around Eddie Mack. Now they spread across the stage, carrying drinks and sandwiches, still wearing the bright garments of Old Heidelberg.

Fisty Fuller came by, dressed as Lutz but looking like Fuller, tapping an English briar against his palm, his eyes filled with ticker tape and daily quotations. When he reached Nick's side, he winked, a violent batting of the eye that struck the right half of his face like a tic and was gone before you could be sure it had been there. "What ho the vintage wine," he cried, wrinkling his strawberry-shaped nose at the paper cup in Nick's hand. Then he clapped the place where his wallet would normally have been, winked again and passed on to join Frederic York.

As low, barely perceptible currents began to move people through the crowd, Nick, riding a minor eddy, found himself next to Andrea. He looked away. He was unhappy because of what he had found out about her, but she didn't know that —and wouldn't have cared if she had. "You were funny," she said. "I was watching you. The way your mouth opened when he hit and your bones danced up and down." She started to laugh, while Nick watched her uneasily. It was, he realized, the first time he had seen her laugh, and there was something unpleasant about the sight, as though laughter were a flaw that might damage this vast and beautiful girl. "I was just telling him how funny he was," she said across his shoulder.

Nick turned when Eddie Mack answered. "Yes, very funny." But the producer's voice was politely vague.

"Is there anything wrong?" asked Andrea.

Shaking his head, Eddie Mack snapped a finger against the telegram he held in one hand.

With a downward glance Nick automatically read the message. LOUD SING CUCKOO SEE YOU SOON LOVE ELFRIDA.

"My wife's coming out to the beach," said Eddie Mack, pondering deeply. He saw the puzzled look on Nick's face and added, "Elfrida Mitchell."

Elfrida *Mitchell?* said Nick to himself in amazement, examining the big man more closely.

50

Eddie Mack began to fold the telegram into halves, quarters, eighths, sixteenths, until he had it down to a hard, square pellet, and then he tried to crush it further between his big, soft palms. "God damn!" he said.

CHAPTER NINE

THROUGHOUT THE WEEK the days were crowded with omens of Elfrida Mitchell's arrival.

You could see the difference now in Eddie Mack—in the way he walked, in the look on his face, in the way he talked. He had the careful air of a man who was going to a great deal of trouble to prove that he wasn't afraid.

"They got along worse than any other couple in the history of marriage," declared Herbert Prager.

"I thought she was dead," said Nick. "Elfrida Mitchell. My God, how old is she?"

Prager pulled nervously at his shirt front. "Sixty," he said. He was annoyed. "Somewhere around sixty," he amended angrily, fixing Nick with a resentful stare. "A great actress. A legend. That should be enough for anyone." And he went away angry.

"That woman must have made his life a hell," said Andrea, her great violet eyes, ordinarily turned so deeply inward, filling with the passion of her discovery.

"Did Eddie Mack say so?" asked Nick.

"No." Andrea conceded the point reluctantly. "He's not the kind. Maybe you don't understand a man like that. My father's the same way. There are things torture wouldn't make him discuss. Even when my sister almost burned down the house, he was as quiet as the tomb about the whole thing."

Examining her face, Nick felt that its beauty was being pinched and eroded by this unprecedented concentration on other people, and he blamed Eddie Mack with a bitterness which he had been concealing from himself for some time. The minute he realized it was all Eddie Mack's fault, he felt a new affection for Andrea. They were fellow victims.

"You know," she said, "sometimes I think I worry too much. It's my nature."

"Really?" said Nick in astonishment. Who would ever have thought that this vast and beautiful girl was a secret worrier? It was always a surprise to him that other people worried, but Andrea was a surprise above all others. He was delighted. As they walked together the knuckles of his hand brushed her leg accidentally and he felt the excitement stir inside him.

"When I was twenty," said Fisty Fuller, "I made a proposal of marriage. I never made the same mistake again."

Nick nodded. He was thinking about the way the galvanized steel pipe of the railing filled his hands as he leaned on it to stare at the sea. It was smooth but veined like a leaf. It was

53

hot from the sun that beat against the side of the theater. Underneath the balcony people moved slowly, stunned by the exploding light.

"You take Benny Wallace," argued Fisty. "That guy's paying alimony to wives he can't even remember."

Nick waited patiently, bent over the steel railing so that he could see the people who crossed the boardwalk in front of the theater. Danielle, the friendly ballerina, passed, walking with Charlie Miller. A certain coolness seemed to have come between them and Nick marveled at it. To have fallen in love so quickly was remarkable, but to have fallen in love and out in slightly more than a week was extraordinary. The shortness of the season accelerated everything.

Renee Wilson, the rehearsal pianist, a dumpy, determined, motherly girl, went by hand-in-hand with Joseph Giuliano, the big baritone, who'd played football at Fordham.

Tony George passed with one of the male dancers. Then a group of singers, male and female, laughing and tossing a beach ball.

Two elderly women in bright cotton dresses disappeared under the marquee to buy tickets. Nick leaned a little farther out to watch them; it was not as common a sight as it should have been.

Far out to sea a small boat staggered across the horizon.

Fisty Fuller turned away to study the façade of the building. On the bald peak of his head the sweat glittered like crystal. "When Elfrida quit show business, she started to drink," he said at last, for this was what he had been leading up to. "Or maybe she had to quit because of the way she was drinking; there are two schools of thought. She drank for three years and stopped. After that she read. Not just normal reading, a book here a book there, but reading like the drinking had been, thousands of books, two, three a day. She has a

54

house in Larchmont, the cellar is full of books, the attic, even the garage."

"She was very beautiful, wasn't she?" said Nick, trying to place a dimly remembered picture of Elfrida Mitchell beside the worn, almost fraudulent handsomeness of Eddie Mack.

Fisty blew a shaft of smoke in the direction of the sea. He shrugged his shoulders indifferently and sent another smoke shaft out to sea.

Old Rough and Ready, thought Nick with some bitterness, fixing his eyes on the comedian's hard belly, which hung like an iron pot beneath the blue linen shirt. The president of the school of hard knocks, Mr. Muscle, Peter Pain himself.

"Three years on the whiskey and two years on the books," said Fisty. "It's five years since she crossed a stage, but the lady's rich, she doesn't have to work another minute in her whole life." Fisty sighed and skimmed a sudden eruption of ash from his pipe. Depressed by the thought of Elfrida Mitchell's prosperity, he sucked on the pipe strenuously and leaned against the wall. He kicked the brick with a rubber heel, scratched his head and stared out to sea. "I wonder what she's coming back for this time. They haven't lived together in years." He stopped and turned as though expecting a reply.

"Who knows?" said Nick.

"A funny dame." Fisty wagged his jowls judiciously. "Once she took up mountain climbing."

"Wonderful exercise," said Nick. "Develops legs of iron."

"On her fortieth birthday," said Fisty, "she disappeared completely for three months."

Standing up, Nick pulled the shirt away from his ribs. The cotton was wet under his fingers. "You seem to know a lot about her," he said.

Fisty shrugged his shoulders. "They washed her dirty laundry in the Sunday supplements for forty years."

55

Just then Eddie Mack came along the boardwalk from the direction of his hotel, walking quickly in spite of the heat. His face was heavy with thought, swollen with worry.

On the beach people slept with arms and legs outstretched in a vast siesta unbroken for miles in any direction. Even the lifeguards had left their white towers to hide in the skinny shadows beneath them.

"Will it be the same way next week?" asked Nick, who had been wondering for three days and was pretty sure that he knew the answer.

Fisty's eyebrows crawled like black caterpillars toward his naked scalp. "I don't follow you," he said.

Nick swung a fist at the open air above the balcony. "The hitting, the kicking, all the rest. Will it be the same in *Naughty Marietta* as in *The Student Prince?*"

"It's never the same," said Fisty, but he knew himself that that wasn't an answer. He thought for a moment and said, "They laugh, don't they?"

In the privacy of his own head Nick had to admit that they did. Fisty wouldn't let them do otherwise. He drove them to laughter, he beat them, pressed them, by the fierce exercise of his energy defied them not to laugh. At those moments when they were sluggish or perhaps merely obstinate in their silence, a kind of madness seized him. Then the first laugh would pop like a cork out of a bottle. Hoo. Ha. Ha ha ha. Hoo hoo hoo. Hee hee hee. What would happen if they ever stopped laughing altogether? Nick hesitated, startled by his own question. Then he realized the answer. It was simple: Fisty would beat him to death.

CHAPTER TEN

NICK INHALED CIGARETTE SMOKE deep into his lungs and thought sadly of how much harm it was doing him. So young, so young, he thought with sympathy, letting the smoke foam out through his nostrils, why I must be harboring a death wish the size of a whale. Death available yet not imminent soothed his ego. He saw Fisty Fuller's rabbit punch under the arch of time and sneered, his pleasure lasting until he reached the concrete plateau where the offices of the Secost Theater were located.

When Nick entered the large square room in which they kept the adding machine and the safe, he heard Eddie Mack's voice from the inner office. "I'm surprised at you, Freddie," said Eddie Mack to the telephone. "Twenty-five hundred lousy dollars."

Nick hesitated in the middle of the empty room, then bent to pick up a piece of paper from the floor, trying to make it absolutely clear that he had no other reason for being there.

It was while he was in this position that he heard from the doorway a woman's voice of a peculiar lowness, yet clear and surprisingly powerful. "Could you tell me where Mr. Mack has his office?"

In the other room Eddie Mack said with as much indignation as he could afford, "There's no question of good money after bad."

Turning, the woman spoke into the hallway behind her. "Bring them in here, please."

Two men followed her into the room carrying between them a hat box, a vanity case and four matching morocco suitcases. They built a small mound of the luggage in the center of the room and left.

"Sure it's going to pick up," said Eddie Mack with the self-demeaning patience of an impatient man. If the telephone had had a neck, he would have strangled it, but in the meanwhile he kept his voice gentle for Frederic York.

"I'm Elfrida Mitchell," said the woman. She smiled. Her hair was a silver helmet and the lines were drawn deep in the flesh of her face, but she walked like a young girl.

She wore a linen dress, oat-colored, and a large deep-green emerald on her finger.

She was what remained of a beautiful woman who had been shedding her skin for nearly sixty years. Juliet and Joan, Millamant, Nora, Candide, Ophelia, Cleopatra, Lady Teazle— each one had taken something from her. Each one had left something behind.

Eddie Mack made the same explanation to his backer for the third time. Always it piled up on a single sullen fact: Frederic

58

York had never gotten the habit of losing money and did not intend to start.

Carefully overlooking the conversation on the telephone, Nick smiled at Elfrida again while they stood with the adding machine between them, waiting for Eddie Mack to finish. "I'm Nick West." Nick pulled out a chair. "Would you like to sit down?" Even as he offered the chair, he knew that everything had already changed, and he began to understand why he had never heard anybody speak of Elfrida Mitchell with indifference.

Elfrida considered the chair as though she might at some future date decide to draw it, then shook her head, but she made no move to go into the other room.

"All right, Freddie," said Eddie Mack, "all right." From the tone of his voice it was anything but all right. "I'll call you back at ten."

The phone hit its cradle with a crash, but Elfrida Mitchell waited a moment longer, not moving until Nick started to leave. Then she held out one hand in a mildly imperial gesture. "Don't go because of me."

Eddie Mack appeared on the threshold of the inner office, carrying his worries with him on his face; they hung there a moment longer while he stared at his wife. "Elfrida," he said, his eyes going to the six pieces of matching morocco and questioning them.

"I reserved a suite at the Florian, but there was a mistake; they expected me next week," she explained.

This time when Nick turned to go, Eddie Mack was the one who stopped him. "What was it? Did you want to see me?" To Elfrida he said, seeming grateful for the opportunity, "This is Nick West. I went to school with his father."

Nick waved the matter aside with one long square-boned hand. "Mr. Prager lost my Social Security number. It can wait until some other time."

They stood together silently in the middle of the room. Elfrida's face changed, shifting meanings so quickly that Nick could not follow what went on behind the eyes. "Gustave is dead," she said.

Eddie Mack shook his head. "He was an old dog."

Elfrida nodded. "Poor Gustave. He's the last of the dogs." Her face changed again, drawing on the sharp edge of bone and lip for a curious mockery. "I can't afford any more commitments."

"You're a young woman, Elfrida," said Eddie Mack severely.

She laughed and went to the window that overlooked the sea. "I closed the apartment. After all these years I cultivate a green thumb in Larchmont."

"Well." Eddie Mack shook his head in wonder and indignation. "I hadn't heard about that. But to leave the city, just cut it off, why that seems strange. You're no gardener. The good earth, rich loam, mulch. Mulch," he repeated and it was a curse. "The only time you went to the country was to rest, and you never needed much rest, Elfrida; you were always as strong as a horse." He paused as though regretting the violence of his words, but was swept away again before he could come to a full stop. "Hollyhocks! Sunflowers! Sweet William! Why, the city was your life. Van Cortlandt Park was Siberia. Beverly Hills was the other side of the moon. What's come over you, Elfrida?"

She smiled ironically, but behind the irony there was a certain pleasure in his excitement.

"My God," he cried, "you're putting yourself out to pasture like an old horse." Suddenly he was possessed of an extraordinary anger—as though he had been accumulating a number of small rages against this moment and was investing them all at once without any regard to the future. "It's ridiculous," he cried, "lace aprons and doilies and a quiet afternoon's tatting.

What are you playing now?"

Elfrida Mitchell studied her husband with an air of friendly interest. "Nothing," she said. "This is me. You're just not used to it."

Eddie Mack's eyes came back to the mound of luggage in the middle of the room. It was clear now why he was afraid of her: even in his moments of bitterest anger or surliest self-interest, she had the power to stir up in him contradictory emotions. "Elfrida," he said, a note of desperation in his voice, "just what are you trying to do?"

As though to give point to his question, Andrea Marston entered the room, talking. "Dinner," she said. "I can't eat but I'll watch. Somehow I've gained a pound." She discovered Elfrida Mitchell by the window. "Oh." She reached one hand out to Nick. "You, Nick," she said, thereby putting the room on notice that it was Nick's dinner she was preparing to watch.

Surprised by the readiness of Andrea's guile, confident it hadn't fooled Elfrida for a second, Nick said, "Ahhh, yes indeed, sure," and saw his stumbling confirm the cynical smile on Elfrida's lips.

Eddie Mack stepped between the two women in order to introduce them to each other. "Elfrida, Andrea Marston. Andrea, Elfrida Mitchell." He paused, added unwillingly, "My wife."

"How do you do," said Elfrida Mitchell.

"How do you do," said Andrea Marston.

In neither case was it a question.

Then Elfrida turned on Andrea a look of magical innocence so brilliantly transparent that it concealed nothing. And at the same time Nick had the astounding impression that in brief, bright flashes Elfrida could still revive the full beauty of her youth.

Perhaps Andrea received the same impression, for suddenly

she began to sulk. A moment later, with a sharp sense of his own disloyalty, Nick noticed that the girl had more nose than she needed, and he wondered why he had never noticed before.

Out of regard to yesterday's feelings, he finally took her to dinner at the Net and Trident, where she continued to brood in that comprehensive way she had, even her knees seeming to participate in a singular monolithic pout.

In the office of the Secost Theater, Eddie Mack was still trying to find Elfrida Mitchell a room for the night. After he had called every hotel in town, he knew he would have to do what he had expected to do from the beginning, and he invited her reluctantly to spend the night at his cottage.

CHAPTER ELEVEN

ELFRIDA MITCHELL and Eddie Mack had remained married for nearly twenty-five years under the most unfavorable circumstances.

At the time of their marriage Elfrida was thirty-five and had been in the theater for all but three of her years. She was famous, she was beautiful, she woke up in the middle of the night, half a lifetime gone, and she was scared. When Elfrida entered the theater the next day, still filled with the memory of despair, the first person she saw was Eddie Mack.

That night, after the performance, the greatest Juliet of the modern stage and her business manager were married by a justice of the peace on the outskirts of a small Pennsylvania milltown. Elfrida did not stop to ask whether she loved Eddie

Mack. When sometime later she finally did put the question to herself, she discovered that the answer was no.

Does this seem strange behavior in a woman whose business was the peculiar anatomy of passion? Not when you understood Elfrida: for as far back as she could remember, the truest part of her life had been lived onstage. Between performances she rested or studied. Between plays, like a hibernating bear, she was only half-alive. She had little need and less time for a private life, and at any rate such a life could not have been nearly as exciting or even as reasonable as the life she led onstage. For all her learning in love, she had little experience of it.

Still, in many ways she had made an excellent choice. A man who had saved for twenty years a rose thrown into a crowd by Sarah Bernhardt, Eddie Mack found it perfectly reasonable that the stage came ahead of him in Elfrida's plans. He was pleased to be her husband, but for years he accepted their marriage certificate as a kind of honorary degree—a distinction that was not to be presumed on too much. In addition, he was an excellent manager of other people's money although rather poor with his own.

Having met and solved the problems of her private life on her thirty-fifth birthday, Elfrida passed a number of succeeding milestones without a twinge. She worked constantly and with an expenditure of energy that would have wilted a prizefighter. When she didn't work she was bored, but she was never out of work long enough to realize this fully.

Possibly, if she had been more keenly aware of her own capacity for boredom, she would have behaved differently on her fifty-fifth birthday. On that occasion, with her flair for the dramatic observance of anniversaries, she announced that she was quitting the stage.

After fifty-two years in a profession which traditionally

kills people young, she was tired—the years had rushed upon her suddenly. She was rich, she was famous. What more did she want?

A great deal more, Elfrida soon discovered. She did not, it seemed, understand the rules of ordinary human behavior, for she had been raised on the fulfillments of dramatic logic. On a stage, if the conjunction of character and circumstance dictates suicide, the hero falls upon his sword. Elfrida could not get it into her head that offstage, oppressed by the same inevitabilities, he might merely pawn his weapon and flee. She lacked all caution.

First she tried to cure the boredom by drinking, then by books. Through it all she suffered greatly from dreams. Finally she took a lover and for a while the dreams ended, but presently they started up again, more horrible than ever.

Eddie Mack was angry. Elfrida could not understand it, for he himself had had many affairs during their married life and she had never complained. With the long periods of separation and the amiably businesslike pattern their marriage had taken, it seemed only natural.

But when Eddie Mack learned about the lover—an aging Shakespearean by the name of John Nichols who had been Elfrida's first Romeo—he moved out of the house. During that same week he scrupulously separated from their common funds the portion of the money that he considered to be his, and during the next three years he spent it on three plays. By the time he reached Secost he had lost all of his own money and a good deal belonging to other people.

He was indeed a desperate man; this was a fact Elfrida kept reminding herself of as she walked beside him toward his hotel.

He wore the black cashmere jacket with the cracked button at the sleeve, and under the jacket a transparent white shirt clung to his sweating torso. The collar of the shirt hung limply

65

over the top of the jacket. A maroon and black tie trailed from his neck like the pennant of a sinking ship. Eddie Mack made no concessions to the sun. They were enemies. His blistered nose bore witness.

How young he was, thought Elfrida in amazement; his hair was grizzled and scarce, his face was running to wrinkle, but the complaints that his eyes made were as direct and heartfelt as those of a child.

"What do you want, Elfrida?" he demanded fiercely, swinging the big feet in their suède shoes in great traveling arcs.

She decided not to tell him just then. "We're husband and wife," she said. For the moment, with the orderliness natural to her, she was inclined to tell him about the lover, whom she had found slightly ridiculous within a week, but a tardy sense of caution kept her quiet about that too.

"Well." He flung an arm out as though to brush away the beach from his sight. "That's a damn technicality."

She conceded the point with a nod and a shrug. "I brought you some caviar. It's packed in ice in the big bag."

"Thanks," he said, trying to restrain his greed. He ate caviar the way other men eat applesauce, but with more enthusiasm; Eddie Mack had princely tastes in everything.

"It's a three-room cottage, two bedrooms and a sitting room," he said.

He turned off the boardwalk down a ramp which led away from the water and she followed him toward a large clapboard castle with a red roof. This was the Hotel Florian. Behind it on a flowing green lawn starred with clover stood the cottages, a series of small red-roofed clapboard castles.

Eddie Mack's sitting room was a jungle of pale brown wicker. The chairs with their great spreading ruffs and finicky, fishbone ribs stood like the skeletons of an extinct species—the giant armachairo, companion of the sloth, playmate of the

66

mammoth. A long, lean coffee table crept along the floor like a crocodile.

"It seems very comfortable," said Elfrida, advancing to the center of the room.

"I don't know what your idea is," Eddie Mack warned her from the doorway, "but whatever it is, I won't go along with it."

She nodded meekly and this made him even angrier. "I mean that," he said, nodding his head as though he were swinging an ax.

"I know." She wished that he would offer her a drink. "It's quite hot," said Elfrida, feeling that this was as much of a complaint as she could permit herself. Under the cottage's low roof Eddie seemed to have grown two sizes. "Why don't you take off your jacket?" she asked. "You look terribly uncomfortable."

"Never mind." Going to the bank of windows, he opened them in turn and stuck his head out of the middle one. "Here come your bags now," he announced.

Suddenly a breeze, rising from the sea, riffled through the cottage. "Ah," said Elfrida, feeling it brush across her neck and forehead, and just as suddenly she felt the weariness that ran like wires through her legs from ankle to thigh.

Tipping the porter, Eddie Mack closed the door and turned to watch the pyre of brown morocco which had risen so quickly in the center of his room.

After three years he was still angry, thought Elfrida. If anything, angrier. As she watched his face, swept by intimations of disaster, she thought perhaps she should not have come after all. He was a great worn and sprawling boy, naïve about everything but money. There was danger in that innocence.

"Why are you so suspicious?" she asked reproachfully, realizing her mistake almost as soon as she made it, for instantly

67

his face began to swell with the thousand good reasons. "Oh, Eddie, Eddie," she said, "things change, people change. Can't you forget?"

But they both knew that she wasn't really asking him to forget, because Elfrida was convinced that he had nothing to remember. "Two old people like us," she said.

They ate in the dining room of the hotel under a giant crystal chandelier which shivered above their heads like an inverted Christmas tree. After dinner he left her, and that night for the first time in nearly a year, she drank herself to sleep.

In the morning when she woke up, the air conditioner had broken down. The slippery air lay heavy on Elfrida, but she remained free of it thinking, cool, cool, cool, and holding her body deliberately still. In a moment the Eskimos would start building their igloos, carving the blocks carefully out of solid air.

Feeling the life go pop, pop, pop inside her, she smiled amiably at the ceiling. Her right knee ached slightly, but her head was as clear as a syllogism. She was Elfrida Mitchell and she was tough. She drifted for a while in limbo, knowing nothing else beyond these two things. Then far in the distance she heard the waves at work and remembered where she was. She listened again but heard no sound in the cottage itself. She looked at her watch. Eleven o'clock. Eddie would still be asleep. He never got up before noon.

In spite of last night she'd gotten beyond the medicinal bottle, she thought; she drank now only for pleasure.

She felt the silk of her nightgown flow along her legs like water as she stood up. Taking her dressing gown from its hanger, she saw at once that Eddie Mack had not come home at all the night before. The door of his room was open, the bed still made.

Lighting a cigarette, Elfrida went to the bank of windows and stared across the lawn, where sprinklers did a silver dance

68

in the green grass. Why had she come? she wondered. But in the hard-headed clarity of morning, she knew exactly why she had come—because she wanted her husband back. It was so simple that she was suspicious. For twenty-five years their marriage had been as calm as a theorem, an arrangement in shades of nothing, a contract born to be breached, and now suddenly she clung to it. If it was simply marriage that she wanted, she could still find herself another man, another husband. So she told herself. And answered that she wanted a man who at least remembered how she was when she was young.

As she watched the dance of the sprinklers, it seemed that the sun was gaining on the water and soon the grass would burn. A dog ran across the lawn, reminding her of the dead dog, Gustave. Her meager ties were snapping one by one: Eddie Mack was now her major investment in reality.

While a great yellow butterfly wandered by on the wind that came from the sea, Elfrida turned away from the window, carefully put out her cigarette in an ashtray and went into the bathroom to take a shower. A half hour later she left the cottage. Still thinking about Eddie, seeing him now more clearly than she had in all the twenty-five years of their marriage, she walked across the lawn to the coffee shop, where she ate breakfast at the counter.

She arrived out on the boardwalk a little after noon. The sun was high, the wood was hot, the sand was a nicotine yellow—the faint odor of sun-tan oil hung in the air. Click, click, click went Elfrida's heels on the smooth pine boards. Seeing the marquee cast its shadow in the distance, she approached more slowly. Click . . . click . . . click. Elfrida, the walking machine, measured out her steps until she came within reading distance. Then she stopped and read. Eddie Mack presents. Et cetera. Et cetera. Turning she walked to the rail and stared out over the sea. Et cetera. Et cetera.

Great gray mother of us all, you are not for me, she thought, blue purple green white-feathered mother, wet, and she turned her back on the Atlantic, snubbing it. In her palms she felt the veined iron of the railing. Where had he spent the night? she wondered.

Across the boardwalk came a fat woman whose fat continued in tiny shivers after the rest of her had stopped. Then blue eyes, bald head, a tall man leaned forward like an unfinished bridge, blowing on his fingers as though they burned. He noticed Elfrida watching, stopped blowing, looked away embarrassed.

Sorry, thought Elfrida, not sorry. This was business. She put away people like a thrifty housewife canning vegetables. Gesture. Inflection. Wink. Pop it in the Mason jar. Her mind flashed back to Eddie Mack, of whom she had stored away shelf on shelf. How he looked at her. Everything you say will be used against you.

Suddenly Elfrida summoned Bartholomew Mitchell from the Mermaid Tavern, where he had tippled canary and the line iambic through England's green morning. Actor, swordsman, adventurer, friend of the poet who died with a dagger in his eye, Bartholomew brave, Bartholomew bold, Elfrida's favorite ancestor.

Nicholas West came out of the shadow into the sun, putting on dark glasses as he walked, all skin and bones and crucified look. What a waste of youth, she thought, giving it to an old man, but as he came closer, there was something about his face that she liked better. A scholar of woe. He seemed to take even the ground seriously the way he walked on it.

"Hello, Miss M-M-Mitchell," he said.

Did he always stammer? she wondered. Or nervous now. Tête-à-tête with the great. He treated her as though she were dead. "Good afternoon," she said, thinking longingly of Bartholomew, who was dead everywhere except in her head. "It's extraordinarily hot."

70

"Average," he said accurately. He raised a bony finger and pointed it at her shoulders. "You ought to be careful. You'll get a terrible b-b-burn."

Suddenly she understood what Eddie Mack was doing. He was pretending that she wasn't there. Pretty soon he'd believe it. Given enough time Eddie could sell himself anything. "Is this your first experience in stock?" she asked.

The skin shuddered along Nick's eloquent nose. His eyes filled with an amazement that made her laugh. "It's my first experience in anything," he said. He constructed a movement with his long bony hands that said his amazement all over again. "You know," he said, "if my father hadn't gone to school with Mr. Mack, I'd probably be jerking sodas." He made another one of his constructions in mid-air. "I did that once when I was in college. After school."

She smiled and turned away from the theater back toward the sea. "When you were coming out, did you notice Mr. Mack?" she asked.

Nick paused to think about it. His forehead wrinkled. "No." His bony fingers twitched. "I didn't see him anywhere all day."

Elfrida started to walk along the iron railing away from the theater. Fumbling through her mind for Demosthenes Mitchell, she picked him up, put him down. Lace at the wrists, steel-tipped tongue. Rapier wit, unkind. Funny. There were myriad Mitchells on the march up and down her head; maybe she should write a book. Poor Will, who had died crying the sky was on fire. Mad. Actors. Life. Alive. Pop, pop, pop.

She shifted toward Nick, who was walking by her side with a hobbled step, cutting his stride to fit hers. When he spoke to her, his Adam's apple bobbed like a cork on water. Was he afraid of her too? Was everybody afraid of her? He was in love with that big girl, that giant child, that immense, improbable beauty. Even in the confusion of the meeting she had

71

noticed that. He had a face that lit up like an electric sign, advertising his most secret intentions between those fanlike ears. And Eddie Mack? What about Eddie Mack? He had looked at the girl too, intentions buried under wrinkle and bone. Enough, she thought, enough, and stopped to face Nick, putting all of the interest she could summon into her eyes, all of her attention bent on him. "West?" she said. "Is your father Franklyn West?"

"You never heard of my father." Nick shook his head and sighed. "He's in Miami now." And as though to clarify this last point, Nick took a letter out of his pocket. "From my father," he explained, unfolding it, looking at the text, then putting it back in his pocket.

"He sits in a hotel lobby in Florida and tells me how to brush my teeth."

The sound of hammers rose in the air—chunk, chunk, chunk —driving twopenny nails into rich pine wood. The skeleton of a bandstand was rising beside the boardwalk where the Indians would welcome the first settlers of Secost to their shores.

"It's the two hundred and fiftieth anniversary of Founders Day," explained Nick.

Chunk, chunk, chunk went the hammers. Now Elfrida could smell the freshly cut pine. Leaning forward on the rail, she saw the golden sap drip along the two-by-fours. Across the beach people slept and ate and stood, staring, while seagulls skidded along the sky. The two carpenters who were building the scaffold dropped their hammers and went to drink a beer under the boardwalk. Turning her eyes carelessly into the sun, Elfrida was blinded. She closed her eyes, but beneath the lids the light sprayed like confetti.

Sally and John Ben Mitchell, she thought, then shook her head in annoyance. Mama and Papa. Let them rest. But they wouldn't stay still in her head as they rode the S.S. *Hesperides* outward bound. The sea was a navy blue, the sky was violet, the moon hung in the sky like an orange about to drop. New York had been a triumph, the whole tour a success, but Mama was crying.

"Do you want me to go back and look for Mr. Mack?" offered Nick suddenly. "If you waited here, it would take me only a few minutes."

Oh, my God, thought Elfrida. Smiling at Nick, she resolved to pay more attention to him. "That's very kind," she said, "but not necessary. We generally get together sooner or later." And she carefully changed the subject. "Is Andrea your girl?"

"What?" He opened his mouth slightly and his tongue moved speculatively along his upper lip. "My girl? Andrea?" His face twitched frozenly, then broke into mounds and valleys of sheer delight. Even as he rejected the idea, it pleased him. "Hardly. She's beautiful, though, isn't she? Really she has a remarkable voice too. But her greatest ambition is keeping her figure."

Nick, who until this point had had trouble speaking to Elfrida, now could not stop. He rushed on desperately as though, having at last discovered the secret of speech, he was afraid that he might forget it. "Really," he said, "in a way she's not very intelligent." He removed his sunglasses and polished them anxiously against the front of his shirt. "No," he said, "that's not true either. She's got brains, she just doesn't use them." He put his glasses back on his nose, but was still not pleased with the accuracy of his analysis.

Nodding a blanket agreement, Elfrida restlessly returned to Sally and John Ben Mitchell, who tossed beneath an orange moon. Off and on for over fifty years, Elfrida had heard the flap and crack of the wind, the rigging creak, the crazy bird shriek, while Sally and John Ben stood black against the rail as though cut out of the sky with a sharp embroidery scissor. Elfrida had wept her childhood away dreaming of their name-

73

less sorrow and now, a little impatiently, she put it aside. Thinking of Will Mitchell, poor Will, the man who made Regency London laugh. Will, anonymous, in the doctor's chambers, seeking relief from the barbarous melancholy which oppressed him. The listening ear, the watching eye, the probing finger, the head that shook, the beard that wagged, the gravity medical, the decision doctoral. There's only one cure for you, sir. See Will Mitchell.

Elfrida shook her head. It was an old story; they told it about all the clowns.

That was the last trip Sally and John Ben Mitchell ever took together, because he abandoned her in Paris, leaving her not for one woman, but for all women. Even at this time, under the Secost sun, Elfrida found the memory painful. Once it had been unbearable.

She turned swiftly to Nick, whose eyes were in darkness behind the glasses. His black hair, twisted by the ocean breeze, rose like a crop of devil's horns. His lips were anxious. Laughing suddenly, she put her arm through his. "Come," she said, walking, "it's too hot to stand in one place."

And as she walked, she felt her strength again—so strongly this time that she felt a moment's pity for Eddie Mack.

CHAPTER TWELVE

ALTHOUGH Elfrida stayed in the cottage the rest of that day and the following night, Eddie Mack didn't show up at all, but on the second morning, while she was asleep, he stole into the building to remove a dozen shirts, six neckties, two pairs of slacks, underwear, socks and a sport jacket. When she woke up and saw what had happened, Elfrida locked the balance of his wardrobe in a closet, and settled down to wait.

Meanwhile the life of the company continued to bubble like an alien stew under the Secost sun. Bert Wishingbird, a young male dancer who had been keeping a secret from himself all his life, even to the point of marriage and two children, finally, unwillingly, sinkingly, but with an overwhelming sense of relief, admitted what he had known all along and went to live with Tony George. Fannie Williams, the wardrobe mistress, finished a banquet cloth with napkins which she had been embroidering for nearly six years and wondered what to start on next. Twenty-three girls fell in love with sixteen boys. Thirty-two boys, including at least half of the sixteen, discovered that they were in love with Andrea Marston. Margherita Hill, star of *Naughty Marietta*, made up her mind at last to divorce her husband. Barton Hughes, bass baritone, looking out to sea, decided that as soon as winter came he would learn how to ski, speak French or play the flute.

Nick West grieved for his father. He was six feet three, twenty-three years old and weighed one hundred and seventy-five pounds. Although given to bone and awkward length, he was actually quite strong and agile. He had flown sixty-three missions in combat aircraft. And still he mourned his father's absence with an unreasonable, unreasoning and largely unadmitted grief. It may seem ridiculous—and possibly it was—but Jake West was his family: father, mother, brother, sister. This was the only human closeness he had ever known except the crew of his plane. So he grieved in a dumb, dim, secret way, while all of the strains of war which he had stood so surprisingly well at the time came back to haunt him. He dreamed unrelentingly of bombing, burning, fire, death and disintegration. And on all sides he was surrounded by Fisty Fuller, for it turned out that the only difference between *The Student Prince* and *Naughty Marietta* was that in one Nick was beaten as a valet, in the other he was beaten as a pirate.

Without warning on the third night of the second week in Secost, Fisty introduced a new item of assault as a kind of counterpoint to the aria "Ah, Sweet Mystery of Life": he caught Nick in the solar plexus with an elbow, tripped him with a cutlass as he bent over and kicked him in the rump as he fell. Heh, cried someone from the audience. Then a halfhearted ha, ha, ha, hoo, hoo, hoo—the forced laughter of obligation. Nick jumped up but the action had passed him by. Marietta was advancing toward the footlights, head thrown back, voice swelling in her throat. A hush fell over the audience, the orchestra crouched to leap on the opening measures of the song and all about Nick actors froze into scenery. What could he do? He let the moment go by. But his sense of outrage continued to grow all night, until at eleven-fifteen he went to Fisty's dressing room.

He pushed open the door without knocking and surprised Fisty at his dressing table, where, stripped to his pirate pants, he rubbed skin food into his plump cheeks. "Yeah?" said Fisty, scowling at the mirror.

Nick discovered that his complaint was too complicated to be put into a sentence. He couldn't say that his father had fled to another coast, or that Andrea Marston stayed away from her room. He could not complain that his nights were ravaged by dreams. "Th-th-this time you went too far," he cried.

Fuller continued to spread the skin food upward past his eyebrows. His heavy shoulders hunched forward over the table, and the muscles moved menacingly in the thick arms. His face, reflected in the mirror, was curiously bare as though he had not yet decided what expression to put on it.

"Wh-wh-what do you say?" demanded Nick, cursing himself for a stutterer, while Fisty Fuller continued to replenish his skin with oils essential to its health.

Two steps brought Nick into the center of the room, where he stopped and stared down at a large mole on the back of Fuller's neck. "Wh-wh-what do you say?" he said.

"Try some skin food," suggested Fisty, pushing the jar along the table top. "It's imported from France."

"Listen." Nick bent a little from the waist and touched Fisty's shoulder. "Don't try to change the subject."

Fisty slid his shoulder out from under the hand. "Cool off,

kid," he said thoughtfully, pumping his right arm until the muscle stood up like an indoor baseball. For a moment they both studied it. "What's grabbing you anyway?" inquired Fuller with that air of intense innocence which seemed to spread even to his strawberry-shaped nose.

Nick, having been bilked of his rage in the same way before, hastily advanced another step into the room.

"It's only fair to warn you I'm a student of boxing," cried Fisty, starting to rise.

As Fisty arranged his arms in the classic posture of defense, Nick, who hadn't known up to this point what he was going to do, hit him and Fisty fell over into the dressing table, shattering the mirror and snapping a spindly wooden leg which had stood in the same place for nearly half a century. Startled by the extent of the destruction for which he was responsible, Nick stared down in amazement at the fallen comedian. He noticed the blood gushing from Fisty's nose, he saw the deep scratch the mirror had made along the cheekbone. He discovered, as though for the first time, the gray hair, the bald head, the grandfatherly paunch.

He went quickly to kneel at Fisty's side. The comedian's eyes were closed tight. Grabbing his arm, Nick tried to pull him out of the wreckage, but without opening his eyes, Fisty pushed him away. "I'm trying to help you," said Nick.

Fisty opened one eye and, seeing the blood smeared on his chest, closed it again. "Go away," he said. One hand reached up to touch the bloody chest. He sighed.

"I'll get a doctor," offered Nick. "I didn't realize I hit you that hard."

This time Fisty opened both of his eyes. "You got a punch like an old lady," he said disgustedly. "I slipped." He sat up, shedding silver powder as he rose. "You hit me while I was sitting down," he claimed, beginning to poke his chest with one cautious forefinger.

78

"I think all the blood's from your nose," said Nick helpfully. "I'll dampen a towel."

Fisty Fuller groaned with rage. "Florence Nightingale," he cried, swinging one arm in wild rejection.

Nick stood up. "I didn't mean to hit you," he said miserably. He started to explain this all over again, but gave up in the middle and ran out the door.

When he reached the boardwalk, a breeze from the water, touching his forehead, made him tremble. He raised his hand to his forehead; it came away dripping. Suddenly he was conscious that sweat poured from every part of his body like some giant act of tears. Forgetting the provocation that had led to the punch, beginning to walk swiftly through the neon-colored night, he thought only of what Fisty Fuller had looked like, gray-headed, bloody and babbling amid the wreckage of his table.

When he passed a bar, he stopped for a drink but could not wait for a second. Down the boardwalk, he repeated this procedure a number of times at a number of bars, drinking, racing and drinking again, until at last his heart became quiet and he felt the weariness flow through his body like warm blood.

Without warning he was hungry. He looked up and before him in the sky loomed a great red haunch, across which had been written in green neon, The Steak Pit.

He went inside, making a path through green sawdust, and sat at a plain wood table. When a girl came to take his order, he gave it quickly without consulting the menu. He thought that the waitress looked at him strangely, but, although at any other time he would have given this his closest consideration, now he thought only of the steak. When he finished it, he asked her to bring him another.

"Really?" she said, examining him with what appeared to be delight. "Really?"

She stared at him, brown eyes swelling, her face thin and

curiously delicate, her body work-strong inside the green uniform. She wasn't pretty, but she was something much more —admiration incarnate. "You're from the show," she said.

He nodded. Ochi chorniye, ochi yasniye. In his whole life nobody had looked at him like this. For a moment he wondered if she were mad. Dilated pupils, he thought, but quickly dismissed the idea. Breasts like a queen, he thought. "Yes," he said.

"I saw you," she said. "Twice. The last time I was in row M."

He smiled at her amiably, finding new pleasures in the delicate face and supple body.

"Did you like it?" he asked.

She nodded. Her pink tongue flicked in and out of her cherry lips. "I love music," she said. "I used to sing in my cradle." Moving closer, she put down her order pad. "You're the first actor I ever knew," she said and went away to get the steak.

When she returned with it, she stood by silently to watch him eat. "I get done in half an hour," she told him.

It was as simple as that. Walking home with her through a rustling labyrinth of back streets, he thought that she was like a child and this made him uneasy, but her admiration was irresistible. "Where do you come from?" he asked her under a poplar tree.

"Oh," she said, "why . . ." Her voice trailed off. She seemed to be unable to concentrate on anything but him. "Oh." She made an effort. "Springfield." One careless hand pointed out beyond the poplar tree as though this might fix the Springfield she meant. "A long time ago. My family just kind of came apart. Seven kids. I go from job to job."

She did not make this in any sense a complaint, for there was a curious serenity to her. She looked on Nick with visible pleasure. "I like a tall man," she said. "My name is Claire."

Nick wasn't used to women on any terms, but most of all he was not used to them as sources of admiration. Now, befuddled by the bourbon he had been drinking, he strenuously turned his mind to the question of what she was up to. Suddenly he suspected her of a vast roster of crimes, some of which had been obsolete for a hundred years, and if he could have thought of a presentable excuse for leaving, he would have done so.

When they reached the front porch of the tall wooden house where she boarded, Claire made him take off his shoes. "Mrs. Collins is very fussy," she said with a note of approval in her voice. "She's been married three times."

Mrs. Collins's boarding house was a large building with a seafaring look. A great balustered quarterdeck fronted the second floor. Lofty crow's-nests peered into the sky at four corners. You had the feeling that Mrs. Collins had only to break out canvas to set her house in motion.

The front hall was lit by a bulb the size of a chicken egg set high in a carved and gilded ceiling. When you stood still, small sounds of life came to you from every part of the house. Beds squeaked, sleepers groaned, floors creaked, pipes whistled, snores rose to uneasy crescendos. Climbing the circular staircase that led to the second floor was like playing an organ with your feet.

There were people asleep everywhere—in the drawing room, in the parlor, behind canvas curtains in alcoves under the stairs. Claire and Nick stole through their midst like spies in an enemy camp until at last they reached her room above the eaves.

It was a room designed for the act of love: you stepped from the threshold right into bed with no place in which to hesitate or premeditate. When Claire closed the door, the room was dark except for a trickle of moonlight.

Claire, who had spent much of her life in her own company,

was not disturbed by silence, and during the next half hour she spoke only twice. On first entering the bed, she whispered in a tone of wonder, "An actor." Sometime later she said the same words again between a gasp and a sigh.

Then she was asleep.

Presently the moon shifted and stripped the darkness from her face and body. The sweat rolled like pearls between her breasts. Listening to the deep, contented roar of her breath, Nick was struck by an extraordinary sense of the life which was inside her. He put one hand out and felt it beating in her wrist. He saw it shudder in her rib cage, pluck at the seal of her eyelids, murmur in her lips. He heard it beat like a tom-tom deep inside her.

Rolling over on his back, he stared up at the rough timbers supporting the roof. In tribute to the bourbon he had been drinking, Mrs. Collins's house rolled slowly from left to right and back again. With outstretched fingers he trolled for his pants in the space between the mattress and the wall. When he found them, he raised his legs in the air and pulled on the pants. He stood up in the hallway outside, while Claire still slept undisturbed in the moonlight. Wanting to say something vale-dictory, he could think only of *amo, amas, amat*, which didn't seem to fit the situation, so he closed the door and stole down through the sleeping house into the street.

He had forgotten his shirt in Claire's attic, and his hand ached where it had hit Fisty Fuller's nose, but he felt oddly content. What next? he wondered, knowing he had the secret of life clearly within his grasp and would be ready to define it as soon as he had a little more time.

In the hotel, he crossed the shadowy lobby—past the clerk who slept at his desk, past the elevator, up the stairs, into his room. Within five minutes he was asleep, but several hours later he was awakened by a knocking on the door.

"Who is it?" he called out of a dream.

82

The answer that came through the door was garbled by wood and rage.

"What?" cried Nick.

A fist pounded, the doorknob rattled. "Grahhh," said the voice. "Come on out and I'll kill you."

It was Fisty Fuller, on fire with whiskey and humiliation. Nick said nothing.

"You can't stay in there forever," roared Fisty. "Come on out and I'll kill you."

CHAPTER THIRTEEN

AT TWO IN THE MORNING the Angel of Death came and stood beside her bed.

"Elfrida Mitchell," he said.

When she opened her eyes, she saw that the room was filled with large black feathers from the center of which came the voice. Elfrida knew immediately who it was. "What do you want?" she demanded, quickly taking inventory of her body and finding heart, lungs, legs, arms, fingers, nose, toes, all well.

The angel gave no answer beyond the rustle of his sable wings.

"There must be some mistake," said Elfrida.

The angel consulted a list. "Miss Elfrida Mitchell," he read, "white, female, age sixty."

"I don't care." Elfrida shook her head. "I'm not ready."

"There is generally a good deal of misapprehension on this point," said the angel.

Could she be wrong? wondered Elfrida, and in her doubt she turned cunning, saying, "Three hours from now the sun will be up. Hot and quiet. Birds are rare in Secost."

"That's very interesting," said the angel politely.

"Feel my pulse," cried Elfrida. "My doctor tells me I have the heart and lungs a woman of twenty might envy."

"Ah, Dr. Jacobs. I could tell you stories about that man. . . ." In the angel's tone there was a note of professional condescension; nevertheless, he was somewhat shaken. "Let me concede for argument's sake that I am a trifle premature. You will grant that it is at best but a trifle."

Elfrida granted nothing.

"Why do you quibble so?" demanded the angel.

And Elfrida, hearing the petulance in his voice, took heart. "I'm Elfrida Mitchell," she said distinctly. "The Mitchells have died of wounds, drowning and disease—never out of courtesy."

The angel sighed and for a moment it was as though a hole had been let into the world and the wind was rushing through. "Mitchell," he said at last, consulting his list again, "two l's or one?"

"Two," said Elfrida coldly.

There was a great movement of feathers in the darkness. "Bringing the record up to date," the angel explained. He muttered softly, "Profession?"

"Actress."

"Name of present employer?"

"Retired actress," said Elfrida with some bitterness.

"Ahh." The angel scratched a note in the darkness. "Children?"

"None."

85

"Hobbies?"

"I used to drink."

"Really?" The angel was plainly interested. "You've given that up too?" Feathers rustled. More notes were made. Time passed. Finally the Angel of Death was ready to continue. "Husband still with you?"

"After a fashion."

"Lovers?"

"None of your business," said Elfrida sharply.

"Think of me as though I were your personal physician," suggested the angel. "Charities? Causes? Political offices?"

"None." The line that the inquiry was taking made Elfrida uneasy. "How many more questions are there?" she asked.

"Well." The angel reflected. "I think in your case the short form will do," he said, then cleared his voice and read from the record. "Retired actress, no children, no hobbies, no lovers, no good works. Husband's status uncertain."

"Now wait a minute." Elfrida sat up in bed. "Brooks Atkinson once compared me to Sarah Bernhardt. Why don't you put that in?"

"Indeed," said the angel. "Sarah Bernhardt?" And there was a pause so filled with inevitable conclusions that for a moment Elfrida thought she had no choice but to die. Solemn music echoed in her mind. A dark procession dead marched beneath a dome of light. Brrrum, brrrummmm. No, she thought quickly, no drums. A column in the *Times*. A passing shudder from her contemporaries. Eddie would buy a black tie. Having known the love of thousands, she would be memorialized in a Sulka cravat.

The hell with that, thought Elfrida.

"According to all principles of Anglo-Saxon justice, the burden of proof is with the prosecution," she declared. But then, suspecting that she had offended the angel seriously, she rushed on. "Actually I'm at the beginning of many things."

"You're sixty years old," pointed out the angel rather testily.

"I don't look it." Even in the darkness Elfrida managed to make herself beautiful.

The angel flourished his feathers disgustedly and said, "A woman's reasoning!"

Elfrida, who had never before considered the sex of angels, realized now that they were male. "I haven't forgotten about my mother," she said with open antagonism. "Every day I think about it a little." She paused, remembering. "Poor Mama believed that there was a curse on the family."

"There's a curse on all families," said the angel, whose point of view was getting darker by the minute. "Some families just keep better track than others."

Elfrida thought of her mother, deserted and dead inside of a year. After the desertion nothing had been important, not her daughter, nor her career, not living. She had received a hurt that invalidated everything—beauty, youth, talent. "I needed her," said Elfrida, "more than I ever needed anybody again and she was dead. It was a cruel thing."

"There are regulations governing these matters," answered the angel stiffly. "Cruelty does not enter in." His presence increased until it pressed back on itself from the walls, filling, suffocating, overwhelming. Elfrida's heart and lungs battled their enemy. "I should like to point out to you that you are not in your mother's position," said the angel with unutterable coldness. "You are neither young nor necessary."

Once again Elfrida had the feeling that she was undone, defeated by a dark dialectic, destroyed by a process Euclidean. Her lips separated and she expected them to say, "So be it," but instead she cried out fiercely, "I have things to do."

"Very well then," said the angel. His tone continued cold and the coldness grew as his presence dwindled with the sound of a hundred thousand feathers disappearing one by one. "I will return," he said in the whisper of a wind.

"So," thought Elfrida, feeling the perspiration turn cold on her skin. Her thoughts began to drift and waver, pleasantly, pleasantly, like a summer breeze wandering from here to there. "Sooooo." The *s* hissed, the *o* rolled along like a hoop. Elfrida slept.

Eddie Mack was having troubles of his own. He had taken up residence in the office above the theater and here he lived surrounded by bills, duns and threatening messages from Frederic York.

Eddie Mack sighed. If the hotels would come to his aid, the whole picture would change in a single night. He turned to Andrea, who sat on the bed examining her nails. "Am I boring you?" he inquired bitterly.

She looked up in surprise. "Why, no." She held out her nails for his inspection. "I'm trying to make up my mind whether I like this color," she said. "They call it Deep Ruby, but it looks more like ketchup."

Eddie Mack grunted and examined her speculatively. He had learned by now that the fact she was sitting on a bed could not be construed as an invitation. Indeed, his relationship with Andrea was proceeding a good deal more slowly than most people would have suspected. They had been paired off in everybody's thoughts for two weeks now, one in the city and one at the shore, yet they had never shared a bed.

Eddie Mack himself had some trouble believing this, but it seemed natural enough to Andrea, who, as a result of a peculiar encounter with a forty-three-year-old portrait painter, was convinced that she was superior to sexual desire. It was a difference, Eddie Mack decided, between two generations which scarcely had an alphabet in common. Passion was dead—killed by the installment plan. Love was going out of fashion along with so many things he had found pleasant.

"I feel sorry for you," he said, "all of you."

"All of me?"

"The accountants have inherited the earth." He swung one arm upward as though he were raising a torch. "Who'd ever drink champagne out of a slipper now?" he asked, aware that he was putting his case badly.

Standing up, he walked around the room. There was something about a bed in an office that bespoke hard times and desperate devices; it struck unhappy chords in his memory. "What the hell!" he said. "I'll bet you never heard of the Great Depression."

Why, he could scarcely pass an apple without remembering those nickel-niggling days, and yet in Andrea's eyes he might just as well have been telling of ancient Chinese dynasties.

Looking at the beautiful girl sitting on his bed, Eddie Mack was saddened, but his sadness never lasted. Optimism was his opium, self-deceit his horse. "God," he said, "with your talent you should be all on fire."

Andrea looked up. She liked to be told about her talent. "Why, what do you think I ought to do?" she asked.

"Ah!" thought Eddie Mack, feeling some of the fire in himself as he crossed the room in two strides. What should she do? he wondered. She had a magnificent body, a face of classical splendor, a considerable voice. When she stood on a stage, you thought how pleasant it would be to sleep with her and then turned your mind to more reasonable hopes. What was it? She was like a cabbage, all wrapped up in herself.

"Listen," he said excitedly, "wake up, stand up," and he began to tell her what her future could be if only she would do these things. For a long time she seemed a little surprised and perhaps even embarrassed by his excitement, but, as it continued to grow, she was infected by it. She had a natural appetite for success. If she had not been too exclusively preoccupied with herself, she might have become a great courtesan. She jumped up from the bed and her voice was like a

89

cello. "Famous," she cried, "it would be so wonderful to be famous."

When dawn finally broke, a large blue bird which had wandered out to the beach from Rumson burst into a strange, wild, chuckling song and Elfrida Mitchell, hearing it, smiled in her sleep.

CHAPTER FOURTEEN

WHEN ELFRIDA WOKE UP on the morning after the angel's visit, she was a rumor, a memory, a myth—alive only by an oversight which had nearly been corrected.

She had been created by Shakespeare and Shaw and Sir Arthur Pinero. A tardy fiction of Aristophanes', a bold stroke of Ibsen's, for three years running she had been the major manifestation of a playwright by the name of Arthur Bourke Smith.

She had lived in the eyes of an audience, she had existed in their ears. Now she was a sight without an eye to be seen in.

She was defenseless against the angel.

And so on a hot summer morning in her sixtieth year Elfrida began to make herself up all over again. She had built people before, bit by bit the way the coral grows, but previously there had always been collaborators.

Where did you start? She looked at her hands. Long and slender and infinitely cunning. They bent, turned, touched; they danced at the end of her wrists. They could work, play, make love. When there was nothing to do, they would sit absolutely still.

That was the kind of character to make, she thought. Classical, noble, and neat. Complications would arise of themselves. Neuroses would accumulate like barnacles.

She jumped out of bed, already pleased with the morning. Four great walls and a roof. She could add the rooms later.

En route to the shower she began to sing "The Bell Song" from *Lakmé*, but quickly abandoned it in the management of the six valves which the Florian supplied its patrons.

She would be good, she thought while her teeth chattered. A warm thought for a cold shower. The good Elfrida supplied her own warmth.

But to be good you had to be good to somebody. Only saints and little children could be good alone. She quickly silenced the ten thousand needles, got dressed and briskly left the cottage. Perhaps she should be good to Eddie Mack, who was, after all, her husband. But he struck her as being a particularly difficult case and better put off until later.

It is harder than you might think to do the smallest bit of good to anybody, even after you've made up your mind that you ought to. This fact was particularly surprising to Elfrida, who had never been faced with the problem before. She had, of course, always been a generous contributor to charities, but this is one of the easiest forms of love, although, unless you are a foundation, difficult to maintain for any period of time.

She had spent her life doing the only thing in the world that she wanted to do or could even think of doing, and as a delightful yet still incidental by-product of this activity she had given people delight, gratification, pleasure, love, perhaps a little courage. Samaritanism had played no part in it at all.

On her way past the tulip bed, she smiled strenuously in the direction of two little girls who were mining the flowering bulbs. At breakfast she left twice her ordinarily generous tip. But these things were trifles and the good Elfrida knew it.

Leaving the dining room she went down to the boardwalk to consult with the ocean. As she leaned against the iron pipe of the top rail, she saw the ruffled seamark on the beach, the last groping touch of the blue-green-silver ocean. The salt smell was in her nostrils.

Elfrida went down the steps that led to the sand, removed her shoes and walked to the start of the water. Standing there on the very edge of the country she had traveled from end to end during all of her life, she felt a swelling nostalgia for a past she had never known—clipper ships and Conestoga wagons, deep green woods and Ben Franklin, Abraham Lincoln, Parson Weems, Thomas Jefferson, Sitting Bull. Suddenly she was in love with Grover Cleveland, Kalamazoo and the Whiskey Rebellion.

The waves licked her toes.

She was enamored of Oliver Wendell Holmes, Molly Pitcher and Huckleberry Finn, the sequoia forests, the ice-blue lakes, the fruitful plain. Speckled trout. The mallard duck. The grizzly bear. Central Park. Harvard College. Susan B. Anthony. Infinitely various. Variety was the thing the label pasters never understood, the beauty truth drudgery falsehood excitement cruelty ugliness north south east west—much to love, much to hate.

The cold waves lapped at her ankles and she danced back gravely out of the way. Across the horizon the fishing boats returned her bow.

Suddenly she thought about the N.R.A. with its blue eagle, Iron Pants Johnson, Franklin Delano Roosevelt. She had wept on a Republican the day that he died. They swung their picks and invented the boondoggle. Doggle. In the distance the horizon doggled. Elfrida doggled back.

The first banana peel of the day slid down a wave. Wonders of the deep. The swift banana leads a sluggish orange.

What had happened to the good Elfrida? She paraded solemnly backward through the sand like an Anglo-Saxon queen. At the foot of the stairs she tapped the sand off her feet and put on her shoes. Along the beach the people ran and stood and slept worshipfully under the sun.

The good Elfrida, climbing the stairs, began to walk toward the theater. She passed the Gypsy Tea Room, the Pokerino, the Louis XIV Auction Chamber, the Home of the World's Biggest Hot Dog, the Cameo Custard Parlor, Ski-Ball Alley. In front of the Palace of Skill stood Nick West, watching a nine-year-old boy toss pennies at a target.

"Too much elevation," said Nick.

The boy stepped back and nodded. The next time he threw the target buzzed.

"There," said Nick. A small shine of pleasure entered his dark brown eyes.

"Hello," said Elfrida. Why, yes, hello, she thought, and her eyes, too, began to shine as she looked on that strangely rueful face. Samaritan armies could stay busy here from morning until night.

"Hello, Miss Mitchell." His Adam's apple was an instrument of expression as fluent as an extra tongue; now it bobbled a worried greeting.

He was wearing a dark blue sport shirt from which his arms dangled bonily.

"How is Andrea?" she asked, knowing what the question sounded like and regretting it the minute it had passed her lips.

"I don't know. She doesn't talk to me. She says I'm juvenile." His lips took on the petulant disdain that Elfrida had seen on

94

Andrea's. The long bony fingers of his left hand did a kind of dance of rejection.

Suddenly Elfrida saw Andrea's head-to-ankle pout. She smiled. "The taste for older men doesn't last," she assured him.

Turning together, they started to walk down the boardwalk toward the theater. Nick put one hand through the air in a slow roll, flew it on its back, then returned it in embarrassment to his pocket. Wanting to confide in Elfrida, he fumbled among his memories for a suitable gambit.

"When I was in the air force, my pilot's name was Timothy Timothy," he said. "His father was a drunk from one of the finest families in the South. A man with a singular sense of humor even when sober. He was the family bum and when he died Tim took his place. At twenty-two they had him holed up in a little town somewhere on a kind of pension. All he had to do was stay out of sight of the family. He drank a little, hunted a little. Once he had a wife, but she left him. Then the war came along and Timothy enlisted in the air force. It turned out he was a genius at flying airplanes. He flew a hundred and fifty-six missions without a scratch."

Nick examined Elfrida's face. She was listening carefully. "I was with him the day he left the army," he said. "He was going back where he'd come from, and all of a sudden he looked as though his clothes were too big." Nick sighed. "Timothy Timothy. He was like my brother. I'll bet he's busy drinking himself to death right this minute."

Nick turned to Elfrida, his Adam's apple signaling wildly. "I hit Fisty Fuller," he said, "made him bleed." And seeing that she still didn't understand, Nick explained, "I knocked him down in his dressing room after the show."

"But why?"

Nick shook his head. Rubbed it. Cracked his knuckles one by one. "You've never seen the show. That's Fisty's act. He beats me." Suddenly Nick was ashamed of this complaint which he made incessantly to himself. "It's not so much that I mind being hit. When I was a kid, I used to average a fight a day because I was so tall it was a challenge to all the pugilists in the neighborhood."

Elfrida was sure now that her instinct had been right: this was a young man gloriously in need of help. Although he was trying to hide it, his hands were trembling.

"I shouldn't have hit him," said Nick. "An old man with blood on his nose." And the really shameful part began to press to the front of his mind. Once or twice he managed to push it back, but then it came on again. "You can imagine what he'll be like now," he said bitterly.

Putting out one hand, she touched his right elbow with her fingers and felt the bone tremble. "*Coraggio*," she said with more sharpness than she had intended.

He stepped away from her. "I'm not afraid of being hit. I just don't want to be humiliated."

She bowed slightly in acknowledgment of the distinction. "Misfortune to a comedian is what a violin is to a violinist. In Fisty Fuller you've got all the world's woe wrapped up in a pair of pants and a shirt. With a start like that who knows where you can go?"

"I've got a pretty good idea," said Nick grimly.

But he was strangely willing to be convinced.

CHAPTER FIFTEEN

WHEN FREDERIC YORK was nine years old, he learned the importance of money by studying his father, a gently improvident grocer who in early middle age finally completed the ruin of the family business and went to work as a clerk in a dry-goods store. The boy carried the knowledge with him calmly enough from his ninth through his nineteenth year, at which time, having married the daughter of a minor hair tonic manufacturer, he entered the commercial world under his father-in-law's reluctant guidance. Within two years young Frederic had scrapped the hair tonic and its proprietor and laid the foundation of the Lovalee Cosmetics empire.

Working fourteen to eighteen hours a day, he converted beauty from an accident of birth into a national obligation. In five years he was rich; in ten years there was hardly a home that lacked a Lovalee woman (What is life without a Lovalee wife?) and Frederic York was many times a millionaire.

Throughout his long career familiarity with money had never bred any contempt for it; when Eddie Mack went into the red for the third successive week, Frederic York's sense of outrage was as keen and youthful as it would have been thirty years earlier. Leaning across Eddie Mack's desk, he said quietly, "Close it down."

The fluorescent light sparkled from his sapphire cuff links and glowed in the rich black silk of his suit. The hand which he rested on the desk was a threat spelled out in fingers.

"Why don't you give it a little longer?" said Eddie Mack soothingly. "The season's still young."

Frederic York turned and went to the cell-like window. The back was as neat as silk could make it, the face was pale with rage.

"You've mentioned that before," he said, coming back to the desk. "Do I look like a fool? Every week you've got more to recover and less time to recover it." He used his fist on the desk like a gavel. "Close it down," he ordered.

Eddie Mack, who had developed a certain tolerance toward York's threats, heard the difference now, saw it in the clenched right fist and felt himself sinking, sinking, sinking in deep financial waters. For a moment he clung to his desk as though it might save him; his mind slipped away from the irrefutable fist.

The smell of cinnamon rose from his grandmother's kitchen. Safety. Refuge. One night in Hell's Kitchen he had outrun twenty boys from a hostile block who would have killed him if they had caught him, their mouths open as they ran, their noses tilted forward like spears. They had left him with a cobblestone scar which he still carried on the back of his head. Danger. Abrasions. On the edge of Belleau Wood a piece of

98

shrapnel had permanently marred his shoulder. Far down on his right side ran the jagged line of an appendectomy. Once he had missed by two minutes a Dallas-bound plane that blew up in mid-air.

He had survived mumps, measles and his mother's displeasure. He had been dunned, subpoenaed and evicted, and had accepted all of these things cheerfully as the price of liberty.

Now.

Now Frederic York.

If disaster had chosen a more reasonable form, it is possible that he might have accepted it, but he had survived too much to give in easily now. His mind whirled. An incredible fluency of thought came over him and even before it had found a shape he was filled with the awareness of his own ingenuity.

Then the idea was there. Simple. Beautiful. As undeniable as a certified check. Suddenly he was quite happy.

"You're right," he said. "If the summer were simply the end of it, it might not be worth while to continue. Even though the receipts have gone up steadily." He paused to let this concession take effect. "But of course I have in mind something much more permanent. A year-round repertory theater. It could be a gold mine."

Frederic York raised an eyebrow. He had been known to chill a whole director's meeting with this gesture, but it didn't cool Eddie Mack's ardor in the slightest. "Look at it this way," Eddie said quickly. "The only thing that's held us back so far is the slowness of the hotel owners in co-operating. A permanent repertory would be a boon to them, especially during the winter months when they don't have the sun and the water. They'd have to co-operate. Common sense would make them."

York had returned the eyebrow to its normal resting place. "You never mentioned this before," he said.

"I had to make sure the market was here," answered Eddie

Mack. Market, he thought, now there's the word. Open Sesame!

Frederic York sat down. "I like enthusiasm," he said thoughtfully. "I appreciate it." For a moment he seemed tired and even a trifle envious. "I myself am an enthusiastic man," he added, tapping his chest lightly. He took a cigar from his pocket and carefully pierced the end. "When the facts justify it."

The two men sat quietly in the heat-heavy room while York lit the cigar and sent a few experimental spirals of smoke toward the ceiling. "Facts," he repeated, "facts," and paused. "After thirty years in the traces, sometimes a man needs a change. Diversion. I thought this might be it. Refreshing. But not unless it's sound. I'm not interested in anything that isn't sound."

Now Eddie Mack lit a cigar of his own and they sat together, quietly blowing smoke like a pair of weary old sidemen thoughtfully searching out a melody.

In a moment of sympathy which needed some kind of confidence for its fulfillment, Eddie Mack said, "Did I tell you that my wife is in town? Elfrida Mitchell."

Even as he said it he heard the note of pride in his voice and was startled by it. His wife, Elfrida Mitchell. Was he still trading in ancient vanity? Angrily he hoped that York had never heard of her.

"Ahhh," said Frederic York, exhaling smoke. His lips fondled damp tobacco. He had heard of her and the memory made him think of his own wife, the daughter of the hair tonic manufacturer, to whom he had been faithful as though by oversight for three decades. "Ahhh," repeated Frederic York. Poor fat Blanche. What she didn't know had continually hurt her, and she was convinced beyond contradiction that he spent his days in wild bursts of infidelity. Childless. Talk, talk, talk. Poor Blanche.

Eddie Mack looked at his chronometer. "Show breaks in ten minutes," he said. "Would you like to eat?"

Frederic York consulted his own watch. "I always eat at seven-thirty. But I could use a drink. We can continue our discussion later."

"I'm meeting Charlie Miller and Danielle outside on the boardwalk," said Eddie Mack. "And Andrea Marston. Why don't we go down and wait? Around now there's always a nice breeze coming from the sea."

Leaving the office the two men descended the sequence of ramps which connected the various levels of the theater. On the balcony floor the halls were filled with music, swelling to a finale.

Spotlights placed on the corners of the marquee sprayed the boardwalk with light and overflowed onto the yellow sand. "Do you know I've gotten up at five-thirty in the morning every morning for as far back as I can remember?" said Frederic York thoughtfully.

The front runners of the audience appeared under the marquee—two quickstepping old ladies who had been garrisoned at the shore by their children. A fat man and a fat woman. A skinny man and a skinny woman. Then they came in fours, in eights, in sixteens, and finally like the legions of Rome in solid hundreds.

And yet there were not enough, for on that night, a Tuesday, Eddie Mack Productions lost exactly $562.47.

Eddie, who already had the figures in his inside breast pocket, looked out to sea where the lights of a fishing boat danced in the waves. When he was a boy, he had stood on the shore watching the steamers go up and down the Hudson. A day ago. A day and a night and here he was.

"Good evening," said Danielle in an obscurely Continental tone that fell on the ear like the pouring of rare French wines and the gleam of jewels in palace gardens. With a breath and a hesitation she could turn the simplest sentence into a mazurka. "Charles will be right out," she said.

Eddie Mack introduced her to Frederic York.

"I have observed Mr. York," said Danielle, the *s* in observe hissing softly, the *o* in York like an open door before the rolling *r*. Gypsy violins sang sweetly in her throat.

When Danielle inclined her handsome dancer's body toward you, you were not merely the recipient of a bow but the beneficiary of the most intense interest to which you had ever been exposed. Meeting her was an experience from which even the most modest men came away with new insights into their own charm.

"Miss Danielle," said Frederic York, acknowledging her bow with a courtly inclination of his weighty head as Charlie Miller crossed the boardwalk to join them.

"Charlie you've met," said Eddie Mack and York conceded the point with a half smile, hardly moving his eyes from Danielle, scarcely looking aside even for Andrea, who was the last to come—vastly beautiful in the colored night.

"I've made reservations at the Ancient Mariner," said Eddie Mack and the party moved off down the boardwalk toward Secost's best-known restaurant, which sat on a pier above the Atlantic.

Before they had gone very far, it was clear that Danielle and Charlie had been quarreling. Charlie seemed puzzled by it all. When he was not on the podium, he was frequently puzzled. Once he had been a child prodigy, but the years had taken that away from him, although more slowly than you might think. Because of his smallness he'd been able to hang on in short pants and embroidered silk blouses deep into his teens, well past his first shave and almost up to the day he started to smoke. Then overnight he had graduated into young manhood and mediocrity together, so that sometimes it seemed his whole life had been a steady decline from its fifth year.

"In Europe it is not like here," said Danielle as the head-waiter ushered them to a table overlooking the water. "A woman knows what she is born for."

"What's that?" asked Andrea suspiciously.

"To bring joy to a man," answered Danielle with a stern look at Charlie. "In Europe a woman longs to cook for the man she loves."

Charlie Miller sighed. Love had seemed to him a simple pleasure, enjoyed for a day or a season without any involvement in gourmet cookery or other domestic matters. Music was his wife. He had room left only for casual affairs.

Drinks were ordered and drunk. Appetizers. Entrees. Incidental beers and wines.

There were five people eating and drinking, but the evening belonged to Danielle and Frederic York. The food and the drink and the salt smell of the ocean filled them with life and subdued all of the others.

"You have never traveled abroad?" said Danielle.

Frederic York conceded that he hadn't, though only momentarily with regret, for in the next minute he knew that he would. Through the open windows the waves stood up like minarets, calling only to him. Paris, Venice, Jaipur—the world's fairest cities were beckoning. There he would find new perfumes and rare essences, he would discover the beauty secrets of the mysterious East. He would do all these things and he would do them on the expense account. Wiggling his massive shoulders under their black silk coat, he looked with pity on little Charlie Miller, who sat in his chair as though he had been exiled to it.

"Unless you have been in Paris in the spring, you have never been young," said Danielle.

"You're as old as you feel," said Frederic York a little sharply, looking down at the fist in which he so easily hid a Martini glass.

"Exactly." Smiling, Danielle swiftly spoke of a deposed king who had driven a chartreuse Hispano-Suiza across France at eighty-five miles an hour in order to bring her the first roses from his garden. "The whole car was filled with them," she said, "and he was such a little man. You could hardly see the king for the roses."

Danielle talked. The ocean moved. Charlie Miller drew sharps and flats on the tablecloth with his fingernail.

Eddie Mack and Andrea spoke softly to each other, unnoticed by the rest of the party.

At four o'clock when the manager announced that the restaurant was closing, York remembered what he had been discussing with Eddie Mack in the office of the Secost Theater. "Mr. Mack has an interesting idea," he said somewhat tipsily. "A year-round repertory theater in Secost. Now what do you think of that?"

"Lovely, lovely," said Danielle. There was rapture in her voice. "Lovely," she said again.

CHAPTER SIXTEEN

THE SMALLEST REHEARSAL in town was being held in Eddie Mack's parlor, where Elfrida and Nick were exploring *The Merry Widow*.

This, in case you have forgotten, is the story of the happily widowed Sonia and Popoff, the blustering, bumbling Marsovian ambassador to Paris who is charged by his government with keeping the lady's fortune in Marsovian hands. Popoff enlists the aid of Danilo, playboy prince and man about Maxim's.

In the meanwhile, Madame Popoff is being wooed by a young Parisian, Camille de Jolidon. When de Jolidon decides to disguise his liaison with the ambassador's lady by paying court to Sonia, Popoff is alarmed; he prevails upon his wife to charm the young man away from the widow. Madame Popoff, naturally, is delighted by the opportunity.

Toward the end of the second act, Popoff, beaming from concealment on the prospect of de Jolidon making love to his wife, explains the reason for his approval to Nish, the embassy messenger.

It was at this point that Elfrida and Nick entered the play, Elfrida in Fisty Fuller's role of Popoff, Nick as Nish.

When Fisty played the scene, he used Nick as a form of living punctuation. Kicked, he was a comma. Hit, he was a period. Kicked, hit, tripped and gouged, he served to underline a joke.

Although Fisty had hit him often enough before, there was a difference now; each kick came with a calling card—this is for you; each punch said remember me. Once Fisty had banged on his door and threatened to kill him. Now he met Nick on the street with frigid courtesy, but onstage he beat him for his private pleasure.

The good Elfrida set about changing all this in Eddie Mack's parlor.

First she played Popoff to Nick's Nish, bullying, blustering, filling her slender body with all of Fisty's derisive energy. Her fists were flails. Her eyes stared storms. When she moved, she carried the fat man's belly in front of her like a battering ram.

Nick stuttered, he stammered, he looked on her in amazement and dismay, for now he knew the truth: he was all the world's doormat, every man's favorite victim.

When she reversed the roles to let him understand what it felt like to be Fisty, the part suddenly seemed to shrink. Popoff popped no longer. Elfrida teased and tormented him, she struggled to release him from himself. "Damnit," she said, "forget Nick West. Who wants Nick West? Let him go hide somewhere deep down in Popoff."

Turning away in disgust, she stalked to the other end of the parlor. All right, thought Nick, the hell with it, I'll become a plumber.

Elfrida was coming at him again with a fierceness all her own. No Popoff, no belly, all Elfrida. "Shout," she said.

"What?"

She shook her head impatiently. "It's simple enough. Shout. Yell. Let's hear how loud your voice is."

"The manager'll come. They'll throw you out of here."

"If I don't worry, why should you?" She made no effort to hide her contempt.

He yelled.

She sneered.

He yelled again.

"I've heard better from a boy soprano," she said.

He bellowed now in a rage with her, in a rage with himself, hoping that the chief of police would come, summoning up the National Guard, the Regular Army, the whole wide world, let them all come and be damned. His face turned red, his throat hurt, his body shook.

"All right," she said, "now Popoff. Yell it. But loud this time."

And before he could recover himself, he was launched on Popoff, tearing the lines to shreds, making no distinction among the words, but not remembering himself either.

When he was done, she nodded. "That time you didn't know what you were doing. This time do the same thing but listen to it. And the hell with Nick West. We don't want him here."

He did it. He did it again and again. And now he saw something else happen. Nish was no longer what Nick had made him. In Elfrida's hands, in Elfrida's voice, he was simultaneously anxiety incarnate and a mocking spirit, beaten and yet unbeaten, on curiously confidential terms with an invisible audience across invisible footlights.

When Elfrida handed Nish back to Nick, the embassy messenger was armed. Blows that had previously crushed him ricocheted from a catastrophe-proof core as he invited you to laugh at his own misfortunes.

Nick didn't know exactly what Elfrida had done, but he had seen her do it and he tried to do it too, stumbling and fumbling in his eagerness even as he had previously in his despair. When at last Elfrida stopped him, his shirt had sprung loose from his trousers, lank black hair hung across his forehead, his bony chest rose and fell. "Sit down," she said. "I'll get you a drink."

"I'll be damned," he said, blowing smoke through his nose. "I've never been so tired in my life."

Elfrida glanced at him doubtfully. He sprawled wildly in the chair as though he were leading an assault on rest. There was a grin on his face. "What price glory?" he said.

Peck, peck, the shell was breaking.

Was she wrong? Was she awakening things in him that he would never have the capacity to satisfy?

She went to the refrigerator and took out an ice tray. Responsibility. Tilting a glass, she slid a cube of ice into the bottom. Serving strong spirits to minors was an offense in every state of the union. She slid a second cube after the first. It was like bringing a child into the world. If you brought them in, you had to bring them up. Responsibility doubled. Tripled. Quadrupled.

She started to cover the ice with Scotch. The hell with that, she thought. Blood was meant to circulate. Fret, sweat, be alive. You only get one chance.

"Ha," said Nick, stretching his legs and thinking of the surprise in store for Fisty Fuller.

"Skoal," said Elfrida as she handed him his glass and lifted her own. The ice cubes rattled like dice in the glasses.

To play the part of Prince Danilo, Eddie Mack had imported Brett Haverford—a man of moderate height and regular, rather pleasant features, whose chief talent was a singular flair for selecting small gifts and performing minor services. Coolly aware from the beginning of his career that he had almost no aptitude for his chosen profession, he had at a very early age determined to offend no one and he had consistently offered his courtesy and consideration to the famous, the infamous and the merely unknown. The living rooms of the world were strewn with his carefully chosen but inexpensive presents.

He had flourished in Hollywood for ten years on the basis of such thrifty largesse, becoming in this time a kind of *sub rosa* matinee idol. He played a hundred major roles in minor pictures. When you saw him on the street, he seemed as familiar as your own brother, but you could never remember who he was. Heads turned. Autograph books were offered tentatively and then feverishly consulted to determine his identity.

Eventually he was treated everywhere as a celebrity, although people still rarely knew accurately who he was. Headwaiters greeted him effusively. Porters on trains to and from Hollywood competed to do his bidding. Still unfailingly courteous, he accepted the apparatus of fame with the grace of a man to whom it was long familiar.

When the war came, he enlisted in the army and by the exercise of the same talents which had always served him so well rose to the staff of a distinguished and crotchety general; before long he was as well known in Washington and London as he had ever been in Hollywood.

It seemed that he had lost nothing by the translation into uniform, but in the end it turned out that he had lost everything. His fame, made up of innumerable minor appearances, could not survive five years of absence. His friendships had faded, his presents had been forgotten; he was forty-five years old and getting fat.

This debonair and elegant man, grown tender of his greatness, caused crisis after crisis in the Secost troupe. He pre-empted the dressing room of Agatha Bentley, the Merry Widow, and although ordinarily a sensible enough girl, she commemorated the event nightly by bursting into tears after every performance. He came to rehearsals late, missed all his cues and left early. He insisted on his star's prerogatives in ways so obscure that they could be identified only by the resentment they caused. He smiled, he bowed, he accepted homage from the empty air as he walked. On opening night he skipped three sides of dialogue set to music, throwing everybody but himself into wild confusion, from which they were saved only by Charlie Miller's impromptu adjustment of the score. Benny Wallace was reduced to incoherence, a state so unfamiliar that it doubled his rage. Charlie Miller, who lost weight at every performance, lost two extra pounds. The chorus, never knowing what new disaster it would be called upon to meet, walked among the bright lights of Paris with a gingerly air, sixty country cousins with their hands in their pockets.

But in all of Secost the man who resented Brett Haverford most was Fisty Fuller. Every twirl of Haverford's opera cape, the angle at which he wore his hat, the twinkling gold cap on his Malacca cane—the smallest of these things could raise Fisty's blood pressure twenty points. He took out his bank books and stock statements and read them for solace, but even that could not soothe him. Although not usually addicted to other people's troubles, he became Agatha Bentley's advocate, repeating the story of her wrongs as though they were his own.

But something else was in the air. On Monday it was obscure. On Tuesday it was plain enough to puzzle Fisty without giving him any clear indication of what was happening. On Wednesday the secret was out in the open. The private rehearsals with Elfrida were turning Nick, the perennial victim, into a boldly fearful imp who danced on the edge of adversity —a skinny human mirror who picked up the image of fat, blustering Popoff and reflected it into the audience at a wildly comic angle.

On Wednesday evening Nick heard the first laugh that he had ever consciously produced upon a stage.

It rose from the simple line, "Perhaps she doesn't mean any harm by it, your Excellency," which had never gotten a laugh before.

The difference now came from a glance, a hesitation, a confidential wiggle of the shoulders.

It was not a monster laugh, nor was it a mere titter. It started with a ha in the rear, a hee in the left center, a hoo hoo from somewhere in the middle, and it grew in the flicker of an eyelash into a solid guffaw.

Forced to stop to let it pass, for a moment Fisty couldn't accept its source; convinced that he must have done it himself unwittingly, he glanced down at his buttons to make sure they were all in proper order, then quickly searched the stage for a shivering wall, a slipping gown, a wandering dog.

It was none of these things. It was Nick. Fisty knew too much about the subject to deceive himself for long. "Harm— you jackass!" he shouted. "She's carrying out my instructions! I want you to watch her, and see how a woman can help her husband in the diplomatic service."

Once more the laugh belonged to Nick, to the sly acceptance in his angular stoop, the deferential twist of his hand, the nod of his head.

It was a bad night for Fisty. When he turned from Nick, what could he look at? Brett Haverford, tilting his way across the stage, showing his perfect teeth and tipping his hat that all the world might love him.

Nick came out of the Secost Theater feeling as though he had just discovered the key to the universe and had to confide it before he lost it.

He thought of Elfrida, but to tell the truth he was somewhat afraid of her. Life was in her like acid; it spilled over and burned what it touched. He had already discovered that well enough was never well enough for Elfrida.

Suddenly he was hungry and his stomach gave him a direction—back to The Steak Pit, where he found Claire among her tables, balanced on aching feet, carrying shrimp and steak and strawberry shortcake, the handmaiden of battle-weary kings.

When he sat down at one of her tables, she came to him with a pad flat in her left hand, a pencil poised in the right. Her uniform was green touched with white at the sleeves and collar. Her pencil was an Eberhard Faber No. 2. "Hey," she said softly when she saw him.

"I just finished," said Nick. "I came right over."

Putting the pad and pencil on the table, she leaned over to watch him more closely. "You look tired," she said. "You got rings under your eyes. You ought to eat more."

He touched her hand with a forefinger. "When do you get done?" he asked.

She looked at her watch, big and unbreakable in its steel case, swelling like an onion from a worn brown strap. "Not for another hour and a half."

"I'll wait. If you want to, you can bring me something to eat."

She picked up her pad and pencil.

"You choose it," he said.

She flushed with pleasure. Her lips were swollen under the lipstick. Her eyes were filled with an admiration so undiluted that it forced him to look away. "Hey," she said again, even more softly.

She brought him food that was carefully selected for its nutritional value and two bottles of beer. The beer, she told him, was best of all; it did for grown men what milk did for babies.

By the time she was done, at one o'clock, he was sleepy with drinking and eating, and his moment of triumph had passed, but it revived when the sea air touched him. He wanted to tell her what had happened in the theater that night, but didn't know where to start. He examined the sea, he examined his shoes, he stretched his long arms above his head. "When I was twelve years old," he said, "I was only a half inch shorter than I am now and I weighed twenty-five pounds less."

"You're a nice height," she said, moving closer to him.

Old Napoleon Bonyparts. How's the weather up there? Bongo. Bongo. Bongo. At eight it had been, oh, to be a Cub Scout and wear a hundred badges. At twenty-one, seeing millions of men fall out of brown and blue uniforms into neat gray suits, he had longed to put on such a suit himself and stand on a station platform in upper Westchester, his hair cropped close, his paper folded to the daily stock quotations, in his left hand a package of English doorknobs to be exchanged at Abercrombie and Fitch or Lord and Taylor. For most of his life he had wanted nothing more than to be in no way extraordinary, yet somehow he'd never made either the Cub Scouts or the neat gray suit. "You know how kids grow," he said, "not systematically, but all ears or all nose. I was all ears. They're still pretty big."

"Not too big."

He looked at her with some irritation. His ears were big. Old Elephant Ears. Once he had claimed to hear things nobody else could, and he had entertained his classmates with new insights into the world around them. The sound a wall makes when it's tired. The ceiling that fell in love with the floor. What Mr. Phelps whispered to the substitute teacher. They laughed. He was a funny man. The Nick West School of Social Success. He was making the best of his advantages, but he would have preferred to be without them. "I was a funny kid," he said. "They called me Bongo."

"Like the drum?"

"No, like the antelope."

"Oh." She smiled. Nothing disturbed her.

America's shyest show-off, king of the cards. Entertain your friends and confuse your enemies. The trouble was that they had laughed even when he hadn't wanted them to. You couldn't fight them all; he knew, he'd tried it. You let them laugh, then you helped them laugh. But tonight was different. "You should have been there tonight," he said. "I was pretty good. You should have heard them laugh."

"They always laugh."

"Not this way."

Her face was pale, puzzled and admiring, for she knew that he wanted something from her but couldn't understand what it was. For as long as she could remember she had measured her existence in dishes and dirty linen. She had borne food to anonymous armies, swept the world's bedrooms, cleaned iron and stone, polished steel and brass and copper. Once in Chicago she had spent her nights for a whole year washing the northeast corner of a marble floor as big as a parking lot. In her eyes Nick's life had always been altogether wonderful; he needed no victories, for triumph was his daily bread. "Oh, look how bright the moon is!" she cried. Wush-h-h went the waves on the sand.

And Nick, finally realizing that this was the price of admiration, stopped trying to make her understand. "There's a bright side to everything," he said. But privately he carried his laugh with him like a banner all the way down the boardwalk, through Secost's dark back streets, up to the top floor of Mrs. Collins's nautical boarding house.

CHAPTER SEVENTEEN

EDDIE MACK made no attempt to evict Elfrida and yet he
continued to store his clothing in the cottage as though he
might return to it at any minute. Shortly before dusk on a
quiet summer day he did return—but only to get his onyx
cuff links. At least that was the reason he gave himself.

"Aren't you bored?" he asked, standing in the center of the
parlor from which he had been dispossessed.

She shook her head. Her hair was silver, but her eyes were
the same dazzling green they had always been, and she was
smiling. "I read," she said. "I take the sun. I'm a much calmer
character than I used to be."

He pulled open the bureau drawer with a jerk that sent
socks flying. Calm was for vegetables, a lettuce—like virtue,

bland and limp and drearily damp, and Elfrida was none of these things, never had been, never would be. Fishing the cuff links from the drawer, he put them in his pocket and turned to look at her more closely. She did indeed appear calm and quite content. Healthy. "If you don't watch out, you'll get fat," he said vindictively.

She had no right to deny what she was. The whole damn world was changing, but he'd never expected it of Elfrida.

"Is business any better?" she asked.

"It comes, it goes. The hotels are helping out a little. When they get that damn pageant off their shoulders, it'll be a godsend."

She reached out to touch the broken button on the sleeve of his jacket. "You never used to go around like that. Take off your coat. I'll sew on another button."

"My God, Elfrida," he said, examining the sleeve, "I never knew you could sew."

Going to the bureau, she took out a small sewing kit. "Try me. Take off your coat. It'll just be a minute."

Curious, he did what she told him, and, sitting down beside him, Elfrida went to work with a deftness which he found pleasantly amazing, a singularly graceful dance of thread and steel and infinitely cunning fingers. Did she ever have a sewing part? he wondered, but could not remember one. She must have watched somebody. Of course. If she saw a thing once, she put it away for life; she'd undoubtedly be able to do as well with a riveting machine. "Elfrida," he said, "you should never have quit."

Severing the thread with a pair of skinny embroidery scissors, she felt his amazement and was amused by it. He smoked cigars and bet on horses, called Jack Dempsey Jack, was learned in the language of profit and loss, knew the inside story on practically everything—and lived on miracles. If it hadn't been for the silk shirts and the sophisticated air, they would have eaten him alive long ago. "How's Frederic York behaving himself?" she asked, still holding onto the coat and remembering again why she had come to the beach. The good Elfrida.

"Well." Eddie Mack nodded thoughtfully. "He's coming around. I'm thinking of setting up a permanent repertory in Secost, and he likes the idea. Of course, he has a head like an adding machine. We'll have to show him results before he goes in much deeper."

Eddie was not the man to grasp at straws in any spirit of desperation—give him a straw and he'd set out to sea on it as though it were the *Queen Mary*. "There's a real possibility here," he said, his face glowing with an enthusiasm that had little to do with greed.

Carrying the coat, Elfrida went to the window, where she looked out over the colored lanterns that hung from the trees. There was going to be a dance in the evening and the thought filled her with a cheerful nostalgia, for dancing in gardens was something that belonged to her generation. The spirit of philanthropy was upon her; goodness pervaded her body and rose irresistibly to her tongue. "I hope you're taking your blood pressure pills," she said.

He looked up at her suspiciously. "I haven't taken them in two years. They made me sleepy. Besides I never felt better in my life."

Coming to the window, he took back his coat.

"The hotel people are so important to you," she said. "Who are they? Have you spoken to them in the right way? Do they understand how much a theater can do for them?"

"That's all been attended to down to the last detail," he said stiffly, although as a matter of fact it hadn't been. After the initial pre-season conferences, his relationship with the owners had been fragmentary and marred by misunderstanding on both sides. "What makes you so damn solicitous?" he asked, shocked by this new manifestation of the good Elfrida. "In all the time we were together I've never seen you so interested in the business end."

Putting on the jacket, he examined the button as though still suspicious that her sewing was pure illusion.

Dusk turned to darkness and lights went on in the garden, where they hung like nests of fire among the trees. "There are dances every Wednesday," said Elfrida. "Japanese lanterns, white jackets, and the girls all look so pretty. It's really quite charming."

To Eddie Mack this was merely more of the new autumnal Elfrida, a kind of calculated senescence, a siren song dedicated to hearth and home and the joys of growing old together. If there had been nothing else, it alone would have been enough to alarm him. All his life he had never settled down; he had no intention of doing so now.

"We're husband and wife," she had said when asked why she had come. He turned to watch her as she watched the garden, and this proved to be a dangerous thing to do, for in her face there was the memory of as much beauty as he had ever seen and it still had the power to move him. This was a little late for her to discover monogamy, he reminded himself fiercely; there were bitter things between them that nothing could change. Looking at her face, he was intimidated again by the serenity of it. What the hell was she up to? Did she think she could make him forget by the sheer exercise of her will? Or was he in her eyes so far gone that his forgetting didn't matter? "You think I'm beaten, Elfrida," he said.

She answered without turning her head from the garden. "I hope not, Eddie."

"Hope not?"

"I've always had the greatest confidence in your ability."

Why this sudden yearning to be good to him? he wondered bitterly. Although not inordinately modest in his dealings with women, Eddie Mack still had too much respect for the name of Elfrida Mitchell to think that she loved him. He looked at her quick, youthful body with a growing sullenness, probing for a motive in unexplored mines of vanity, perversity, whimsicality. All during their life together he had never even pretended to understand Elfrida, and until now this fact had always made him oddly happy; it seemed to define her uniqueness more clearly than ever. She was Elfrida Mitchell; there was no need to explain her beyond that.

"If I can be of any help," said Elfrida, but, as the anger strained his dilapidated face, she knew that she had gone too far.

"Is this a game?" he demanded. "A new hobby? Is it what wives are doing this year instead of mah-jongg? If you want to help me, please, just leave me alone. Help!" The word enraged him. At the same time it supplied a curious enlightenment. The shadows of evening swept over her face in the unlit parlor; darkness clung to her eyes and he knew what she was, a devotee of disaster, a hex, a witch who trailed mementos of his past defeats and carried promises of those still to come.

"What's wrong?" he demanded. "Wasn't mountain climbing exciting enough? Now you're playing chess with people."

She moved back even farther into the shadow before suddenly turning on the light. Her face had gone pale, but it was perfectly composed; Elfrida would let you see what she wanted you to see and no more. "That's completely unfair," she said. "If you knew me at all, you'd know it wasn't true."

If he knew her at all? He didn't know her at all. For the first time the fact filled him with rage and despair and a curious desire to hurt her as though by hurting her he might discover what lay beneath that infinitely flexible surface. "You're acting," he said. "This whole damn business is some kind of performance. All I can say is you're going to have to recast the victim. I'm not available."

She turned the emerald ring on her finger three times, while

Eddie Mack watched the action of her hands. The good Elfrida is beyond belief, she thought bitterly. I'm credible only on a stage. The big emerald was hard and real under the pressure of her thumb; she was lonelier in Eddie Mack's presence than she had ever felt when he was gone.

Obliged to justify one unkindness by another, Eddie Mack added brutally, "I'm not Arthur Bourke Smith. I don't destroy easily." And slamming the door as he went, he left the cottage.

Elfrida turned back to the garden, where they were now setting out small metal tables which glinted like shields in the moonlight. The wicked queen, caster of spells, mistress of deadly arts; for nearly half of her life she had been pursued by rumors of curious wickedness and ingenious sins, and she had never cared, but now her reputation was coming home to roost under the improbable sponsorship of Eddie Mack.

At eighteen she had been the innocent queen of love, the Darling of the Decade, a vestal virgin dedicated to the public expression of a passion wild and poignant, yet so chaste that even the most proper young man might have been proud to bring her home to meet his parents. This was the first age of Elfrida Mitchell in the general mind; it lasted until the day she was charged with hitting a policeman while leading a suffragette parade up Broadway. At the police station she called upon the women of America to lock their bedroom doors in protest against civil slavery. Overnight Elfrida Mitchell was something more exciting than the Darling of the Decade.

The press found her quotable; she was amused by the stir she made. In interview after interview she contributed wise cracks, witticisms, irreverences which quickly accumulated into a picture of Elfrida not at all supported by the facts of her own life. She was interviewed on the subjects of love, of American men, of European men. "Love," she proclaimed, "is blindman's buff with blankets. . . . American men look on women as a kind of sleeping pill to be taken before going to bed. . . . To the European a woman is a musical instrument which he himself plays better than any other man in history. They make love to the sound of their own applause."

The new pagan Elfrida marched into the twenties as a symbol of worldliness—undaunted by the fact that her experience lagged far behind her reputation. Her name for sexual malfeasance, inherited in part from every actress ever kept by a millionaire or a poet, now received unexpected support from her father, that fading epicure of love, who, issuing bulletins from London with the regularity of a press service, helped make the family name a synonym for elegant debauchery.

At some point during the twenties, the public Elfrida entered a new, more sinister phase, and it seemed that nothing contributed as much to this as Arthur Bourke Smith's play, *Mrs. Winthrop's Confession*, which ran for four years and brought Elfrida her greatest popular success.

Mrs. Winthrop is a great lady, the widow of a prominent military and political figure, who returns in her old age to the village in which she was born. Sick and old and with her mind wandering, she confides the story of her life to a young servant girl.

In a series of brilliant flashbacks she appears onstage as a gaudy adolescent, as the young woman who had been the greatest beauty of her time, as a wife, mother and widow. At first this appears to be the chronicle of a noble and successful life, but as the old lady continues to peel back the successive layers of her past, it becomes apparent that something very different is involved. Running through her history is a steady strain of catastrophe for which Mrs. Winthrop calmly accepts responsibility; however, there is the chance that this is an exaggerated sense of guilt or perhaps the figment of a failing mind. It is not until the final scene, when she reveals the circumstances behind her husband's death, that it becomes undeniably clear she is indeed a kind of female Iago, who, in her raging appetite for life, has destroyed everything she has touched—including at the very end the faith of the young girl who has been listening to her.

During the run of *Mrs. Winthrop's Confession* a rumor began to circulate that Elfrida was a narcotics addict, and although she had never been in any of these places, she was reliably reported to have been sighted in cocaine frenzies in Rome, in Hong Kong, in Budapest. She was observed drunk on the Eiffel Tower, naked in Piccadilly, under charge of murder in Madrid. In the thirties her sins were wrapped in ermine and gold; during the forties they turned political. Whenever a Restoration comedy was to be revived, her name came up automatically. The floating gossip of the world attached itself to her with a persistence that would have defied denial even if she had sought to deny it; by the time she reached Secost she had toured the Decalogue interminably.

This was the history of the good Elfrida; this is what she had seen in Eddie Mack's eyes. Leaning against the window sill and looking out over the garden, she thought that her reputation was singularly old-fashioned; the century in which Auschwitz and Belsen flourished had given private wickedness an amateurish flavor. It was the day of the mushroom cloud. In the quiet night sky she saw flame like a sword raised to destroy the world. Children dying in public squares. Tanks rolling, bombs drifting. Starvation had a million faces and the whole world suffered from nightmares.

Going to the door of the cottage, she began to walk through the part of the garden that was still dark. Arthur Bourke Smith, she thought. How many people would remember that name? On her finger she twisted the emerald ring which he had given her, and, leaving the garden, she started up the street toward the boardwalk, where the bright lights of evening colored the sky. *La belle dame sans merci*, the eternal succubus, she thought, feeling a sensation of sorrow so sharp that she confused it with physical pain and did not know what hurt her.

CHAPTER EIGHTEEN

WHEN NICK RETURNED to his room after the performance that night, he found a bundle of dispatches from his father, whom distance had made unusually articulate.

Oranges grow on trees [said Jake West]. Big skinny dogs chase each other around in circles. Old ladies dance like Little Egypt and everybody's the color of the chair in the living room your Aunt Bessie broke. You wouldn't believe the gambling. They laugh at me and say you should see Havana, Cuba, that's where there's real gambling, here's just for pikers. Besides it's summer, who's in the summer anyway? That's how it is with everything. If you don't drive a Cadillac car, nobody figures you're poor, they figure you're peculiar. If I say my what a lot of Cadillac cars, they say you should see it in the winter, now it's all shut down, Cadillac cars like pebbles on the beach. Only the beaches don't have pebbles. What's with you you don't write letters only a post card? I suppose you're too busy. That's all right. Your father, JAKE WEST

P.S. Some of the things go on down here it's a disgrace, old ladies they should know better, young girls their mothers should know better. Bathing suits so small it's bound to lead to trouble. Your father, JAKE WEST

This second Jake West concluded with a flourish running halfway down the page, a kind of exuberance which in itself was an indication Jake's mind was troubled. The next P.S. started at the bottom of the page and was particularly cramped as though in apology.

A funny thing happened I met two ladies. One of them is named Mrs. Little and she's very fat. Little ain't little any more, she says and then she laughs. I never heard a lady laugh so loud. I think she drinks. She's kind of a fresh lady. The other one is named Mrs. Martin and it's funny they are friends, she is very quiet, I think she must be embarrassed, this Mrs. Little tells dirty jokes all the time like a truck driver, not that I got anything against truck drivers they work hard but an old lady should know better, especially an old lady like Mrs. Little everything she says you can hear it in the next state. Mrs. Little and Mrs. Martin are both widow ladies, their husbands are dead, Mrs. Little's husband no wonder, it must have been a blessing for the man. One thing you see down here a lot of, widow ladies, you start to wonder what's going on with the men they're all dead. Anyway this Mrs. Little comes up to me and says how come a good looking man like you is running around loose? Mrs. Martin looked very embarrassed like she always does. I didn't know what to say, nobody ever called me a good looking man before, I mostly sit in the lobby 95 per cent of the time, a big place with marble and more chairs than Macy's furniture department. Mrs. Martin is skinny, small only not too small, her husband had a chain of cleaning stores and now she has them, she dresses very nice. I think about your mother a lot. I never told you that. What was the use? I tried to have a philosophy about it, but sometimes I think a philosophy isn't what it's cracked up to be, it never changed anything yet. Your mother was a beautiful woman, maybe that will surprise you, the pictures don't show it but the cameras were old fashioned in those days. She was a quiet spoken lady you didn't have to say anything she understood without talking. It's a lucky thing to have a mother like that. Maybe you don't know it, you never saw her to speak to, but it's a lucky thing, take it from me. Your father, JAKE WEST

Nick read this letter several times, for he felt that it asked a question and not only didn't he know the answer, he wasn't sure of the question. Sitting down at the rickety desk in the corner of the room, he placed some letter paper in front of him. He held the pen above the paper, put it down, picked it up, changed his position on the chair, but no words came. After a while he started to draw a sea horse with a thousand scales and a triangular head.

Some time later, carrying the still unanswered letter, Nick left his room for the boardwalk. Turning left, away from the theater, he walked along the curving shore, watching the people and the booths and the rolling sea as though these things might phrase his answer for him. In front of Mulligan's Home of a Million Curiosities he saw Elfrida examining pictures of the curiosities with an expression of mild distaste.

He put his hand against the breast pocket of his jacket and felt the letter crackle. Perhaps he could read it to her, he thought eagerly, but in the very moment of his eagerness, even as his right foot moved out toward her, he paused to consider how he might ask the question. What question? All around him shadows leaned forward to listen. Excuse me, ma'am, I have here a letter stating that my father wanders in orange pastures. Yes? I'd like to ask you a question about it. What is the question? That's it exactly, I don't know. Nick looked down in irritation at the right foot which had betrayed him. If it hadn't stopped, he would never have worried about what he was going to say, he would just have said it, but now he was lost. He kicked his right foot with his left—a wise man with foolish feet.

Thinking, my God, even my problems have problems, he moved up gloomily to inspect Mulligan's Million Curiosities. Now Mulligan's outside wonders were of a relatively minor kind, for Mulligan was not disposed to give too much away free, and Nick settled down between a picture of a two-headed calf and a genuine replica of King Arthur's sword. What's your line? asked the calf gravely. I'm in the laugh business, said Nick. Really? said the calf. With *your* problems? It always rains on my side of the street, Nick assured him. Maybe you ought to look for another line of work, suggested the calf. Perhaps, said Nick politely. Perhaps indeed. He lived in a universe where even shoes and chairs and tables rose in rebellion against him. Two-headed calves insulted him. He looked at his feet in despair. What could you do with a disposition like his? He sweated, he grunted, he saw a glimmering. Oh, funnyman, funnyman, learn to dance in the forests of the night, and that fertile paranoia will be your treasury.

When Nick had been engaged with the calf for about five minutes, Elfrida, turning to go, noticed him. Engrossed in study, she thought, as he bent away from the calf to study King Arthur's sword. His shoulder blades pushed against his pale jacket like stubby wings, oh, woebegone angel, a cluster of hairs stood up in back like a feather duster. She thought of that other angel and, feeling her body move in a sudden tremor, she walked toward Nick, her companion in rue, thinking two greater curiosities Mulligan never had.

"How did it go tonight?" she asked.

He acknowledged her presence with a start and a smile.

127

"Pretty good." One hand drifted upward to smooth the feather duster. "I found a new laugh in that place where Danilo tells me about the girls at Maxim's and I write it down in a notebook."

"Good," she said.

They stood side by side, examining Excalibur.

"Would you like to go in?" he asked. "K-K-King Arthur slept here."

"Not really. I'd rather keep my own ideas of the Round Table. Do you have a cigarette?"

He produced one and lit it for her, cupping his hand around the flame against a nonexistent breeze.

"How about Playland?" she said, sucking the good gray smoke, letting it swirl, dear and deadly, into her lungs. "I passed it down on the boardwalk. They've got a roller coaster and crack-the-whip and a Ferris wheel."

Nick, his sense of propriety younger and livelier than Elfrida's, was a little shocked on her behalf, but he accepted the suggestion gladly. Walking quickly, they soon reached Playland, a fortified city of light guarded by an old woman in a golden booth. Nick bought thirty tickets from the old woman and they entered the city. There, strapping themselves into a red roller coaster, they rode invisible mountains into the sky with the sea on their right hand and the sleeping town on the left, falling each time from a black pinnacle into the gaudy phosphorescence of Playland, only to be swept upward into the night again. In the car behind them a girl squealed steadily. The wind tore at their hair.

In the midst of life, thought Elfrida, exhilarated by the sweep and swirl of the little red car and pleased by the chock, chock, chock of the wheels. Up they went into darkness, down, down pulled the light. She saw the ocean's last wave, she saw the town asleep. Beside her Nick fought gravity with his long legs, pushing the car up each time from the valley until they were flying once more. Tail gunner, he had said, oh, the sky was full of improbable warriors; under the ground they burrowed in caves; the sea was alive with submarines, while somewhere deep beneath the water they searched for a flaw in the globe. At the hotel they would still be dancing in the garden.

When they came to earth for the last time, Elfrida and Nick wandered back into the center of Playland, where a whistle blew, smoke puffed, a girl screamed. The world was full of screaming girls that night. "It's the F-F-Fun House," said Nick doubtfully. "A-A-Air jets."

"I'll be careful," said Elfrida.

In they went under a horseshoe arch on which cracked wooden gargoyles smoked plaster cigars. They passed through the Hall of Mirrors, saw their bodies shrink, spread, twist and attenuate, and they advanced into the Chamber of Horrors, where a stuffed gorilla roared at them. In Catacomb Cave they heard their third scream of the evening, a rather gentle, well-modulated sound followed by a soft Continental whisper. "Freddee, I saw it move!"

"Of course, you saw it move" was the answer. "There's a string pulling it."

"I am frightened anyway," insisted the Continental voice.

"Go ahead," said Freddee coolly.

Around a corner, in front of a shivering skeleton, Elfrida and Nick discovered Danielle, the prima ballerina, and Frederic York, huddled together in a tangled group, four arms and a big brown cigar. When Frederic York saw strangers in the room, he started to light the cigar.

Freddee, thought Elfrida, Mister Doom, the lord of all their destinies. Fending off Danielle with one hand and trying to ignite a cigar with the other, he did not look nearly as ominous as he did during the day when his tie was always straight and his hair shone with a scientifically compounded oil. "Oh, Mees

Mitchell," cried Danielle, who had met her in a corridor of the Secost Theater. "Always such a pleasure to see you! Freddee, Mees Mitchell."

"How do you do?" said Frederic York. "I've heard a lot about you."

I can imagine, thought Elfrida. "And I've heard so much about you, Mr. York," she said. "I'd like to introduce you to Nick West, who does the comedy parts."

The skeleton started to glow softly, but Danielle had forgotten that she was afraid.

"Are you enjoying yourself at the beach?" asked Elfrida.

"It's different," admitted Mr. York, glancing at Danielle. "I find theater people very different. If you'll forgive my saying so, they're a bit like children."

What did this forbode? wondered Elfrida. "It must be quite a change from the business world," she said.

"In business you know where you are all the time. Otherwise you don't stay in business." The skeleton made a sound like a hiccup and Danielle remembered to grab Frederic York's sleeve. "It's not like the old days," he continued. "It's a science now, the most modern of all sciences. You got market research, you got laboratories. I have psychologists on my staff know more about what women want than women do themselves. Now that's a remarkable thing."

"It certainly is," said Elfrida politely. "What do women want?"

"Ah." Frederic York was pleased by the question. "Women want to be whatever they're not. If they're brunettes, they want to be blondes. If they're blondes, they want to be redheads. If they're skinny, they want to be fat. If they're fat, they want to be skinny. The whole damn country's going around in disguise."

"It's stopped moving," said Danielle, pointing at the skeleton.

"Are you aware of the statistics," asked Frederic York, "on

how much money is spent in this country every year on falsies alone?"

"No," said Elfrida.

"It would amaze you," Frederic York assured her. "That's the wonderful part about my business. Every year there are more women and every year they get more dissatisfied. My market-research department estimates that by 1965 there won't be a woman in the country wearing her own eyelashes."

"Let's get out of here," said Danielle. "I've had enough skeletons for one night."

"A woman nowadays has an obligation to be beautiful," continued Frederic York, ignoring the interruption, "a moral obligation. A woman lets herself go to pot should be shot."

"That seems a little extreme," said Elfrida.

"Just a manner of speaking." Mr. York diluted the statement with a deprecatory wave. "Beauty is the new frontier."

My God, thought Elfrida, poor Eddie Mack. He doesn't stand a chance, he's the oldest frontier in the country.

"Keep your market expanding," said Mr. York as they passed into the Tower of Tortures, "and you're in good shape." He kicked an Iron Maiden with a pointed Italian shoe. "How about a drink? I'm dry as a bone."

"A drink would be very pleasant."

Next to Playland was a café known as the Hanging Gardens, with tables out front under a red-and-white striped awning. Here they settled down to drink. "There are still a lot of people on the boardwalk," said Elfrida, looking at her watch.

"Every one of them a consumer," Frederic York assured her.

"That's why it's such a wonderful location for a theater," said Elfrida, who had re-enlisted in Eddie Mack's cause at some point during the conversation. "Thousands and thousands of people all in search of fun."

131

Frederic York smiled. "Who should know better than I? I had a complete rundown on this place before I put a cent into it." Nodding, he tapped the side of his glass with a swizzle stick. "Only one problem. How do you talk to the people?" He looked at her sharply.

"I don't understand," she said.

"They're on vacation. They don't read the papers, they don't listen to the radio, they don't watch TV. How you going to tell 'em you have a product they want?" He tapped the glass again and it rang like a bell. "That's the crux—find a way to talk to the consumer. Now how do you do that?"

Elfrida hesitated, but Frederic York already had the answer.

"The hotels, that's the only way. They go to the hotels to eat, they go to the hotels to sleep, they go to the hotels to ask directions. It's like the man said, Give me a place to put my lever and I'll move the world. You give me the hotels and I'll move Secost into your husband's theater."

"Well, they are co-operating, aren't they?"

"Nah! All I hear is pageant, pageant, pageant. Give me posters in the lobbies, give me notices on the menus, give me tickets for sale near every desk clerk, give me little stickers on the mirrors over the washbasins. You give me these things and I'll back Eddie Mack Productions right up to the hilt because they got to succeed." He looked at Elfrida closely. "Maybe you heard I'm a hard man. I'm not a hard man, I'm a business-man."

As Nick walked Elfrida back to her cottage, he took Jake's letter from his pocket and tapped it against his hand. "My father's still in Florida," he said.

"Oh?" Elfrida heard the statement but didn't absorb it, for the evening had acted on her like Benzedrine, burning away the shadows of the past, reviving the good Elfrida, who knew Eddie Mack's cruelty was merely the measure of his desperation and had the strength to overlook it. "Oh?" she repeated. This time she saw the letter. "Do you want me to read that?"

She studied it under the light of a street lamp. "I see," she said when she was done.

"There's something bothering him." Nick scowled, he squinted at the sea, he examined the darkness. "I know him like a book. He wants something, but I'll be damned, I don't know what it is. Do you think he's in some kind of trouble?"

"He doesn't say he's in trouble."

"They could be lighting matches between his toes and he wouldn't say a word. He'd just be surprised it hadn't happened sooner."

"Maybe he's having a good time," suggested Elfrida.

"Not my father. He doesn't believe in it. He's in some kind of trouble. He never asked me my advice before and now he doesn't know how to go about it."

But Elfrida's mind was back with the problem of Eddie Mack. The pageant, she thought, always the pageant.

All over Secost that night a kind of midsummer madness seemed to have descended on the troupe. They drank, they quarreled, they made love as though on the edge of their last tomorrow; even those who were asleep had strange dreams.

On the twelfth floor of the Hotel Bowman, Fisty Fuller, having spent several hours plotting the ebb and flow of the stock market, sat down to clean his guns, a pair of pearl-handled, thirty-eight-caliber Colt revolvers with which he practiced his fast draw in moments of high emotion. He had been doing this ever since he was a boy, starting at first with a weapon whittled out of an egg crate, graduating to a water pistol, to a cap gun, to a Police Special found in an alley and finally to a series of Colts. His present guns were nickel-plated and beautifully balanced; he wore them in handmade holsters especially designed for the fast draw.

Fisty's hands were thick-fingered, but they moved skillfully over the gleaming metal, swiftly breaking each gun down, cleaning, oiling, polishing, then affectionately reassembling it. When he was twelve he had pointed the Police Special at his father and seen that big longshoreman's body come to a lurching halt, one meaty hand still dangling the brass-buckled belt with which the head of the family traditionally celebrated the end of his Saturday-night drunk.

"Put that down," said the father.

"Make me," said the son.

The big man lurched forward a single contemptuous step, took another look at the gun in the boy's firm hand and stopped. "Git out, yer punk," he said.

Fisty got out, leaving Chicago that night on a fast freight; by the time he returned ten years later his father had died of pneumonia in an icy gutter.

On the twelfth floor of the Hotel Bowman, Fisty stood up and buckled the holsters over his pale-blue pajamas. Billy the Kid with notches on his gun butts, Doc Holliday, Wyatt Earp, the Barker Boys, Jesse and Frank James, pow, pow, conquerors of plains and barrooms, notches, notches, notches. Fisty Fuller, the fastest man alive, went to the closet and opened the door, baring a full-length mirror. Belly sagging, eyes cold, he retreated backward across the room. His head was bald and his stomach wobbled under the gun belt, but his step was catlike, his hand was as steady as it had ever been in Chicago when he held the gun on his father. Five times he drew on Brett Haverford and five times the top-hatted actor staggered, grabbed the place beneath his boutonniere which Fisty never missed and turned his face up in the incredulity of death.

When Fisty had finished with Haverford, his heart beat a little faster. The sweat washed down his neck, but his hand was still as steady as a rock. I know you're in there, he called to the mirror. Come on out and fight. Although he used every taunt in the ritual of gun fighting, Nick West wouldn't come out and Fisty went in to get him. At last the stinking coward drew, only to go down before the blazing pow, pow, pow of Fisty's guns, three shots so closely spaced you could cover them with the ace of spades.

For a moment Fisty contemplated repeating the ordeal, but the effort of forcing Nick into a fair fight had exhausted him. Putting away his guns, he went to bed, where he quickly found the best night's sleep he had had in weeks.

While he was being gunned to death, Nick sat in his hotel room still trying to write the letter to old Jake. He had already covered several pages with Andrea, Claire and Elfrida, but he knew perfectly well that he wasn't going to send them. He couldn't write about himself; he didn't know what to write about Jake. Am I my father's keeper? he inquired and, filled with an uneasy sense of responsibility, assured himself that he was.

Standing up, he started to pace off the tiny room, one two three four five six seven eight wall . . . one two three . . . He measured his room as carefully as Andrea measured her body. Mountains made out of molehills: our specialty. Inward, inward, inward, he had spent his youth searching out the petty places of his soul and discovered only that they were petty. The Magellan of the navel, he had circumnavigated his own small seas of woe until they rose in angry oceans against him. How to get seasick without leaving home. By the late Professor N. W. Mal de Mer.

But he couldn't tell this to Jake either and in the end he returned to the desk, destroyed what he had written and wrote, "Is there anything wrong?" on a separate sheet of paper.

The next morning, including the note in a box of salt-water taffy, he sent it to his father.

CHAPTER NINETEEN

ALTHOUGH the town of Secost was due to flirt with obscurity for most of the next two hundred and fifty years, on the hot summer morning of its founding near the dawn of the eighteenth century, it seemed destined for a future as bright as the sun itself. That, at least, was the judgment of Sir Henry Bowman and he was not a man given to being wrong.

Lean, shrewd, ruthless, with a taste for power and a flair for profit, he planned to raise from the wilderness the greatest port of the new world. To this end he had brought with him a well-balanced company of shipwrights, sailors, farmers, traders and fighting men as well as substantial capital, both in goods and coin. During that first false summer the Secost shore glowed with the promise of prosperity. Trees fell, houses rose, the skeleton of a ship took shape like a declaration of intention on the bank of a sandy cove.

Even that year Secost's troubles started with the passing of the summer sun. First it was pestilence, then the Indians. Although Sir Henry had carefully purchased his holdings from the Leni-Lenape, the original owners did not understand the nature of real property and continued to roam the land as though they had never surrendered title. Sir Henry's chief lieutenant, Captain William Frisbie, was employed full time in small but nasty wars. Shipbuilding lagged. Food turned wormy. Discontent infected the company.

When at last the long-planned-for vessel was finally launched, it disappeared during the night in an unseasonable storm. Now discontent came close to rebellion, but Sir Henry held his colony together by force of an indomitable will and an uncertain temper. Nothing, it seemed, could break this man; yet even as his followers prepared to take shelter in his strength, he was carried away by a bout of the flux. Then the timber that had been cut for the second vessel was converted into a tavern and Secost settled down to a century and a half of slumber. While the ships of Salem and New York circled the globe, Secost became one of America's earliest ghost towns. The strong and enterprising moved away; the sick, the weak, the listless remained behind. Soon Secost was little more than a personal and not particularly prized holding of the Bowman family.

During the Revolution the Bowmans were Tories and continued privately to stand with the king long after the issue had been settled everywhere else. During the Civil War, in tribute to their Loyalist sympathies, they favored the Confederacy, although they did nothing about this either, beyond occasionally toasting General Robert E. Lee in the family port.

Toward the end of the nineteenth century Secost was reborn as the summer place of a prospering merchant and industrial class; it was then that the big, rambling houses in the center of town were built. Several decades later the great gambling casinos came to town, and at this time a few of the older hotels were erected; the owners of the big, rambling houses began to move away.

With Prohibition the validity of Sir Henry's vision was confirmed from an unexpected quarter; at night Secost became a haven for a fleet of remarkably swift fishing boats engaged in rumrunning. At about the same period the great hotels began to rise into the sky along the curving coastline—some of them financed, it is rumored, by the proprietors of the swift fishing boats—and the Secost Theater was built, not primarily as a theatrical enterprise but in order to attract the convention business which held so much promise for the winter months.

During the Depression many of the great hotels stood empty. In the early 1940's they were taken over by the army and navy as processing and recreation centers, and finally after the war, as a new leisure came upon the land, the period of Secost's greatest prosperity began.

By now the Bowman family had one hotel and many memories. In this they were far ahead of the other founding families, who had only memories, for with the exception of the Bowmans the hotel owners and managers were neither Secost-born nor Secost-bred. They had come to town to buy hotels, to build them and to run them. When they discovered that Secost had a history, they were mildly surprised and pleased only insofar as it might help the tourist trade.

The founding families had not been much luckier in holding on to political control of their town than they had been in holding on to the land. The mayor's name was O'Grady and he was an emigré from Pittsburgh. The voting strength was in the hands of the people who had arrived in town to staff the hotels and build the small businesses that served them. The rambling white mansions had been converted into boarding houses or cut up into apartments or turned into public buildings. Two of them had become flourishing bordellos.

The old Secosters, who for one glorious moment had seen themselves as hosts to the world, were now visitors in their own town—tourists from another century. What they had was memory and they clung to it.

Elfrida, once more a volunteer in Eddie Mack's cause, had put together most of this information from a variety of sources, for she was now convinced that her husband's future was inextricably tangled with Secost's past. Having discussed the matter first with Miss Felicity Bowman, president of the Secost Historical Society, she appeared at the next meeting of the society.

The meeting was held in the town library, formerly the tavern built by the Secosters in place of their second ship and used at various times as a fort, a trading post and a school. Its walls were a foot thick. The roof was bound in copper. Long and low-slung, notched for rifles, it looked as though it could fight off time itself; in fact it was the only one of the original buildings left, the others having all given way to fire, to defects in workmanship or to progress. In her own lifetime Miss Felicity Bowman had seen three of them go under the bulldozer's blade, and each one she had fought hopelessly to save but could not because they stood on land now valuable beyond Sir Henry's most piratical dreams.

On the inside the library was one long room, surrounded shoulder-high by books. The walls, where they could be seen, were yellow with age and crusty with determination; you had the feeling that blood had been spilled on them. They were still covered by an arsenal of antique weapons, ranging from muskets to tomahawks; in one corner, under a globe of the world, stood a small cannon.

At the head of the room Miss Felicity Bowman sat on a

dais, examining some papers while she waited for the society to assemble. Even sitting she impressed you with her height and the way she handled it, for, unlike her brother Henry, she had inherited the Bowman build, that erect, spare, soldierly bearing designed for the leading of cavalry charges. Her face was long and so was her nose, which, as elegantly curved as a parenthesis, now lent her a certain air of command, although in her youth it had seemed merely ridiculous. Her eyes were gentle, brown and tired with much reading. Around her neck on a silver chain she wore a pince-nez like a royal order. Her dress, purple and old, hung from her lean body like a toga. On the infrequent occasions when she grew angry, you understood a little better how Sir Henry had held his colonists together during the long winter of their discontent.

Walking swiftly to the dais, Elfrida introduced herself. "How do you do, Miss Mitchell?" said Miss Felicity. "We are honored to have you with us tonight. It's so rarely that anybody from the outside shows an interest in our history." Her tired brown eyes examined the almost empty room. "The others should be here soon. I am expecting a full meeting, for we have some rather difficult matters to discuss."

A man opened the door of the tavern and stepped inside. A monstrously fat man. Although his head was at least of normal size, it was as out of place on that enormous body as a billiard ball on a butcher's block.

"Captain William Frisbie," said Miss Felicity, "Sir Henry's adjutant." Catching herself, she smiled. "Rather he's descended from the Captain Frisbie who was Sir Henry's adjutant. He's still addressed around here as captain, although actually, of course, military titles are not inheritable."

A tide of flesh, irresistible, Captain Frisbie proceeded down the long room. His eyes were pale, incongruously small, diminished by overhanging brows and swollen cheeks. His skin was mottled by the sun. His lips were always apart as though no nose could supply the demands for air and oxygen of that great bulk.

He came to a halt, vast and deadly, enjoying the drama of his own flesh. "Empty," he said, rolling his head to indicate the bare benches.

"It's not even seven o'clock," replied Miss Felicity sharply. "It's still quite early."

"Maybe." The captain tolled out the word ominously. In everything he did or said there was a hint of violence in reserve, waiting a time of need which must surely arise. He surged toward a barrel-backed chair and sat. Wotan, waiting.

Miss Felicity sighed. "This experience with the pageant has been quite instructive although somewhat trying. Really it's given me a clearer idea of the problems of leadership." She waved the word aside apologetically. "In the smallest way, of course, but I think I know better now what it must have been like for Sir Henry during the early days in the colony. I've been trying to do a book on him, you know. In a way it's the righting of a wrong. Perhaps not so much a wrong as an oversight." Putting her pince-nez on her nose, she examined Elfrida. "This may sound like a form of ancestor worship, but I don't think it is. Sir Henry Bowman had the equipment of a great man. He was brave, intelligent, resourceful. He had a sense of history and his place in it. If he had chosen another point on an unknown coastline, there might have been a state or a great city named after him today. A small error in navigation might have gained him immortality."

As Miss Felicity had forecast, the hall was beginning to fill up now. "I think I'll take a seat," said Elfrida. "You should be ready to start soon."

With a nod Miss Bowman returned to her papers while Elfrida sat down in the back of the room, feeling a twinge of sympathy for this lean and earnest lady, so intent on salvaging her ancestor from history's neglect. The Mitchells themselves, practicing a profession not always highly esteemed, had passed on their name with a pride that had survived more than three centuries.

The Secosters were arriving now in pairs and threes and family groups and the library's massive oak benches filled rapidly. In ten minutes more Miss Bowman was able to bring the session to order.

When the secretary had read the minutes of the previous meeting, Miss Felicity rose to deliver the president's report. With speed and clarity she ticked off the arrangements that had been made for transportation, refreshments, costumes, publicity, advertising, boats, viewing stands, police, tickets, the placement of props and the issuance of ancient weapons from the library's walls and a supplemental storage place in the cellar.

"We have a great opportunity before us," she said. "My brother Henry, as president of the Hotel Owners Association, informs me that their enthusiasm is greater than ever. There is even some talk that our pageant may become an annual event, taking its place eventually as one of the country's great historical performances. However, we have problems that still haven't been solved and we must solve them tonight if the pageant is to go on at all. It's as urgent as that."

"Hear, hear," said Captain Frisbie grimly.

"Now we have all the major participants," continued Miss Felicity. "My brother Henry, who was not able to come tonight, will be Sir Henry. Captain Frisbie will be Captain Frisbie."

"Point of order, Madam Chairman." A small, knobby man with a weather-beaten sailor's face stood up. This was Sy Puckett. His eyes were bloodshot. He wore his head at a contentious angle. Fish were his business, dissent was his life's work. For ten years he had been Secost's most skillful rumrunner.

"Yes, Mr. Puckett," said Miss Felicity.

"It's my personal opinion we hadn't ought to run over this business of the major participants so fast."

"Why not?" demanded Captain Frisbie.

"Because it ain't regular procedure, that's why not. We oughta hold an election."

"I'm afraid I don't understand," said Miss Felicity patiently.

"I think we should vote for who plays Captain Frisbie and all the others irregardless of who's whose ancestor. Just because my family was boatbuilders, does that mean we gotta be boatbuilders forever?"

"But it's all been decided," said Miss Felicity.

Mr. Puckett bowed. "You'll pardon me, ma'am, but I didn't decide it."

"You want to come outside?" inquired Captain Frisbie. "We'll decide it in two shakes of a lamb's tail." The captain was a butcher by trade and his speech was filled with references to slaughterable animals.

"Any time," said Mr. Puckett.

"Gentlemen, gentlemen." Hammering her gavel for order, Miss Bowman turned to Sy Puckett. "But it *has* been decided, Mr. Puckett."

"All right." The ex-rumrunner hunched his head forward, his sharp little eyes performing obscure acts of aggression against the captain's great bulk. Sy Puckett appeared to be laughing. "Just put it in the record. That's all I ask. Just put it in the record."

The secretary put it in the record.

"That brings us to the chief subject of the evening," said Miss Felicity. "Indians. May I remind you that without Indians we're lost, there just can't be a pageant? Now I'll ask again. Who'll volunteer to be an Indian?"

Faces turned away. A prolonged whisper traveled through the audience like a hostile wind. Not a single hand was raised.

143

"We're all entitled to be there as the representatives of our own families," called out a Mr. Cartwright from the rear, and he was supported by a quick murmur of assent.

"But, of course, it'll be understood you're not really Indians," Miss Bowman assured him.

"Don't make no difference." Once more Mr. Cartwright was seconded by a murmur from the members.

Sy Puckett stood up. "If I can't be Cap'n Frisbie, I might as well be an Indian. I volunteer."

"Outside," said Captain Frisbie.

"Any time," said Mr. Puckett.

"Thank you, Mr. Puckett," said Miss Felicity. "Now are there any more Indians?"

There weren't any.

"But Mr. Puckett can't be the whole Leni-Lenape nation," protested Miss Felicity.

There was a moment of silence, a stubborn hiatus which seemed as though it might last forever. Then Elfrida had an idea of dazzling simplicity and brilliant promise; it could easily solve everybody's problems, including Eddie Mack's. Rising, she addressed Miss Bowman. "May I make a suggestion?"

"Please do," said Miss Felicity.

"In the Secost Theater now, as you all know, there is a large troupe of actors. I'd like to suggest that the chorus would make excellent Indians."

"Do you think they'd agree?" asked Miss Felicity eagerly.

"I'm sure that if I speak to Mr. Mack, he'll be delighted to co-operate in every way he can."

"That would be wonderful and most obliging," said Miss Felicity gaily. "It would solve our last remaining problem." She looked over the audience, from which came a mutter of agreement and acceptance. "Since we're all in accord, I'll be delighted to arrange this with Miss Mitchell."

The meeting dissolved in an atmosphere of attainment, and

as the old tavern floor creaked to the sound of departing feet, Elfrida thought she heard all of the summer's ill-assorted gears slipping into place.

Indians made a happy hunting ground of her head, red-bonneted and fierce, swift, silent ghosts on the trail of spectral buffalo, swooping across prairies that had long ago been consumed by concrete, solemn at cold conference fires. War whoops echoed in her inner ear. The Five Nations charged their dappled ponies across the barrier of the years. There were dances of jubilation. Arrows twanged. Pocahontas joined hands with Captain John Smith and Elfrida walked the boardwalk in the middle of an Indian renaissance.

Nick West could be a chief, she thought; he'd look fine in feathers.

CHAPTER TWENTY

As ELFRIDA entered Eddie Mack's office, the rain descended on Secost. Falling on the sea, on the bathers, on the boardwalk in fat, lazy drops like tears, it ruined permanents, took the starch out of pretty summer dresses, dissolved picnic lunches, dribbled in ice cream, trickled down submarine sandwiches, halted a thousand expeditions. It swiftly emptied the sea, cleared the beaches, stripped the boardwalk and cost the merchants of Secost seventy-five thousand dollars in business they would never recover. Hotels, boarding houses, private homes and parked cars were filled with people drying themselves while they turned their thoughts to pinochle, bridge and other indoor sports.

Only Eddie Mack in all of Secost was pleased by the rain,

146

but he was sufficiently disgruntled by private matters so that his disposition was not much improved by his pleasure. "What can I do for you, Elfrida?" he asked, at the same time regretting the harshness of his tone. He was still ashamed of the way he had spoken the last time he had talked to her and the memory put him temporarily at her mercy. Even when he insulted her in the privacy of his own mind, it was a little like profaning a household god; he was afflicted by premonitions that the ridgepole might fall in.

As she explained what had happened at the meeting of the Secost Historical Society, he was delighted to discover that the purpose of her visit was not more personal. He agreed at once to co-operate with Miss Bowman in every way he could.

"She's quite a forceful woman," said Elfrida. "If you help her, I'm sure she'll persuade her brother to help you. It'll make for a better feeling among the town people, too. They don't seem exactly happy with us right now."

"I know." He went to the window and looked out gloomily. "The bastards." Taking a cigar, he sought comfort from the rich Havana scent. "Sit down, Elfrida. This looks as though it's going to keep up for a while yet."

Presently he sat down beside her, raising his feet to rest them on the desk. Aware that he was unusually thoughtful, Elfrida waited for him to start talking. Eddie Mack was one of those people who need an audience to think; until an idea was spoken aloud, it had no real existence for him.

While she waited, Elfrida listened to the rain which was coming down with a driving force, banging against the slanted roof and rattling the windows. Somewhere a steady drip, drip, drip had started. Water swished through copper gutters with a silky sound; it gurgled on the turns and slup, slup, slupped through the mesh that had been set to strain it. Forty days and forty nights, two by two we sit in the ark.

"You take all this talk about juvenile delinquency," said

147

Eddie Mack, "hotheads and hopheads and hotrods and rumbles and all that jazz, hell, we used to have street fights in Hell's Kitchen would make these things look like Boy Scout rallies." Now that he had it out, he understood that he was not yet near the center of his subject. Sliding his shoes down from the top of the desk, he tapped the right one against the floor. "What I mean is this, it isn't any violent generation. Oh, maybe some on the fringes and it makes a lot of noise, but the majority sit home thinking what's for dinner. Now you take, for example, what they called the lost generation. I guess you and I were just a little old for it, but you have to give them credit, they got themselves good and lost. Now it's all half measures. Maybe a detour every once in a while, but they damn well don't get lost, the roads are too well marked. When they're good, they're only pretty good, and when they're bad, they're not so very bad. These days you get to be twenty-two years old, you start worrying about your pension. They must sow their wild oats when they're fifteen. By the time they're freshmen in college, they're already settling down."

"You forget," said Elfrida, "the ones who were in the army first were already pretty old by the time they were freshmen in college."

"The hell with that," said Eddie Mack, not caring to have his theories upset by minor problems of chronology. "It used to be all the bankers' sons ran away and became poets. Now all the poets' sons run away and become bankers."

Eddie Mack was not normally addicted to generations. If he belonged to one at all, he had joined up only recently and Elfrida suspected that even now the younger generation he attacked consisted of Andrea Marston.

"I'm damned if I understand them," said Eddie Mack. "Sometimes I think I'm getting old. Then I think that I'm young and *they're* getting old. It's like talking a language all

148

your life and then finding out all of a sudden nobody understands what you're talking about. You take the Depression. Some ways it was a better time. Even the theater was a livelier place. So help me, Elfrida, I've been in show business all my life, and I'm not even sure I understand that any more. The accountants are taking over the world. There isn't room for a little success now, nobody can afford it; you got to be a big success every time out or you go broke. Hell, if you don't have a million-dollar advance sale, you're a bum. Who ever heard of advance sales? Pretty soon there'll be only one play on Broadway and they'll run the whole country through it on conveyor belts."

"Eddie, you're getting to be an angry old man," said Elfrida, touched by his anger, pleased with it too. He had at times a forlorn look which disturbed her beyond measure.

"Damn right," said Eddie Mack. He leaned back in his chair and, freed from the flow of his words, grew sad again. "Wasn't it a better time, Elfrida?" he asked.

She hesitated, resisting the pressure of his nostalgia. "We were younger," she said. "We digested our food better. Our bones didn't ache. We had plans." She found his mood infecting her, but she fought it. "Look, Eddie, I don't feel any fidelity to a generation. Whatever they are now, we helped make them. Maybe they like pensions, but it was our generation that set up the pension funds."

"I don't care," he insisted. "No matter who's responsible, it was better then. Life had flavor."

"Now is what we have to live in," said Elfrida.

"Unfortunately."

Elfrida shrugged her shoulders. Time went by in the ticking of a watch, the beat of a pulse, the sound of rain on a roof. Now was now or never. Why use the past to kill the present? She listened eagerly to the sound of the rain, trying to hear all of it, but the sound went dead as she was swept away from it on the tide of ancient memories.

The first time Elfrida saw Arthur Bourke Smith he was a big redheaded boy in his early twenties with immense hands and an expression of cautious arrogance. A coal miner's son who had been at various times a dishwasher, sailor, boxer, hobo, college football player and soldier of fortune, he had read *Crime and Punishment* under a palm tree and taken a new look at life. Emerging with the conviction that he was meant to be a writer, he went to Paris because that was where writers went. In Paris he taught a prominent novelist how to box, but it turned out that that didn't help much, so he retreated to an attic to write—and destroy—a twelve-hundred-page novel. He returned to New York, was advised by a man in a bar to go to Hollywood and did so, winding up first as a porter, then as an extra and finally as a bit player. Still not a writer, he came East again to enroll in a famous course for playwrights. It was then that he wrote *Mrs. Winthrop's Confession*.

Eddie Mack bought it, Elfrida starred in it. *Mrs. Winthrop's Confession* ran for two years on Broadway and two more on the road and the coal miner's son, the ex-boxer and dishwasher, swiftly became one of the leading literary lions of his day—as indispensable at parties as the gin. When his play went to London, he repeated his success there.

During all this time he wrote nothing longer than an occasional letter to his mother. He didn't need to. If he felt the impulse to tell a story, a crook of his finger would assemble an audience. He spent his talent over cocktail glasses and collected his rewards on the spot in free drinks, free food and free women. In certain circles of international society, sleeping with Arthur Bourke Smith became a kind of tribal initiation rite.

Unfortunately, he had the physical endurance to keep this up for a long while. By the time he was ready to stop, his fame had a flavor of fraudulence to it, for from the very beginning there had been people who said that without Elfrida the play was nothing, and in the end Arthur wasn't sure himself. He started his second play a number of times, fled from it into parties that seemed to run all month with only a change of locale to distinguish the hosts from each other. On more than one occasion he awoke on a boat in mid-ocean, not knowing in which direction he was headed. He spent twelve weeks in Hollywood as technical consultant on a screen version of his own play, but he never saw the script. He was the guest of a royal personage on a yachting trip in the Mediterranean. He went boar hunting in the Balkans, drove a Stutz-Bearcat roadster from coast to coast without stopping to sober up, attended a costume ball in the nude as the Spirit of Physical Culture. He was Arthur Bourke Smith, the world-famous playwright, and the cognoscenti understood that Elfrida was the only reason for his play's success.

Now when he approached a typewriter, his hands shook, his armpits grew moist and his throat dry. He suffered from dizzy spells curable only by gin. Even the characters he created had no respect for him as an author, running away and winding up in cul-de-sacs from which he could not rescue them. In Paris to attend the first performance of his play there, he met again the famous novelist whom he had taught to box. By now everything he had ever done was coming back to haunt him and the novelist knocked him down during a Pernod-flavored discussion of the merits of the Russian ballet.

At this point he returned to New York. Suddenly seeing Elfrida as the key to all of his problems, he watched her for two weeks in every performance, trying to decide where his part in the creation of Mrs. Winthrop started and Elfrida's ended. Each night the verdict changed. Sometimes he came away in a state of abject depression, feeling that he had contributed practically nothing. On other nights his part was everything; he had created not only Mrs. Winthrop but the actress who portrayed her and he toasted Elfrida proudly in the nearest bar as the figment of his imagination.

Although the verdict changed, in every instance it revolved around Elfrida; absent or present, she had become the center of his existence. He sent her flowers, not in corsages or in bouquets or bunches but in overwhelming imperial profusion, squads of messengers staggering under a burden of roses, panel trucks heavy with the scent of gardenias. He bought her pictures and books and rare lace, a chess set that had belonged to Napoleon, Marie Antoinette's fan. Like a belated Tamburlaine he pillaged the capitals of the world for curious treasure; he spent his imagination on the searching out of gifts.

When she returned his presents as too extravagant, he besieged her with reasons for accepting them. If she would concede no other relationship between them, he fell back on the bond between playwright and actress to which he ascribed an extraordinary closeness, for neither was complete alone.

Except upon a stage, Elfrida had never been the object of such a passion before. Arthur brought excitement to an area of her life in which she had not expected to find it—and hadn't wanted it. Now that it was there it was not easy to resist. Although in the past she had rarely gone to parties, Arthur, the Baedeker of ball and binge, began to show her something of his world. He taught her to ski and sail. He escorted her to museums and showered her with arcane information about swords and armor and sarcophagi. The world was her oyster; he had dedicated himself to opening it for her.

By this time he had stopped writing completely, but every once in a while an idea for a play or a scene would wheedle its way into his head with irresistible grace and for a half hour he would entertain it; at the end of that time, if it hadn't disappeared of itself, he could always talk it away.

On at least a dozen occasions Elfrida tried unsuccessfully to snap the tie between them. From the very beginning she had insisted that there was a limitation on what she would give him in return for all his bounty. She had been married to Eddie Mack for five years; while their union was conducted largely at long distance, she remained faithful to it. In the beginning, fidelity had been a convenience, for it had helped her resist the playwright's demands of time and interest and energy. In the end, when she was in love with him herself, it had become an inescapable burden.

What she tried to give Arthur instead of love was the ability to write again, but it turned out that this was not hers to give. At last, after two years, she left *Mrs. Winthrop's Confession* in the hope that she might release it to its author; three weeks later the play, starring Elfrida's successor, closed in New York for want of business.

The next night Arthur came to see her. While he had been drinking, he wasn't drunk, and although liquor usually made him gay, he wasn't gay. His eyes were clear, his hands were steady, he was full of unspecified resolutions. In his left hand he carried a large package; his right hand was in his coat pocket.

"A ream of unsullied bond," he said, putting the package down on a table. "Twenty-four pencils and a typewriter ribbon, virgins all."

Under the lamp his hair was a brilliant red, his eyes a gleaming blue. "I'm going to lock myself up and come out with a play," he said. He took the right hand out of his pocket. There was a small white velvet box in it.

She shook her head slowly, watched him lift the burning emerald from the box and shook her head again. A pressure in her chest, a stirring in the veins, the shadow of a memory at the bottom of her mind. Afraid.

"We could be married as soon as I've finished the play," he said. "It'll be your wedding present."

He held out the ring to put it on her finger. "No," she said. Afraid.

"Look," he demanded, "how long is it since you've seen Eddie Mack?"

"He's in California."

"I know where he is. I asked how long since you've seen him."

"When we were married, we knew it would be this way. We both work in the theater."

"That's no marriage," he said harshly. "If it were, I'd walk out of here in a second and leave you alone, but we're closer now than you and Eddie ever were. We understand each other better. We mean more to each other. Divorce him, Elfrida, and he'll never notice the difference."

Divorce. Two syllables sharp as knives. She looked at his face and thought that it was all sharp edges too. He couldn't understand her marriage; weakness was its strength, it was a fortress built of cobwebs. She was angry. Or was she afraid? It didn't matter; anger was fear turned inside out. "Go write your play, Arthur," she said.

That was the last time she ever saw him alive, for late the next day he was found in his apartment, dead from an overdose of sleeping pills, two empty whiskey bottles by the bed and the ream of paper scattered across the floor. Dozens of sheets were filled with unfinished sentences and broken paragraphs. On the bed by his side was a script of *Mrs. Winthrop's Confession*, which, as though attempting to remind himself of what it had been like once, he had started to copy. At some point after the first few pages he had dropped the pencil and abandoned the attempt.

The next day the emerald ring arrived by mail, wrapped in a note. "In memoriam. A. B. S."

Although officially the death was listed as accidental, the newspapers were not willing to let it go at that; for several months feature writers were busy with the story and what they guessed to be Elfrida's part in it.

A month later she started an extremely successful tour in *Antony and Cleopatra*.

In Eddie Mack's office in the Secost Theater Elfrida turned the emerald ring on her finger. She wore it now for the reason that it had been given—as a memorial. In spite of its great initial success, *Mrs. Winthrop's Confession* had never been revived; it was a lost play from a forgotten year, and the name Arthur Bourke Smith was hardly familiar enough now to revive old scandals.

Eddie Mack watched her twist the ring on her finger. "Why do you wear that damn thing?" he said.

"I'm sorry, I didn't realize it bothered you." Startled by the violence on his face, she covered the ring with her right hand but didn't remove it.

"You've got other rings. I've given them to you myself." He got up and went to the window to watch the slackening rain. "Any minute now, the sun'll be out again," he said disgustedly. "My competition. In my time, I've had some strange competitors, Elfrida."

Nodding she looked down at the hand with which she had covered the ring. "You won't forget about the Indians, Eddie?"

"No, I won't forget."

"They need a chief, too. I thought Nick West would do fine for that."

Eddie Mack's face was heavy with a dozen discontents. Coming to anxiety late in life, he was not equipped to handle it. "Nick West," he said. "There's trouble between him and Fisty Fuller. I don't know what it is. Nick. That face of his.

Sometimes he reminds me of Buster Keaton, so help me God."
As he thought of Buster Keaton, Eddie Mack's own face
changed, grew cheerful, flickered with delight. "Now there
was a talent if they'd only known what to do with it. One
thing you've got to give me, Elfrida, I never had any talent
myself but I could recognize it; I could smell it a mile away
before anybody else knew it was there. And in my whole life
I've never done it any harm."

"I think that's true, Eddie," she said quietly.

"You take Andrea Marston." He dropped the name freely
in the enthusiasm of the moment. "God gave her a voice and
He gave her a body to match it. Maybe that's what's wrong.
If she had been born ugly, she might have had more respect
for the voice. What good is talent unless you use it? She thinks
it's something you can bring out and dust off when there are
visitors, like the porcelain bowl Grandpa brought back from
China." He smacked one big-knuckled hand into the palm of
the other. "That's what I mean," he said angrily. "People lost
their souls as well as their shirts in '29. All they've gotten back
is their shirts. Hell, they think we were silly, but they don't
take themselves seriously any more. The whole damn world's
gone fishing."

"All right, Eddie," she said with a conscious irrelevance. She
had rarely seen him so moved before and she knew that the
state of the world had only a little to do with it. Andrea
Marston was his world, Frederic York was his fate. What
could she do or say? They had been married for twenty-five
years, but they had never been close. You could not change
that in minutes or seconds or hours. Danger. Danger. If she
said the wrong thing now, it might be the last wrong thing of
all. You wandered among people like a blind man in a field
of land mines.

"Don't forget about the Indians," she said, standing up
to go.

CHAPTER TWENTY-ONE

NICK SLEPT until the fifteenth ring before reaching over to pick up the phone. It was Andrea.

"Is that you, Nick?" she said anxiously.

Mumbling, he swung halfway between sleep and waking. When he tried to sort out the reasons why she might be calling he couldn't find any, for he hadn't spoken to her in days. It was hot. Although he'd opened the window as far as it would go, there was no breeze, no air, only sun. Through the heat came Andrea's voice. "I've been looking for you everywhere. I have to see you. It's vitally important."

Vitally? A pleasant word. He wiggled his shoulders against the sheet. "Where?" he asked.

"I'm calling from Whipple's Stone Pier. Where they have

the shooting galleries. I'll meet you next to Madame Wanda's booth."

When he arrived there, Nick discovered that Madame Wanda had a face of deadly pallor, nylon hair and steel gears and sat in a glass case. If you put a quarter in the appropriate slot, she dispensed your fortune through a small trap door. To the right of Madame Wanda a little boy was firing an electric machine gun at a swarm of Messerschmidts that whirled and flamed across a blue tin sky. "What's wrong?" asked Nick.

"I have to talk to somebody," said Andrea, moving toward him. "You're my only true friend in the company." She tugged on his arm. "There's a bench in back of Madame Wanda."

While he was a little skeptical by now of the rights and privileges that went with being Andrea's only true friend, he was delighted to sit beside her. She had put on, either for this occasion or another, a dress he had never seen before, a pale lilac appliquéd at the low-cut neckline, and she was as fresh and fair as the sea beyond the horizon.

Feeling singularly debonair, he lit a cigarette in the manner of E. Phillips Oppenheim. Raffles. D'Artagnan. Tarzan of the Apes. All of his life since the days when he smuggled aristocrats out of the living room into the kitchen, he had wanted adventures. The only trouble with the average adventure, as he had discovered, was it scared hell out of you. Kneel, Nicholas West. I dub thee Sir Cowardly Adventurer. Rise, mighty trembler, and prepare to do battle with your fears. He was better off next to Andrea; just sitting beside her was adventure enough for any man. "Brrrp, brrrp, brrrp," cried the boy with the machine gun.

"We are friends, aren't we?" said Andrea.

"I certainly hope so," said Nick.

"A person doesn't have many friends," said Andrea. "It's a

rare thing. Until I was twelve years old my only true friend was my dog."

Nick's sense of privilege diminished rapidly. "What happened when you were twelve?" he asked.

"Frisky bit a neighbor. We had to give him away. But that's not the point. All of a sudden when you have to talk, you realize how few true friends you really have at any time, people you can tell anything and they'll understand."

As she turned on him the full architectural splendor of her face, it seemed that she might be about to cry. "Life is full of loneliness," she said.

Every time Andrea spoke of loneliness or anxiety, she filled Nick's heart with hope; he was like a man wandering through an alien city who suddenly receives the grip of the secret society in which he is a charter member. "Have a cigarette," he said and lit it for her.

"We live in a large house on five acres of ground," she said. "I don't want to mislead you. It was always very comfortable. Daddy does quite well in the automobile business. Of course, my mother is not an easy woman to live with. I suppose it comes from not having enough to do. She has plenty of time to drive everybody crazy, including Daddy, except he has the business and nerves of steel anyway. I think I told you he was a flyer in the Lafayette Escadrille."

"I was a flyer too," said Nick, "a gunner."

"Well, Daddy flew in a plane all by himself. Later he was a racing driver. He came in second at Indianapolis in the old days."

"He must have been good."

Andrea nodded. "The cups are in the attic now, because Mother doesn't think they're quite respectable. Mother's family has money. They helped Daddy get started in business in the first place."

On the other side of Madame Wanda a short, muscular man with hairy arms fired at a parade of white ducks. The ducks went down in order.

"What started me on this?" asked Andrea. She glanced about in surprise as though she might find the explanation in one of the neighboring booths. The man with the rifle had stopped shooting to watch her. If she noticed his stare, she gave no sign of it, for admiration was the air that Andrea breathed. "I didn't ask you here to listen to the story of my life," she said.

"If you want to tell it, I'll be happy to listen."

She shook her head. "I have a problem that concerns Mr. Mack. That's what I want to talk to you about."

It was the first time she had ever referred to Eddie Mack as Mr. and Nick's ear, suddenly alert, picked up the difference. He examined her face, looked at the fullness of her arm against his. Flesh touched, but their minds had no place to meet. She was a goddess, marvelous marble, caught in the act of meditation as she presided over the mysteries of her cult.

Mr. Mack, thought Nick, the hell with Mr. Mack, the young belonged to each other. What should he do? If he had had a guitar, he would have played it, but instead he tapped his feet. How could you make love without music? "I have something to tell you, too," he said.

"Oh." She turned her wonderful body toward him. If she was the goddess, Nick was the high priest. She nodded thoughtfully. "I'm interested in your opinion, but first you have to hear what I have to tell you."

"We're practically the same age," said Nick, "except that I'm a little older and that's the way it should be. It's the law of nature."

"I'm sure it is, but you're making me lose track of what I have to say. How can you advise me until you know the facts?"

"All right, tell me the facts." Nick glanced at Madame Wanda and scowled. He'd been right in the first place, you had to have music. George Gershwin, Jerome Kern, Richard Rodgers. Without them how could you tell you were in love? He put his hand in hers and she let it stay there, skin communicating to skin. Vincent Youmans, he thought, Cole Porter, Irving Berlin, they should erect statues to them all in the Bureau of Vital Statistics, Washington, D.C.

"Mr. Mack thinks I have a great natural voice," she said.

"Well, there I agree with him." Her hand twitched under his, but he held it firmly.

"He wants me to settle in New York, to take an apartment there, so I can work and study with the very best people."

"That's not a bad idea, under the right conditions, of course."

"Just listen to the facts," she said. She seemed to have forgotten about her hand, lying quietly now under his. Her eyes took on the deep, inward look with which she consulted the past. "All my life I've known that I could sing, even when I was a little girl." She hesitated. "I have a sister, you know."

"I know."

"My sister can't sing at all."

"It happens that way in families, one sister has talent, the other doesn't. It's not unusual."

Andrea turned her face toward his. "This is unusual. She's my *twin* sister."

"Your *twin* sister?"

"We're identical," she cried bitterly.

He could not keep the amazement from his face, for it was beyond belief that somewhere in the world there was the exact double of all this magnificence.

"Even our little toes curl up the same way," said Andrea, seeing his amazement and finding in it the confirmation of all her woe. "The only difference is that my sister can't sing."

161

She took back her hand as though this was something she had to bear alone. "You hear about twins that love to dress alike. I never did, I hated it. My mother thought it was cute. I used to fight with her all the time. How do you think it feels to be a carbon copy?"

Nick didn't know. It was a contingency that had never been covered by Rodgers and Hart. "It doesn't make me feel any different about you," he said, and, after the initial shock, this was true. Although there was a duplicate concealed in the Midwest, for him she was still the nonpareil.

"Oh, that's the one who sings, they used to say, but only after I'd opened my mouth. It got so I used to sing everywhere, there wasn't a wedding or a cornerstone laying in Kansas City without me. I could sing 'The Star-Spangled Banner' in my sleep. I made up my mind that one day I'd marry an important man and move to another state. Everybody would know who I was."

"If you became a great singer, everybody would know who you were."

"That's what Mr. Mack says." With a smile Andrea granted Nick the most unqualified approval she had ever given him. "You walk in the street and people know your name."

Her face grew blissful with dreams of greatness; she wandered in a land where even the wind murmured her name, and, stirred to ecstasy, she let Nick take her hand again. "I have an important decision to make," she said, scarcely interrupting her dream. "That's what I want to talk to you about. Should I marry Mr. Mack?"

This time Nick was the one who broke the twining of their hands. He had fallen in love with her, given her up and here he was again. Boy meets girl, boy loses girl, boy— Something had gone wrong with the formula. His eyes catalogued the exquisite ears, the harmonious brow, the immortal nose, the lips created for kissing, the eyes that shone with vitamin A, the toothpaste-perfect teeth, the skin to which all of the natural oils had carefully been restored. Where had he seen such perfection before? The two-dimensional Lorelei of his youth beckoned from a thousand silver screens. He was their slave. When you met a beautiful girl, you fell in love with her; this was the law of the City of Angels and he had merely obeyed it. But where were the yachts, the Swiss châlets, the blue lagoons, the bedrooms like bank lobbies? He had been seduced by the brothers Warner, victimized by Metro-Goldwyn-Mayer.

He could not say any of these things to Andrea; instead he answered her question with another. "Has he asked you?" he demanded.

"No." Andrea shook her head. "But he would if I wanted him to. Women have ways of managing these things."

"He's got a wife now."

Andrea glanced at him in surprise. "You are old-fashioned, aren't you?"

Wound on wound. Nick kicked the floor with a crepe-soled shoe. "Wh-wh-what makes you so sure he would?" Stuttering.

"You know how men are," she said coldly. "He'd like to sleep with me."

"You mean he hasn't!" cried Nick in surprise.

"Don't be vulgar." Andrea rose imperially from the bench. Beneath its coating of pale lilac her body flowed in delightful curves, but her face held a goddess's wrath. "You ought to be ashamed of yourself," she said, "really you ought to."

In spite of her indignation, she lingered a moment longer, for Nick had still not answered her question.

"Well, now look," he said, "maybe it's not as simple as all that. Eddie Mack's not just some kid; he's an important man, a big producer."

"That's what I thought," she said, shook her head and left. He had, after all, answered her question.

Stretching his legs, Nick lit another cigarette. My l-l-luve is l-l-like a r-r-red, r-r-red r-r-rose. Even his thoughts were stuttering. Duplicate letters for a duplicate maid. M-m-maid? Oh, stutter mine, companion in crisis—it came and went, but more and more at his bidding. Once he had fought it, now he had grown almost affectionate. You could lie in wait behind a stutter, prolong a moment, defer a joke until the instant yearned for it. He had seen Fisty Fuller becalmed in a sea of extra syllables.

Nick scratched his back on the bench. In the shooting gallery a man and his girl sent a barrage against the ducks, while the cowardly adventurer yawned, put his hands in his pockets, tapped his feet. Leaning toward Madame Wanda, he dialed his birthday, then dropped a quarter in the slot.

Madame Wanda dipped her head reflectively. The brocade shawl slipped over her ears; a green light glowed in her eyes; machinery whirred in meditation, coughed and shot a pink slip from madame's interior into her hand which transported it arthritically to the outgoing slot. There Nick retrieved it.

"Don't start anything new today or tomorrow," it said. "Intimate relationships of a romantic or marital nature may be under a strain. Anticipate an emotional week with possible changing weather bringing moods and vagaries. Seek out congenials. Be jolly with associates. Good luck, Pisces!"

CHAPTER TWENTY-TWO

THE CHORUS had assembled under the boardwalk to receive their first instructions from Miss Felicity Bowman. Standing on an overturned rowboat in sneakers, a flowered dress and a straw hat that sheltered her long, distinguished face like a giant mushroom, she blew three blasts on a silver whistle.

"Ladies and gentlemen of the chorus," Miss Felicity called through a megaphone, "it gives me great pleasure to welcome you here to participate in the two hundred and fiftieth anniversary of our founding. Thanks to Miss Mitchell and Mr. Mack and your own good selves we now have a full complement of the Indians so vital to our project." She inscribed a benison on the air with her silver whistle, declaiming, "Oh, welcome, Leni-Lenape, first people of this place, our red brethren of the woods and the streams and the forests, long gone now to your eternal rest but ever present in our hearts."

"Dirtiest Indians in the country," whispered Captain Frisbie to Sy Puckett in the shadow of a concrete pillar.

Side by side they stood like opposing principles, vast Frisbie, small Puckett; there was nothing about which they could not disagree.

"There's more important things than bathing," said Sy Puckett.

"Hunt them by their smell," said Captain Frisbie.

"The first item on the program will reveal the ways of the Leni-Lenape before the coming of the white man," explained Miss Felicity. "The stalking of the deer, the curing of the hides, the keeping of the wigwam, the dances of war and hunt and celebration. Mr. Tony George, your choreographer, has already studied the original Leni-Lenape dances with me and has many interesting things to show you."

Tony George, in lemon jacket, pink shirt and dove-gray trousers, bowed from the forefront of the crowd.

"One of those," said Captain Frisbie, his breath making noises in his nose like a tea kettle. "There's something for your Indians."

"My Indians?" demanded Sy Puckett.

"Your Indians."

According to Secost legend, an early Puckett had taken a Leni-Lenape maid to wife, and indeed the ex-rumrunner's profile would not have been out of place on the back of a buffalo nickel. "Go to hell," said Sy Puckett calmly.

"The ladies of Secost are working on your costumes right now," continued Miss Felicity. "I am sure they will please you. They are authentic down to the last detail. Right now I'd like to invite you all to fresh lemonade, most kindly supplied by the Secost National Snack Bar."

While the chorus crowded around the lemonade, Nick joined Elfrida, who had taken a seat on top of a pile of discarded life preservers. The stay at the beach was doing her good, he thought. Her body was brown, her face had lost its lines of weariness and she seemed to be getting younger. He sat down beside her.

"What do you think?" she asked.

"It should be great. Just wait until Tony George gets hold of those Indian dances. It'll be the first time he's had a free hand all summer."

Elfrida smiled.

How could he tell her about Andrea? Yet he had to tell her. "Andrea Marston called me yesterday," he said awkwardly.

"Yes?" Elfrida turned to watch him. He had a way of starting even his most casual conversations as though he were falling off a cliff.

"She wanted me to meet her right away out on the stone pier." He hesitated, crouched on the life preservers, his long arms drooping to his ankles. Although they were sitting in the shade of the boardwalk, he took his sunglasses out, polished them and put them on.

He was still in love with her, thought Elfrida, but it wouldn't do him any harm; in his own dim, fumbling, easily injured way, he had the endurance of a tiger.

Concealed behind the sunglasses, he tried again. "She seems to have elected me her father-confessor. I didn't ask her to tell me these things. If I did, she wouldn't; that's how she is." Removing the glasses, he polished them again. "Next time she wants to tell me something, I swear I won't listen."

"What is it, Nick?" asked Elfrida.

He examined the glasses scrupulously, but could find nothing more to polish. "She's from Kansas City, you know. Well, Mr. Mack wants her to go to New York to study." Elfrida would have to understand this, for he couldn't say it any more plainly. "I hope you're not sore," he said. "I thought I'd mention it."

"It's all right, Nick." Elfrida stood up. "Let's get some more lemonade before it runs out."

He was trying to warn her, she thought dispassionately. He was a good boy but naïve and perhaps he'd never get over that, perhaps it would be better if he didn't. Everything happened to him for the first time; his days were full of discoveries. What did he want her to do that she wasn't already doing? She looked down at the emerald ring. If she took it off, would that change anything?

As they reached the lemonade, Tony George began to divide the chorus into squads. The girls were going with Miss Felicity to learn the duties of a Leni-Lenape housewife; the boys were assigned to Tony himself to receive instruction in dances of the war and hunt. "Mr. West," explained Miss Felicity, "you will be the chief in charge of all negotiations with Sir Henry. I've typed out everything that you'll have to do. It's quite a bit and I thought you might study it." She handed him a sheaf of papers. "Since Mr. Puckett is an experienced hunter and tracker, he will be in charge of the young braves on the warpath. Is that all right, Mr. Puckett?"

"You're the skipper," said Sy Puckett.

Adjusting her hat, Miss Felicity considered her arrangements thoughtfully. "The settlers know their parts already," she explained, "so we don't have to worry about them at all. It was the Indians that had me worried and Miss Mitchell has solved the Indian problem beautifully." She grasped Elfrida's wrist in her strong hand. "Thank you again, Miss Mitchell."

While the sun ate at the shadow beneath the boardwalk, the squaws learned to sew with bone needles, the young braves mastered the bow and arrow. War whoops and signal fires rose along the sleepy beach. Tomahawks split the innocent air,

168

scalping knives flashed, the pipe of peace was passed from hand to hand. Costumes arrived, wigwams were erected, ugh, ugh, ugh went the braves as their moccasined feet beat the sand.

Sweating, grunting, dragging his three hundred pounds relentlessly through the sand, Captain Frisbie brooded over home fire and hunting trail like some vast, venomous god. His pale, slippery eyes frisked the boys for signs of effeminacy; they clung squidlike to the breasts and thighs of the girls as though at last in this land of seminudity he had found a special license to stare and lust and stare again. He could not take his eyes from Andrea Marston; her size fascinated him at the same time that he was infuriated by it; he was a god deprived, trying to possess with his eyes what every law of nature said should be his, yet never would be. If you had asked him what he felt for these people, his answer would have been contempt. He despised their strange underworld of artistic affectation and improbable sin with a vigor that made his bowels groan. He was judgment. He was vengeance. He was Captain William Frisbie.

Late in the afternoon the Hotel Association's publicity man brought a photographer who took pictures for release to the newspapers, and finally Henry Bowman came himself, a slender man, shorter than his sister but with somewhat the same look of bone and determination, turned sour in his case by a lifetime spent in scorn of his fellow men. "I hope you know what you're doing, Felicity," he said.

That evening, however, Henry Bowman, who had never passed more than an hour under obligation to anybody, telephoned Eddie Mack to make certain specific promises of cooperation. Item, he would place tickets on sale at three points in his own lobby. Item, he would see to it that his clerks sold an absolute minimum of one hundred tickets a day. Item, he would post appropriate notices at places still to be decided on in his own mind. Item, the places would include some mention in the menus, which of course represented his most unfailing line of communication with his guests.

When he had finished ticking off these commitments in his precise, rather high-pitched voice, he paused. "You will notice," he said, "that I have made no mention of any hotel other than the Bowman. Although I am president of the Hotel Owners Association, I cannot undertake any such steps on behalf of the association until the matter has been brought up in a formal meeting. You may depend on it, however, that the matter will be brought up." He cleared his throat carefully. "You may also depend on it that I will not be ignored."

What a wonderful man, thought Eddie Mack, suddenly finding things to admire in Henry Bowman's nasal voice that nobody had ever admired before. It was frequently said of Eddie Mack that he would give you the shirt off his back. Now in his moment of jubilation there was nothing good enough for Henry Bowman, and he tried to shower on the hotel owner items of human haberdashery in the form of musicians, singers, stage hands. His mind glowed with gratitude, his voice grew heavy with it. Perhaps he could get a big bass drum to boom Sir Henry off his ship. Would there be anything added by his personal presence at the rehearsals? Did Mr. Bowman care for cigars? What was his taste in whiskey?

Mr. Bowman did not either drink or smoke. As for the other matters, they would have to be taken up with Miss Felicity, who was in sole charge of all arrangements for the pageant. "Good evening," said Henry Bowman, charging the three syllables with their exact portions of disapproval, and even in that vinegary farewell Eddie Mack found something to admire.

When the final click terminated their conversation, Eddie Mack was like a commander who has lost every battle only to find himself miraculously in possession of the war. His desk seemed to have grown a foot and it displayed a rich mahogany grain he had never noticed before; his office was large and pleasant and delightfully square; the savage Secost sun was gentle on his skin.

Elfrida had done this for him, he acknowledged with a forthright gratitude which was one of his most endearing characteristics. What could he do for Elfrida? He called her on the telephone to explain what had happened. "Thanks to you, Elfrida," he said generously. "Every bit of it was your doing. If I ever forget it, all you have to do is remind me."

They both thought about this offer for a moment, but Eddie Mack was the first to annotate it. "I'll be perfectly frank, Elfrida. This summer is my last chance. I hope I've done better things and more important things, but there was never one as important to me."

"I think you're exaggerating," she said. "There are plenty of opportunities ahead of you." But it occurred to her with a sharpness she found a little terrifying that he was probably appraising the situation more shrewdly than she was. "Anyway I'm glad it's working out."

Eddie Mack lit a cigar. Tobacco had never had a finer taste. "Your Indians were a sheer stroke of genius. Whatever happens, I hope we'll always be friends."

"I'm glad everything's going so well, Eddie," she said. Whatever happens? she thought.

The next person he called was Frederic York, who had taken to spending more and more time at the beach in the company of Danielle. York was nearly as pleased as Eddie Mack had been.

He enjoyed the role of Maecenas. The people, the music, the theatrical flavor were the fulfillment of youthful dreams he had never before had the opportunity to acknowledge. A kind of princely yearning was on him; champagne, the waltz, swirling skirts, these were the things his dreams were made of, but the dreams had been haunted until then by unfavorable profit-and-loss statements. "I'll give a party to celebrate," he said. "We could have it on stage. I'll see to everything."

That night after the final curtain had fallen, Maxim's echoed once more to the pop of champagne corks, the cry of fiddles and the sound of soprano laughter. Danielle was unusually gay, for she was the unacknowledged queen of the occasion. She danced, she issued recipes for rare Hungarian dishes, she sat at Frederic York's table, scarcely glancing at all into the outer darkness where Charlie Miller languished. If he wasn't suffering, she was convinced he was and that was just as good. "You are a man who knows the grand manner," she confided to Frederic York. "I have known only a few such. All of the others had noble blood in their veins."

"Just call me Count," said Frederic York.

"As a matter of fact, you bear a remarkable resemblance to Count Miklos, whose partner I was on the night he broke the bank at Monte Carlo. Have you ever thought of wearing a monocle?"

There are two more events of this night that must be recorded.

At two-thirty Nicholas West, unaccompanied and wearing a raincoat and sneakers, penetrated Mrs. Collins's boarding house, stole through its jungle of grunts and groans and impassioned squeaks up to the attic where Claire slept in the light of the full moon. He rapped on the door sharply with what appeared in the darkness to be a tomahawk.

"Who is it?" called Claire sleepily.

"The chief of all the Leni-Lenape."

"Leni who?" asked Claire. "Oh, Nick, is that you?"

When she opened the door, he dropped the raincoat to the floor, leaving himself appareled only in breechclout and red paint; then he danced the Rain Dance of the Leni-Lenape.

Claire, for whom nobody had ever before danced a Rain Dance or, indeed, anything else, began to weep with pleasure. "You're crazy," she said.

"That may very well be," he acknowledged gravely as he entered the room and her bed in a single bound.

Lastly there was a large post card with a sailfish and a bearded man standing shoulder to shoulder on the picture side. "You ask me is something wrong?" wrote Jake West in the space provided for the message. "I answer you when isn't something wrong? Only now nothing special. Your father, Jake West.

"P.S. Thank you for the salt-water taffy, but next time don't waste your money."

CHAPTER TWENTY-THREE

JAKE WEST'S POST CARD was followed on the next day by a letter which revived all of Nick's fears.

When I first got here [said Jake] I sat in the lobby eighteen days and eighteen nights except for sleeping. I thought life what is it? You are born alone, you die alone and in between you sit in a lobby alone. At least in the lobby it's comfortable. I sat and watched the people, I never saw so many before. Living in New York all my life I should be used to lots of people but there I never looked at them. Here you got to look at them, women in little pants, men in shirts like the Bronx Botanical Gardens, and everybody carrying something, tennis rackets, golf clubs, spears for killing fish. So this is life, I thought, women in little pants and fish spears. Where you been Jake West you never killed a fish? These are the things that make people happy. So who says you got to be happy? No place is there such a law written. Besides who knows what is happiness? My father, may he rest in peace, said that it was to do good and be clean in the sight of the Lord, blessed be His name. When I was a boy in the hotel business, I knew a man who collected string. He had a box for long string, for short string, for medium sized string, even a box for string that was no use at all. Maybe he was crazy, but every time he found a piece of string he was happy. While your mama, may she rest in peace, was alive, I was happy.

Here the letter broke off temporarily. When it started again, the ink was a different color and the mood had changed.

Mrs. Little drives us all over in her car. Everywhere she knows people. If she ran for governor, nobody else would have a chance. She says she's so loud nobody can stand her for long except Mrs. Martin so she has to keep moving. You would like Mrs. Martin, her favorite book is Shakespeare, there she says is a man who knows life. I told her you were an actor. She says you must be a very sensitive boy. I didn't tell her what you act in. We went to a place named Venice, Mrs. Little has friends there, a Mrs. Gunnerson and her sister both retired schoolteachers. Being retired is a regular profession in Florida. Mrs. Gunnerson said I looked like some movie actor who is always the banker, her eyesight isn't so hot. You wouldn't believe it, your father played shuffleboard. I had a drink of whiskey. Very relaxing. Mrs. Little's husband Big Bill Little was in the construction business in Akron, Ohio. They drink a lot in the construction business to keep warm on cold mornings. You'd be surprised how many widows there are, America is hard on husbands. All of the widows say I'm a young man. What do you think of that? You wouldn't believe it, maybe it's the air, the other morning I felt so young, I jumped out of bed like a crazy man and sprained my ankle. That's why I'm writing such a long letter I'm laid up with bandages. Don't worry, it's nothing. Mrs. Little has a business proposition she wants me to invest in. $8,000. She says you only live once. Your father, JAKE WEST

P.S. I miss you but don't worry.

How could Nick help worrying? His poor wounded father lay beleaguered by profane and devious widows in a false paradise. Nick was overwhelmed by intimations of responsibility and worldliness. What did the old man know about widows or shuffleboard or whiskey? Adrift in that strange, lush, orange-heavy world, he couldn't even get out of bed without personal injury; at the very least he would be swindled of his life's savings.

Nick thought of taking the problem to Elfrida and rejected the idea as an evasion of his own responsibility. He thought of writing, of phoning, of sending a telegram, but all conventional methods of communication seemed as cold as they were ineffectual.

Aimlessly he started to review his schedule for the next twenty-four hours. That evening would be the first performance of *New Moon*, in which Fisty Fuller was Ribaud, the great detective, and Nick was Fouchette, his assistant. The night and morning after that were free and so was the afternoon. He had twenty, perhaps twenty-one hours to himself; he could fly to Florida and back in six or seven. Even allowing a total of ten hours for travel, he would still have another ten with his father.

Surprised and considerably impressed by his own capacity for definitive action, he made the reservations immediately and that night, after the curtain fell on *New Moon*, he headed by taxi for the nearest airport. Taking off in bright moonlight, the plane flew peacefully over the silver land while Nick dreamed that he was back in the air force again, watching shrapnel unfold like deadly flowers in the sky.

At six in the morning he called his father's room from the

hotel lobby and tried to convince the startled old man that he was downstairs. Five minutes later he was in the room.

"So?" said Jake with the familiar air of a man who was not to be taken in by subterfuge or misled by affection. Jake West in a state of siege: he wore new blue pajamas of a military cut; the grizzled hair had been cropped close to the skull; his skin was tanned, his leg was taped. Six o'clock in the morning and all's wrong.

"I wanted to see you," said Nick, searching his father's face for the mark of the devious widows.

Jake settled back in the chair with a caution that seemed to extend beyond the painfully injured leg. He used his body with a tentative air as though it were an unfamiliar instrument, capable of who knows what eccentric behavior. "For three cents I could have sent a picture," he said, but there was an unguarded pleasure in the turn of his lips and the movement of his eyes. "Stand up straight, it's bad for your liver to slump." Reviewing his son from top to bottom, he shook his head. "Did you have breakfast yet?"

"Coffee on the plane."

"Ahhh." The carriage of Jake's face and body took on a new precision. He frowned, picked up a pencil, raised the phone; Jake West, patron of room service, commenced the ordering of breakfast. He added juice and fruit, cereal and wheatcakes, eggs, toast, muffins, pastry, coffee with the satisfaction of a man putting bricks in a wall, and when he was done, he capped this edifice with a double order of hashbrowned potatoes. "A solid breakfast is like the foundation of a good house," he proclaimed, "you can build on it all day long."

It was an aphorism as sound as the Laws of Nutrition—yet somewhere a syllable rang false, a consonant and a vowel conspired to betray Jake's air of confidence. What was it? Nick looked at his father again and saw the white stubble along the hinged jawbone, saw the uncertain flesh of the neck, the question in the innocent eyes. Mortal. Fragile. Vulnerable. Nick examined the room and did not like it. At least in the apartment each article of furniture had had a personal history; here there was nothing, the furniture had grown old through some anonymous process as though they aged it by machine in the basement. Nick looked back at his father. Vulnerable, he thought, endlessly vulnerable.

"How long can you stay?" asked Jake. "I'll show you the sights. I'm an expert."

"I'm on the two o'clock plane."

"Today?"

Nick nodded.

"What kind of crazy business is this? You use airplanes like they were the Van Cortlandt Park Express."

Nick smiled uneasily. Suddenly conscious himself of how little time he had left, he cast about anxiously for a way to begin. "Did you ever think of coming back to New York?" he asked.

Jake hesitated, reflected, shook his head. "When I was sitting in the lobby, that's all I thought about."

"But now it's different?"

Jake leaned forward to rub his ankle. He had not indeed decided just how different it was, for he was still a questioning stranger in this land where the Fountain of Youth was a piece of real estate. Why did the boy ask him about New York? As he looked at Nick, all of his sense of life's infinite entrapments rose in him again. "Is there something wrong?" he said, searching his son's face for signs of difficulty. The left eye was bloodshot. What did that mean? There was something in the boy that was new and a little wild and with that look in his eyes there was no knowing what anything might portend. "Speak out," he said. "Don't beat around the bush. I'm your father. You can tell me anything." And Jake sat straighter in his chair, feeling the old familiar armor grow around him, prepared to do battle for his son against the most whimsical demands of destiny. When the boy remained silent, Jake ran through his ready catalogue of misfortunes and selected one from the top. "What is it, a woman?" he demanded fiercely.

"Hell, no," said Nick, startled to find himself on the wrong side of the questioning. "I'm doing fine. I'm learning a lot."

"About what?" asked Jake suspiciously.

"About acting."

"What's to learn?" Sure and subtle inquisitor, Jake ignored the pain in his ankle in order to lean forward for a closer inspection of his son's motives. "Are you going into debt?"

Nick shook his head.

"Do you have much to do with Eddie Mack?"

"Not really. I see more of Elfrida Mitchell."

"So they're still married." Jake scowled. "She's a dangerous woman." Danger signs glinted in his eyes. "Tell me how you spend your time."

"The way you'd expect." Nick shrugged his shoulders vaguely, kicked off his shoes and leaned back on the bed. When he lay with his head on the pillow, he read the story of his father's innocence in the alien ceiling. Over the coffee cups he seized control of the conversation. "Are you really thinking of going into business with Mrs. Little?" he asked.

The name brought an expression of surprise to Jake's face —as though he had mentioned it by oversight in his letters and had forgotten the occasion. "Mrs. Little," said the old man obscurely, "Mrs. Little's got all kinds of ideas."

"Do you know anything about her? The world's full of peculiar people."

"A philosopher," said Jake. But there was no force in the remark, for he was thinking of other things, other times. "To you it's a lifetime—to me it's only yesterday your mother was alive. She wasn't much older than you are now when she died." This fact, known but never phrased before, turned yesterday into today. "We could have had a whole lifetime together," he cried, then restrained himself. "Sometimes I thought I should get married again," he continued more quietly. "A little boy without a mother is not a natural thing, but Jake West got married once and for always. Maybe it wasn't fair to you."

"I've got no complaints," said Nick.

"So." Jake nodded fiercely. "You were a good boy." Disturbed by this display of emotion, he pulled the pajama leg back from his injured ankle. "Look at that. I never sprained an ankle in my life before. Not even a finger."

Above the bandage the skin was white, the leg frail. It seemed to Nick that some mysterious partnership of time and distance had acted incomprehensibly to shrink his father; he had never remembered him as being so small.

"Mrs. Little says I'm the life of the party," said Jake West.

This statement seemed so improbable to both of them that they stopped to consider it for a while, Nick looking at the ceiling, the old man continuing to investigate his ankle. "That's just the way she talks," Jake said at last a little apologetically. "With Mrs. Little nothing's halfway. She's the life of every party she ever went to and if the neighbors have their windows open, she's the life of their party too."

"Could I meet her before I go?"

Jake shook his head. "She went to Sarasota. She won't be back until tomorrow." He looked at Nick strangely. "Why do you want to meet Mrs. Little?"

"She sounds like an interesting woman."

"No, she doesn't," said Jake with a flash of shrewdness; "she sounds loud. But sometimes it's good to have noise. She's a good-hearted woman."

Viewing his son from the newly won clarity of this statement, Jake wondered what the hell the boy was up to anyway. If he was in trouble, he was keeping it a secret, but, to tell the truth, he didn't look as if he were in trouble. When at last it occurred to Jake that the child whose nose he had wiped and tears he had dried had come to take care of him, the idea was so pleasantly absurd that he began to laugh.

"What's so funny?" asked Nick.

"Nothing." The old man shook his head. "Sometimes I tell myself jokes," he said, gasping.

"Why don't you come back to New York?" asked Nick.

Jake stopped laughing. "Don't worry, your papa can take care of himself. When it comes to taking care of himself, Jake West Esquire is a regular fox."

"Are you really going to invest all your money with her?" demanded Nick of the innocent fox.

"Don't worry," said Jake, putting on an expression of cunning so transparently false that even he didn't believe in it. "There are cards in the top drawer there. Get them. We'll play rummy."

They played, slipping with relief into the easy rituals of the game, and amid the congregation of kings, the fluttering of queens, Jake spoke more freely than he had yet. "How old do you think I am?" he asked.

"Well—"

"Fifty-seven." Jake flicked a card with his finger. "When I was a boy, that was an old man. Now there are societies down here I can't get into because I'm too young. Old Jake West. In my whole life nobody ever said I was too young for anything."

He smiled—tentatively. He did everything tentatively, as though the process of being reborn at the age of fifty-seven had left him infinitely uncertain. He was like a child learning to walk with all of an adult's knowledge of how painful it was to fall.

"It's a whole new kind of people," he said, "old people.

When they wouldn't let me in, I got mad. Who ever had a better right than Jake West? Mrs. Little thought I was crazy. She laughed so hard she had to run out of the room."

Jake smiled himself in memory of that laughter, a tentative, exploratory smile. "I got rummy," he said, putting down his cards.

"What are you going to do?" asked Nick.

"I don't know. Maybe I'll go into business out here."

Vulnerable, thought Nick, capable of endless wounds. His father had built his defenses early and lost them late, he was adrift in a strange land with strange yearnings.

"I'll find something," said Jake.

What could he do? wondered Nick and he knew he could do nothing. If Jake was going to be hurt, he was going to be hurt. And so they played rummy throughout the morning, stopping only for lunch.

At one o'clock, as they awkwardly made their preparations to separate, Jake said with an air of deliberate obscurity, "I might have something to tell you soon."

There was no time left for discussion. Seeing the ironic gleam in his father's eye, it occurred to Nick that this was the way Jake had planned it. His father was embarked on an adventure of his own from which no one could save him and from which perhaps it was better not to be saved. "Good luck," said Nick.

They shook hands, then finding that this was not enough, embraced. As Nick went through the door, Jake had the last word. "Don't play cards with strangers."

CHAPTER TWENTY-FOUR

THE HOTEL OWNERS were finally co-operating; they had even shown some interest in Eddie Mack's idea of a permanent repertory theater. By the end of the week Eddie Mack Productions had shown its first profit and Elfrida was a publicly acknowledged heroine.

Now Elfrida was constantly busy.

Nearly every afternoon she tutored Nick; things that she had forgotten were knowledge were knowledge again when he heard them for the first time. The sweet arcana of wig and make-up rose in her mind and she presented them to him in an unassorted treasury. She gave him the way a lion walks, the turn of an old woman's head, a young girl skipping. One day when he arrived her chair was occupied by an ancient sailor who whispered chanteys in a voice that had worn itself out on gales in the China Sea. For ten minutes she was Cleopatra, or, limping like a wounded dog, Lear's faithful fool. Lady Macbeth followed Saint Joan, Ophelia sang her rue, Millamant filled the air with crystal arrows.

"At eighteen," said Elfrida, "the first thing I knew every morning was that I was Elfrida Mitchell and that was exciting. When I stood on a stage, they looked at me and knew I was Elfrida Mitchell and it was exciting for them too. I never disappeared into a part—whole plays disappeared into me. I was young, I was famous, people loved me because of what I was. Then one day, after five years of it, I was tired of Elfrida Mitchell, even though no one else seemed to be. I decided to become an actress again, to be a thousand people and never Elfrida Mitchell."

She looked at Nick who sat cross-legged on the couch, a bony Buddha contemplating nothing but her. "It's not just a trick," she said, "copying a walk or picking up an intonation. You have to perform the rarest feat of imagination—believing there is life outside yourself and trying to understand it. The closer people are to what you are, the easier it is. The further away the harder it is, until at last I suppose it's impossible."

Getting up from the couch, Nick walked across the room. When he came back, he was Fisty Fuller, filling his pipe and adjusting his hat and assaulting the world with his belly.

Elfrida laughed. Uneasily. Wondering what she had started. Nick's performance with Fisty grew from night to night, play by play, its continuity leaping across the boundaries between Act 5 of one operetta and Act 1 of the next. In a way it was the most natural thing in the world; they were filling the vacuum that existed in what they had been given; it was the thing they were filling it with that made Elfrida uneasy. Fisty was what he had always been,

In comes I, Beelzebub:
In my hands I carries club,
On my head a dripping pan.
Don't you think I'm a funny old man?

A mechanical demon, whipping and driven to get laughter, he was now attended by his own private devil, Nick, a shy, confiding, infinitely dexterous familiar spirit who quietly filched the hearts of the audience for which they struggled.

Borrowing Fisty's swagger, Nick spread it over his own gaunt body like an oversize suit of clothes. When he was hit, he exploded. When he was afraid, he lived in a paradise of paranoia; a wink could stagger him, the blowing of Fisty's nose struck him like a cannon ball. And without ever looking at the audience he seemed to be entrusting them with what he was—terror unterrified, gentle anarchy, proprietor of lost causes, an indomitably unsuccessful warrior who had the grace not to bleed.

"Does Fisty speak to you any more?" she asked.

"In the past few days he's gotten quite polite." Nick smiled. He moved his hands fluently. For all his boniness he had the easy, supple air of a man who was nourished on laughter. "Sometimes I find him looking at me like a surgeon trying to decide where to start the incision."

Fuller, Fisty, man of violence, swells and swells and grows polite. Elfrida picked up a book that was wrapped in sunlight, held it golden in her hands. Fisty Fuller. Timeo Fuller. "Be careful," she said, turned the book, groped for a bit of wisdom. "Never let an audience cough," she said. "A tickle in the throat is the actor's worst enemy."

"How do you stop them?"

"I don't know, you just stop them. If you don't, you have an epidemic on your hands before you can say God bless you."

The life of the company proceeded at a peculiarly intense pace as though governed by a special clock. If you marked off the days in terms of what happened, they were weeks, and yet they went so swiftly that they might have been hours. Romances born on Monday died on Friday. Careers that were swollen with promise on Wednesday were black with defeat on Sunday. Time stretched, contracted, passed. A few weeks before Elfrida had been a stranger to the troupe, a legend perhaps, an item of theatrical history but distant and dead; outside of Eddie Mack and a few others no one had even realized that she was in Secost; then suddenly she was in their midst, Elfrida Mitchell, wisewoman and wonder-worker. If you had a problem, what better place to take it? Overnight she became a kind of guru by the sea, Dorothy Dix of the rolling waters.

Wisewoman. Leaving the stage, she had been spilled into a world without a discoverable pattern and for three years she had sought the solution in a bottle. Old Grand-Dad. Come to me, child. Fatherly bottles, grandfatherly bottles clustered around her in the darkness and whispered forgetfulness, but she could not forget what she had never remembered and so she turned to books, reading at first the way she had drunk—in order to forget what she couldn't remember. Books now rose in the darkness, filling her head, cluttering tables, stuffing rooms with millennia, ages, infinity, the decline and fall of practically everybody. She traveled from the Acropolis to the nucleus of the atom, crossed wastelands, entered bleak houses, saw the whiteness of the whale and of Molly Bloom's thighs; she floated down the Mississippi, marched to the sea, tasted hemlock and a little crumb of madeleine, sat in Plato's cave, escaped from the Farnese Tower, rode out from the village of La Mancha, watched one man die in a swimming pool, thousands more at Waterloo. Humphrey Chimpden Earwicker dreamed, Icarus fell and Elfrida fled to the governmental town of N. Ulysses burned Elpenor's armor, Helen walked the walls of Troy, a fiddle scraped in Odessa, Dr. Johnson fought his amorous propensities, Jonathan Swift saw the future in a blasted tree. In weeks Elfrida consumed a world that Balzac had built in a lifetime on genius and black coffee, and when she was done, she wept as though she had lost a friend.

While she devoured centuries, days passed unregarded as though time spent in Provence or St. Petersburg did not count in Larchmont. She asked the sages of the East and West who she was and received a variety of answers, some taking away her liberty, others returning it most painfully. Metaphysical skyscrapers reached their logical splendor into the heavens. She pursued yesterday's certainties down a thousand avenues, traveled the royal road from Eden to Id. She was wise in the ways of the Trobriand Islanders, the Arapesh and the Manus.

Wisewoman.

"You know about love," said Danielle, "you know about life," and Elfrida listened, aware by now that her petitioners sought from her not solutions but rather the opportunity to be heard.

"The trouble with men," said Danielle, "is they don't know what's good for them." When she spoke to Elfrida, she lost her accent almost completely. She was, as a matter of fact, the daughter of a locomotive engineer in Duluth and had acquired the accent along with her wardrobe during a tour of the Continent. "I offer them gourmet cooking; they look at me and think only of beds. How will I ever get married?"

Danielle was always unfortunate in love; she had been abused by a whole series of men whom she had sought to serve. A homosexual ballet dancer, a much-married painter, musicians, writers, penniless noblemen, a dispossessed king; she had tried them all and been disappointed in every case, for while her heart was filled with domesticity, she invariably brought it to the wrong door.

She had turned to Frederic York in the hope that he would make Charlie Miller jealous, but Charlie, if anything, had been relieved. Now what was she to do with Frederic York, who was married to the daughter of the hair tonic manufacturer? "It is all a waste of time," she said sadly. "Soon I will be twenty-eight, then twenty-nine. How much time can I waste?"

Elfrida nodded; there was nothing else to do, for Danielle would continue wasting time until there was no more of it to waste. I see a tall, dark stranger, a long journey, a great fortune from an unexpected source; oh, we are sisters under the skin, she thought, roving the world in search of domestic treasure.

Standing up to prepare a drink for the girl and for herself, Elfrida thought of Arthur Bourke Smith, the playwright whose plots would never come out right. Her golden moment of triumph started to fade. She had seen Eddie Mack with Andrea on the beach, and Eddie hadn't been in swimming since he'd jumped off a pier into the Hudson River when he was twelve years old. He was wearing cerise swimming trunks bought in a moment of temporary blindness or as some obscure flag of passion. His body was thick but still surprisingly well kept, although the hair on his chest was turning white. Oh, guru, guru, guru, she thought, gur thyself.

That night Elfrida was revisited by the angel.

"Go away," she said.

"So few people talk to me that way any more," he replied reproachfully.

There was a sureness about him that Elfrida found unsettling; from the amount of rustling in the darkness she suspected that he had found a whole new sheaf of documentation. What now? She had invented the good Elfrida in answer to him, making herself up afresh each morning, but she was no longer sure of her invention. You could change your hat, the way you looked, talked, moved. You could find a thousand faces and for a moment, for an hour, you could borrow the emotions that went with them, yet in the end you always came home to Who's that sitting in the darkness? Fancy meeting me here. There she was and there she wasn't. Who's that?

"You have heard, of course, of the method," said the angel.

"What method?" Scarcely bending her mind toward him, Elfrida searched for herself in endless night. When it came time to put together the good Elfrida, she had turned always to other people. Nick. Eddie Mack. To those like Arthur and her mother, now alive only in her memory. Was she indeed nothing but a mirror?

"The Method," repeated the angel, adjusting his capitals.

The big *M* attracted Elfrida. "I was a friend of Stanislavsky," she said sharply.

"We gather that the Method has rendered your technique somewhat obsolete." Soothingly. Oh, what worlds of ironic sympathy there were in that professionally courteous voice.

"Good acting is never obsolete."

"There are fashions in everything," said the angel gently, "and, of course, they die."

This subtle irrelevance caught Elfrida on its hook. Her work was what she was: obsolete, she had outlived her time. She gasped. The angel's irrelevance held her fast.

"Farewell, sweet prince, now they've put the Method in your madness," muttered Elfrida. Wrath was her support. Anger was her salvation. Let the Methodists have their hour. Let them scratch and stand on each other's toes, mumbling. With all their spiritual setting-up exercises, they came out looking alike, sounding alike, acting alike. Cobbling O'Casey to fit, shaving Shakespeare. Obsolete. Give her a year, two years, five. If you fell far enough behind your times, you were bound to be in the forefront of the next revolution.

I grow old, I grow old, I wear my crotchets bold, she thought, feeling a little amusement at her own anger, then putting it aside as inappropriate to the occasion. Somewhere, dimly, she heard the sound of the Atlantic rolling. How many years ago the cable? FATHER DYING COME AT ONCE. She went, wondering, across the Atlantic; arrived, wondering, not having seen him in thirty years; and there he was, dying in a great, gold, bargelike bed in Paris as he had lived, reigning monarch over a nation of women, holding his subjects to the very last, the brow marble, the eyes a blue command, but the voice only a memory of the instrument that had once been able to place a whisper in the rear of the most remote balcony. "So," he said, "you came," and somewhere, remotely, on some profoundly inner level, that seemed to give him a certain satisfaction.

The large white hands were folded sculpturally on the coverlet. Outside a breeze murmured in the chestnut trees. His face had the perfect serenity of a man who had never denied himself anything. By the next morning he was dead.

Moving uneasily in the darkness of her bedroom on Secost's shore, Elfrida heard a foghorn call and knew that across the water people were awake and watching. The salt smell of the sea was in her nostrils. Her heart was steady. Under her hands the sheet slipped pleasantly by. She was filled with the sweet unreasonableness of life. What other defense did she need? The foghorn called again, hoarse and unadorned, steady as her heart. "Go away," she said to the angel again, but he had already gone and suddenly she knew that this was indeed a personal angel, long resident inside her and in need of constant exorcism.

CHAPTER TWENTY-FIVE

TOWARD NIGHTFALL two Leni-Lenape stood side by side under the boardwalk and looked out over the beach.

"If I ever thought I was going to wind up in a Pocahontas suit, I might have listened to Daddy," said Andrea sullenly, rattling the beads on her imitation buckskin jacket. She hurled a handful of sand at the disappearing sun. Although normally she dressed with great precision, her displeasure with the Pocahontas suit seemed to have extended to the way she put it on. "Captain Frisbie has eyes like oysters. You can feel them sliding down your back."

Nick glanced at her curiously. Could oyster eyes be the source of all that displeasure? He tapped the concrete pillar beside him with his tomahawk. "You've got to understand him," he said.

"No, I don't. That's the silliest thing I ever heard. If Daddy were here, he'd punch him in the nose. Daddy isn't afraid of anybody." Andrea swung one hand out in a protest that included the sea, the sand, the sky itself. "Daddy never wanted me to go into the theater anyway. He said it wasn't dignified. Right now my sister's putting away her tennis racket and wondering if she's got enough energy left to go to a dance tonight. I haven't danced anything but a minuet since I came here. Sometimes I think I ought to have my head examined."

"There are lots of places to dance around here. All the big hotels, and the Shipmate is supposed to have a good band, Larry somebody and his Rhythm Rumanians. Do you want to go tonight?"

Ignoring the question, perhaps not even hearing it, she bent to reflect on the line of her thigh, while Nick contemplated the fact that he was a fool. "In Kansas City two drunks insulted my mother," said Andrea. "Daddy beat both of them up. One had a broken jaw."

Nick twirled the tomahawk thoughtfully. "Nobody's insulted you."

"If you don't stop turning the other cheek, you're going to run out of cheeks. Daddy says you don't get anything in life unless you fight for it."

What would Rodgers and Hammerstein do now? Nick scratched his head. He had abandoned Andrea because she had been beyond his reach, and now she seemed to be telling him he had stopped too soon. There was venom in the violet eyes, contempt on the raspberry lips. Oh, who could know the heart of a woman? Nick decided to investigate. "Let's sit on the boat," he suggested. "My feet are sore from all that jumping around."

He sat down objectively, put one arm around her experi-

192

mentally and kissed her scientifically, a student of love. His mind was an instrument of analysis, her lips were smooth and full and tasted of raspberries. He added his other arm to the formula and heard the beads on her blouse rattle. Her eyes were clouded by a sulkiness that might have passed for passion. Her lips responded and the student of love was lost.

"Oh, stop it," she said at last, "you know I'm practically engaged."

Sitting there in the wreck of his experiment, Nick groped for lost detachment. His pulse was high. His face was angry. Lips that tasted of raspberry. He was a fool, he decided, confirming a previous conclusion. He looked at the sea and it was dark as wine. He looked at the sand and it was gold, fool's gold. A goddess with raspberry lips and obscure intentions. What the hell did she want? "Then why don't you tell Mr. Mack about Captain Frisbie?" he asked.

Her face tightened, her eyes grew stern, she started to adjust the collar of her Indian blouse. "There's no telling what he might do," she said. "He paces back and forth like a tiger. He bites his nails. He smokes cigars end to end. He has a million plans. I never saw such an excitable man."

"Eddie Mack?"

"Eddie Mack." She shook her head. "You don't see him the way I do. Nobody does. One thing on the outside, another on the inside." Reaching down to dust the sand from her feet, she glared out over the darkening ocean. "I'm not used to people like that. He confuses me. I thought he was such a calm man, but when he starts that pacing he's like a tiger."

Eddie Mack, who had finally settled in a suite at the Bowman, invited Andrea to his quarters that night for a serious talk. It was time, he felt, to put his life in order and, as he waited for Andrea, walking back and forth across his living room, a big, worn, still-handsome man full of plans, he tried to clarify in his own mind just what that order was. First there was the Secost Theater, which he now saw clearly established as a flourishing all-year-round venture. From the Secost Theater flowed a series of independent and as yet not fully specified enterprises which he would be in a position to undertake as soon as he had a substantial source of money at his disposal. Then came Andrea's career, a constantly enlarging vision, a dream as fresh as borrowed youth, a glory to be shared and a promise to be kept; this was his own special genius, for he was a dowser of talent, a diviner of other people's hidden gifts. Last of all came Andrea herself—a tractable Elfrida, a sweet and loving Elfrida, an Elfrida who owed him everything she had.

When Andrea came in, wearing her gloom like a sandwich sign, he did not notice it.

"Look at what I've found," he said. He held out a pair of Victorian garnet earrings she had once admired in a local shop; they dangled in his hands, red as blood, fluid as a waterfall.

"Why, they're lovely," said Andrea, regretting her delight as soon as she revealed it, for she had planned an evening of steady discontent, calculated to slow Eddie Mack down and give her time to think. She went into the bathroom to try on the earrings. When she came out again, her face was once more composed in accents of neutral woe.

Eddie Mack, who was back with his plans again, had no time for the changes passing over her face. "I've been thinking it would be a good idea for you to do a small part in *Blossom Time*. You're never going to be much of an actress, but the experience will do you good."

"I never pretended to be an actress," she said indignantly. "I'm a singer."

He smiled. "I know it."

Andrea shook her head in a slow, solemn act of resistance

194

against forces she had not yet defined for herself. On her ears the garnets seemed to whisper, Go slow, go slow, there are better things in life. "That's something I wanted to speak to you about. You're always trying to make me what I don't want to be. It's not very fair."

"What's wrong?" Noticing her demonstrative sullenness for the first time, he interpreted it as physical discomfort. "If you don't feel well, you ought to lie down. Suppose I get you a glass of water?"

"I don't want to lie down and I don't want water. Just because a person doesn't want to be an actress doesn't mean she's sick."

"All right," said Eddie Mack. "We'll discuss it some other time."

She sat down with a deliberate lack of grace. Andrea expected to be understood even when she did not understand herself; she regarded Eddie Mack's obtuseness as merely one more burden she would have to bear through what was bound to be a difficult evening. "I suppose you think because your wife's an actress I have to be one too," she said defiantly.

"No." Eddie Mack's voice was brusque. He had little desire to discuss Elfrida; he did not in fact care for the tone in which Andrea mentioned her. "Would you like some sherry?" he asked sternly.

Andrea considered the question with care, for she knew by now that every step she took in the course of this evening committed her to another; however, she could see neither harm nor advantage in the sherry, and so she accepted it. "I was talking to that Nick West," she said a little more amiably. "I think he's in love with me."

"Oh." Eddie Mack looked up from his bottle. "What makes you say that?"

"There are ways of telling those things." Andrea pulled at the strap of her sandals. "He wanted me to go dancing."

Eddie Mack handed her the glass of sherry. "We've never been dancing, have we? I could take you sometime, if you want."

Andrea sipped the sherry thoughtfully, taking pleasure in the soft, golden warmth as it rolled on her tongue. "Wait'll you see him with his feathers on," she said.

Shaking his head, Eddie Mack advanced stubbornly along the course he had ordained for himself. "There's a man in New York I want to listen to you. Da Vinci. He's probably the finest voice coach in the country."

"Um." Andrea sipped and thought of Nick, who apparently had the power to make Eddie Mack angry. "One crazy Indian," she said, kicking a hassock into position for her feet.

In concession to her mood, which had finally penetrated the barrier of his plans, Eddie Mack fell silent, studying the sherry in his glass, examining his blunt, freshly manicured fingernails, inspecting the Moorish cloister that was his living room. Andrea continued to sprawl over the hassock and chair with her conscientious gracelessness. Although he had been exposed to her sulkiness before, it had never been this overt; dull, dim, consuming, it filled the room with its special pressure, an open invitation to brutality. He stood up, went to her side and touched her with unloving hands.

When she turned her face up to him, there was neither alarm nor interest on it but instead a kind of chilly *savoir-faire*, as though she were prepared to ignore practically anything he might do. "Why don't you turn the radio on?" she said.

Reaching across her chair, he did.

While she maintained a rain of irrelevant comment, his hands moved over her, searching for a response they could not find; she made concession after concession without excitement until finally, as though taken by surprise, she slid into an instant of passion, her eyes suddenly veiled by it, her breath coming in gasps. Lifting her from the chair, he carried her into the bedroom.

There is nothing like a bed to encourage the illusion of intimacy. Surrounded by the splendid geography of sheet and pillow, Eddie Mack lost himself in an ecstatic communion with somebody he called Andrea. Gentle now, tender in thought as well as act, he murmured his delight in their joyous collaboration, thinking it was never like this before and saying it too. Love was youth, he was young; happiness had a name and it was Andrea. Eddie Mack, who had spent his life in rose-colored glasses, saw visions of the future now that even he did not dare put words to.

And meanwhile Andrea, having recovered from that initial moment of self-betrayal, the transient stab of passion that had taken her by surprise, peopled the bed with substitutes for her partner in ecstasy, replacing him first, experimentally, with Nick, then with a roster of discarded suitors and finally with a screen star of international fame. None of them pleased her much, but at least they helped her to the knowledge that Eddie Mack pleased her even less. The multiple uncertainties of the past few weeks coalesced into perfect clarity. She was Andrea Marston, who, everyone agreed, was beautiful. In Eddie Mack she had sought only the confirmation of this fact—and its just reward; instead this wild, panting, aging man offered her a prospect of infinite toil, a life of labor set to music. His very enthusiasm offended her; the man she had imagined him to be would have no reason to be that enthusiastic about anything. She could scarcely believe she had ever intended to marry him, and the accident of their being in bed together confirmed her doubts, for somewhere Andrea had acquired as basic wisdom the principle that the man you most certainly didn't go to bed with before marriage was the one you intended to marry.

They could not have been closer together—or further apart. When they separated, they were perfectly clear in their own minds what they planned to do, so clear that it didn't even occur to them to discuss the matter.

Eddie Mack went to Elfrida to demand a divorce. "I'm sorry," he said firmly. "It's something we should have done long ago."

There was conviction in his eyes, in his walk, in the new jacket which she had never seen him wear before. If she had had more time to think, perhaps she would have been less gracious, but at the moment the only thing that occurred to her was, "All right. If you feel that's the way it has to be. I suppose you know how to go about it. I wouldn't even know where to start."

In an outburst of relief at this easy accomplishment of an interview he would have avoided if possible, he bowed, he touched her hand affectionately, he assured her that she would have no trouble at all.

She felt his gratitude more plainly than she felt any emotion of her own, thought Elfrida, smiling pleasantly, all tolerance, balance, goodness, understanding, nothing. On a stage she had always been able to rise to the big moment; now she met it with a nod. Nothing. How could she be so empty? Then she understood that this was an event for which she had been waiting all her life.

"Would you care for some tea?" she asked automatically.

"I'd like that very much, Elfrida." He was obsequious in his desire to please her now, deferring to the merest shadow of a wish. "Nobody could ever pour tea the way you do. People have made ballets out of less."

"Thank you," she said, going to the door that hid the sink. As she filled the kettle, she wondered briefly what would happen if she emptied the pot on his head, and for a moment she held the image of him in her mind with water trickling through the sleek hair and cascading over that generous grin, but instead she maintained the ordered dance into which this interview had turned so swiftly. "I saw Miss Bowman a little while ago. She said that everything was going very well. They expect an extraordinary number of people at the pageant and the mayor's going to make a speech."

"You did a wonderful job there. It was very good of you," he said humbly.

Good good good-by. She took out a cigarette and he sprang to light it. How pleased he was to leave her. Going to get the teacups, she remembered—no, it was so sharp that it was not memory at all—the child she had been was alive in her again without regard for the years that had come between.

When her father left her mother, the severance was so unexpected and catastrophic that the child Elfrida invented a dozen explanations of the disaster, as though trying to make up by sheer quantity for the fact that she couldn't believe in any of them. She dreamed of secret missions, international plots, kingdoms in jeopardy. When each dream wore out, the child awoke at night, convinced that she had merely misunderstood; in the morning her father would be seated at the breakfast table.

At last Elfrida tried to join her mother in an alliance against the man who had hurt them both, but Sally Mitchell had little capacity for self-defense. She spent what remained of her life wondering what she could have done to change it and died unexpectedly and without regret of a relatively minor ailment, leaving her daughter to the theater.

Elfrida poured the tea. Eddie Mack accepted it as he had accepted everything else she had seen fit to give him—with gratitude.

"The girl's awfully young, isn't she?" she asked, thinking this was the summer of which she was the author; even her successes were operating against her.

Eddie Mack paused with the teacup in his hand, his eyes

watchful, the gratitude slipping a little. "She's a grown woman," he said, "a very mature person."

Poor Eddie, he had no gift for picking brides, but there was no point in telling him now. "Some more tea?" she asked.

He shook his head. "I've got to go, Elfrida."

She hesitated and, as he stood up, said, "Eddie, I want to apologize."

"For what?" he demanded in amazement. "You've got nothing to apologize for."

"Oh, yes, I have," she said, but since there didn't seem to be anything to be gained by specifying the things she had to apologize for, that was all she said.

CHAPTER TWENTY-SIX

THE MORNING of the Secost pageant a single cloud hung in the sky above the beach like a lost balloon, but by ten o'clock the sun had burned it away, leaving a day as bright as a knife. The sea was quiet. The sand where the pageant was to be held was freshly raked and as smooth and pale as a bridal sheet.

On the section of the beach reserved for the women of the tribe, wigwams were being erected under the supervision of Miss Felicity Bowman, who had been up before dawn to make a final survey of her arrangements. Tall and gaunt in her purple-flowered dress, wearing her giant straw folded back like a campaign hat, she stalked the Secost shore, oppressed by strange anxieties and shapeless premonitions. Her long, nobly parenthetic nose investigated the breeze in search of meteorological phenomena incalculable by any other measure. Her eyes doubted the intentions of the sun. Her ears strained for the solemn music of storms beyond the horizon.

The day continued to shine. The Indian village rose. Now new anxieties stirred beneath that lean, impassive face, and posting a city policeman to guard the village, Miss Felicity drove off in the cab of a red pickup truck.

With two and a half centuries roaring in her ears, she leaned from the cab to motion traffic out of the way. "Hurry," she shouted to the driver, "we must get the Treaty Table."

Her voice was sharper than she had intended, for the table disturbed her; it could not possibly have figured in the original ceremony. Massive and unwieldy, its oak surface scarred by the thud of tankards and the ingenuity of whittlers, it was not built until a hundred years after the original landing. You had to have a table, she argued with herself. Where else could you put the beads and the cloth and the documents? Where else would the pipe of peace rest? But she was not satisfied, for this was a final concession piled on innumerable others in a step-by-step betrayal of the past. The fact was that, after having lived from early childhood with a brilliantly clear picture of the original ceremony in her mind's eye, she had found in practice that she really knew very little about it, and she had been forced to constant and disillusioning invention. "Can't you go any faster?" she demanded fiercely of the driver.

By two o'clock the stage was set. Pouring in for the day from neighboring cities and towns, emptying out of the giant hotels, stripping the back streets and porches of Secost itself, a crowd estimated by the chief of police at fifty thousand lined the boardwalk, while fifteen hundred honored guests sat in bleachers along the sand. Within ten minutes twenty-seven thousand freshly ironed dresses began to wilt, nine thousand pairs of sunglasses smoked up, one hundred little girls began to whisper urgently to their mothers, three thousand frankfurters were eaten, eight thousand bottles of pop were uncapped, twenty thousand toes were stepped on, three small boys were lost, four expectant mothers felt faint, an out-of-town pickpocket by the name of Freddie the Dip went to work on the edge of the crowd and Sy Puckett began to fortify his braves with strong waters under the boardwalk.

His Honor the Mayor, in top hat and tails, was escorted by a police honor guard to a bunting-draped box where he joined Miss Felicity Bowman, nine members of the Hotel Owners Association, the president of the City Council, four dignitaries whose names have been lost, Elfrida Mitchell, Eddie Mack and Frederic York. The high-school band struck up "Secost Supreme," which the head of the music department had adapted from "Ten Thousand Men of Harvard." In the Indian village the Leni-Lenape squaws started to practice their native crafts.

When the band stopped, the mayor stood up to make a speech, but was heard only imperfectly because of a malfunction of the public-address system. A large pot-bellied man with a big voice and a red face, he belonged to the school of political oratory known as silver-tongued, in which the audience is sung to without musical accompaniment. It was said that, awakened from a deep sleep, he could talk for two hours on any subject without pausing for breath or offending a voter. Now, endowed with the largest audience of his lifetime, he wooed them one by one, lauding in turn the Irish, the Jews, the Italians, the Hungarians, the Poles, the Swedes, the veterans, the nonveterans, the American Legion, the Bowmans, the library committee, the Hotel Owners, the Chamber of Commerce, the Rotarians, the Lions, the Elks, the Oddfellows and, in case he had left anybody out, all good Americans, past and present. He spoke well of the Lord. He gave his praise to the sand, the sea, the sun and the stars and concluded with a veiled but stirring denial that his brother-in-law had gotten rich on the garbage concession.

Beneath the boardwalk Sy Puckett in breechclout and feathers, his small, hard body streaked with red and yellow and black paint, his eyes bloodshot from the sun and three hours of preliminary drinking, felt again the fierce joy of command, dormant since his rumrunning days. Although the Indian blood in the Puckett veins had long since been diluted, if it ever had existed at all, for this one afternoon it flowed unadulterated. "There's one thing I want you guys to remember," he said, pausing for effect, the bloodshot eyes examining his braves with a ferocious enthusiasm that was the closest he normally got to affection, "Indians got plenty to complain about."

The personification of all grievance, sworn enemy of Volstead and the Internal Revenue department, opponent of the W.C.T.U., neckties and continence, defendant of Indians, atheists and anarchy, he raised his tomahawk above his head and glared, seeing who knows what strange allies in that feathered host. They were all dancers—the singers had wound up with Nick—and the male American ballet dancer is himself a special form of rebellion, following a trade that by and large parents do not select for their sons, pursuing what has become the most feminine of the arts at a time when every one of them is more than ever under female custodianship. A number of the dancers were homosexuals and many of those who weren't had given some consideration to the matter.

When the tomahawk fell, they headed out onto the sand, stalking invisible buffalo, sweat making rivers on their painted bodies, the sour mash whiskey bubbling strangely in their bellies. Moccasined feet stole through the gripping sand, bright feathers wagged against the wind, notched arrows hung in their bowstrings.

On the boardwalk another thousand frankfurters disappeared into hungry mouths, two thousand bottles of pop were swallowed by thirsty throats, Freddie the Dip pocketed an alligator wallet. "Splendid," said the mayor to no one in particular.

Under the boardwalk Nick West stood with the main body of the Leni-Lenape, awaiting the arrival of the colonists, while far out to sea Sir Henry Bowman and his party lay becalmed in a retired ferry which had been disguised with wood and canvas as the original *Sea Sprite*.

Sir Henry's starched ruff had worn a bright red collar of irritated skin around his neck, his eyes twitched from the unrelenting glare of the sea. "Don't just sit there," he said nastily to Captain Frisbie.

Captain Frisbie shrugged his shoulders with a vast indifference which made his stomach roll. He was himself suffering from gas pains and a general malaise. "It's not my boat. The captain's fixing it." But Frisbie, unhappily aware that there were times for cowardice, remembered the size of the Hotel Bowman's meat bill and went to confer with the vessel's master. "They found the trouble," he announced, returning with a bottle of beer in his hand. "Now all they got to do is fix it."

Huddled under an awning, Sir Henry watched Captain Frisbie and catalogued his vices, beginning with gluttony and coming back to it at frequent intervals. The engine coughed despondently. The sea moved like a huge, rumpled hammock. Sir Henry was not well.

On the beach Sy Puckett raised his tomahawk once more, starting a chorus of whoops and a rain of arrows; invisible buffalo dripped invisible blood into the sand.

"Splendid," said the mayor.

Miss Felicity glanced at her watch, scanned the horizon, wished suddenly that the whole thing were over. In the middle of the beach the Treaty Table stood as though it had grown there, a massive irrelevance belonging neither to the Indians nor the settlers, an item of landscape so improbable that for one desperate moment she contemplated having it removed.

"Ekki rah," yelled Sy Puckett, who had just made the pleasant discovery that he was fluent in the language of his ancestors. "Brak um punty wah." Pointing his tomahawk at the boardwalk, he led his braves into its shelter, where they joined the main force under Nick West.

"Any signs of the boat?" asked Nick.

"Likki akki fut," replied Sy Puckett smugly.

Nick looked at the watch he had concealed in his breech-clout. "We're not supposed to start the ceremonial dances until the boat's in sight."

"Speak Indian," said Sy Puckett.

Tony George, wearing the canary-yellow jacket over one arm like a buckler, joined the two chiefs. "What the hell do you do when a boat misses a cue?" he said plaintively.

Up above on the boardwalk there was only a limited awareness that something had gone wrong. The spectators, disposed to be pleased by whatever was offered them, ate and drank and contentedly watched the empty sand, cheerfully unaware that they were sharing their pockets with Freddie the Dip. The mayor thought bitterly of his brother-in-law, who talked too much, and the Indian village, which had lapsed into somnolence during the hunt, began to hum again with domestic activity; at a sign from Miss Felicity the band embarked on a medley of Sousa marches.

Miss Felicity herself, leaving the box, came down under the boardwalk. She had put aside the floppy straw and the purple flowers; her dress was silver, her hat bore the name of a famous designer, she moved eloquently. "Something must have gone wrong with the boat," she said. "Please go ahead with the ceremonial dances."

Obediently they ran out on the sand where they danced to the rain, they danced to the sun, they danced for good crops, for fat buffalo, for victory in war; at one point they danced something suspiciously like a ballet Tony George had prepared for *New Moon*. When they could dance no more, they retreated under the boardwalk and the band returned to Sousa.

Then a murmur rose from the crowd as the *Sea Sprite*, sails limp and figurehead awry, chugged wearily into view. All over the boardwalk fathers raised their children as though in salute. Freddie the Dip for once put his hands in his own pockets. Miss Felicity stood up. The mayor said, "Splendid," and the newspaper photographers, who had been shooting the Indian village and the dances, began to jockey for position on the beach.

While the *Sea Sprite* hove to with a shudder of its limp sails, Nick West led his tiring warriors onto the sand for the dance of welcome. Colonists rushed to disembark in small boats. As Sir Henry, Captain Frisbie and their chief lieutenants headed toward shore in the first boat, the band blared "Secost Supreme," the crowd underwent a giant tremor that shook the railings of the boardwalk and the Indians howled a wild hello.

The first wave of colonists clustered in some embarrassment at the edge of the sea, shouldering muskets and blunderbusses, disengaging swords from between their legs, adjusting ruffs and smoothing breeches.

"Assemble the troops," said Sir Henry.

"Yessir," said Captain Frisbie, who no longer trusted himself to say more.

Struggling out of the sea, colonists hurried to line up four abreast behind Captain Frisbie. For two minutes they were wandering civilians with water in their breeches and sand in their shoes; then, harried into place by the captain's military monosyllables, they straightened ranks, stiffened backs, denied their bellies and adjusted the instruments of war. "It's a long long way to Tipperary," said the trumpets to the tuba. "For'd harch!" roared the captain. Through the sand, across the centuries they went, the immemorial sea behind, the Leaning Tower of Pizza aslant in the sky ahead of them.

Nick West lifted one arm sweepingly, mournfully, greetingly and the dancing stopped, the band fell silent; Nick and Sy Puckett led the Leni-Lenape to meet their destiny at the Treaty Table.

On the boardwalk the crowd was quiet. Even the sea stood still, green marble veined with white toward the shore, a single gull drifting above it in the distance. The sun was out of Genesis, the sky was light undefiled. As the white tide met the red, history was in the making again and even Felicity Bowman, who had become more and more uneasy about what she had done, felt with a rush of gratitude that at least this fragment they had recovered truly from the past.

The solemnity of the moment hung over the beach like a canopy. Henry Bowman accepted the silence of so many people as a physical confirmation of a glory he only infrequently remembered he possessed; life briefly had a simplicity far beyond bills and mortgages and recalcitrant cooks; for two hundred beats of his heart there was absolutely nothing of which he disapproved. Behind him the men of Secost, feeling their sand-clogged shuffle turn exact, grew pleasantly aware of the dignity they had put on with a suit of ancient clothes. The single exception was Captain Frisbie; to him the moment was something lost rather than something gained; born to be a hunter of men and beasts, he knew in his bitterness what life should have been and was not.

As red and white met on opposite sides of the Treaty Table, Sir Henry picked up the microphone waiting for him there and by that simple act terminated the eighteenth century. "Oh, red-men of the forest and the plain," he said into the wavering public-address system, "across the many waters I have come, leaving the land of my ancestors to bring the blessings of civilization to this great new land. I come with guns, but I come in peace, for I come to buy your land, not to steal it. Where there is nothing but a vast and teeming wilderness, soon will be heard the sound of the ax, the adze and the saw, carving out the place for great cities. The land will know the plow and will bring forth grain. The wheel will master the earth and boats floating like great swans will come over the waters. Wonders will be seen in the heavens. All of the arts of industry and culture will flourish."

The words were Felicity's but the delivery was Henry's, and that high, supercilious voice, sharpened on generations of cooks and chambermaids, somehow converted the promises of peace into threats of war. For a half hour the glories of civilization turned sour in his mouth, while his one gesture, a stiff projection of the right hand at shoulder height, invariably came to rest on the Leaning Tower of Pizza, which in turn stood for the plow, the wheel, the boats floating like swans, the wonders of the heavens, the arts of industry and culture.

The Indians saw the sea, the settlers faced a giant Coke bottle in the sky, dreams of liquid refreshment raged among them.

Then at last Sir Henry was done. The band began to play "Auld Lang Syne." Nick West, accompanied by a small band of warriors, moved around the table to present the pipe of peace, walking quickly, hot, tired, eager now to bring the ceremony to an end. His mind on the ocean, on frozen liquid and interminable shadow, he did not notice the large foot which Captain Frisbie had left negligently extended in his path. Nick stepped on it heavily.

All day long the captain had suffered from heat, thirst, digestive infirmities and Sir Henry's insolence. On the happiest day he had ever lived he had hated at least one person well. Now he could bear no more and, using his immense forearm like a club, in one sweeping motion he brushed aside the pipe of peace, Nick West and the last hope of the pageant's success.

The pipe spilled red coals in the sand and shattered. Nick, staggering, saw the coals; he saw Frisbie's face spread across the sky. The incredibly dainty nose, suddenly articulate, twitched its disdain of Indians and actors and all the lesser races of man. The lips smiled scornfully. An intolerable vanity shone in the oyster eyes.

The captain folded his mighty arms. Implacable, glorying in the majesty of his own flesh, he presided over catastrophes still to come.

Nick sat in the sand, felt sand, tasted sand. For a moment, looking at the irresistible arm that had delivered him there so casually, he wished only that he could pull the beach up over his head like a blanket. Then he felt his legs. They were intact. He touched his buttocks. They had survived. With increasing pleasure he examined himself part by part and found no damage. He rose to his feet, he stooped to pick up his battered war bonnet. He straightened it tenderly, he glanced at Captain Frisbie reproachfully. In a moment of defiance he started to fold his arms on his chest too, but thought better of it. A single feather floated downward from the bonnet. In mid-air he caught it, studied it fondly. He looked at Frisbie, he looked at the feather. Then the wonder of it all dawned on his face. Wotan had moved. Wotan had struck. Wotan had broken a feather.

Frisbie heard laughter. Indian laughter. Actor's laughter. His breath roared through his nose and his already enormous face began to swell. For a moment his whole body shook like some vastly inefficient machine which had mysteriously gone to work upon itself; then he hurtled down the beach toward Nick West.

At this point Sy Puckett stuck out a leg and deftly tripped the captain. As that vast body toppled majestically, the melee was on.

Mr. Cartwright hit Sy Puckett behind the ear. Captain Frisbie, stranded on his stomach like a beached whale, groped for a red ankle. Mr. Prentiss, suddenly fearful, started to fend off the nearest Indian with his blunderbuss. Two Indians, racing for the shelter of the boardwalk, ran over a kneeling photographer. Three more photographers headed into the heart of the struggle and Captain Frisbie, catching one of them, smashed his camera. The girls in the Indian village began to scream.

"Splendid," muttered the mayor, who had fallen asleep in the middle of Sir Henry's speech and awakened to what he construed as cheers.

On the boardwalk the crowd, confronted with a spectacle beyond their most extravagant expectations, struggled for positions along the rail. A Mrs. Furness went to her husband's assistance with a beach umbrella. Mrs. Waters, who had been a physical-education instructor, hauled Mr. Waters away by the back of his breeches.

In the bunting-draped box Felicity Bowman rose to her full height and stood in enigmatic contemplation. Her silver dress hung from her lean, strong body like armor. Her hat was a helmet. Her face was the face of a captain of armies, watchful, stern and curiously serene. She noted dispassionately that Sir Henry, who had been sickly as a child and was still disinclined to athletic endeavor, had retreated under the Treaty Table.

Although there were officially only two sides in the battle, many were the strange private banners under which war was waged. Some fought boredom, others fear. They battled sin, strangers, themselves. They fought fathers, mothers, siblings, fate. A Mr. Frazier struck out against long-hair music. A blond dancer was there because he hadn't received electric trains for Christmas when he was six years old. Giuliano, the big baritone who had played football at Fordham, enjoyed the exercise. There were men there of gentle hearts and peaceful ways who fought out of a sense of social obligation. Several photographers, cameras demolished, fought indiscriminately on both sides in the name of freedom of the press.

Nick West, who in his own judgment was to blame for all this, went to rescue Sir Henry. "I want to help you," he explained, poking his head under the Treaty Table.

Sir Henry sat with his shoulders around his ears; his pale, thin lips were clenched as though nothing would ever make him talk again.

"Just tell me what you want me to do," said Nick, wondering what word or act of his could unseal those frozen lips. "If you want, I'll make a public apology to Captain Frisbie."

Sir Henry's narrow face twitched; one eye remained fixed and staring while the wrinkled eyelid fluttered alarmingly over the other. "Go away," he said.

"Let's discuss this like rational human beings," suggested Nick.

It was then that Sir Henry kicked him.

Nick went away. He stopped to speak to Mr. Prentiss about the use of the blunderbuss and was hit with it. He took an arrow from an Indian who was thoughtfully fitting it to his bow. Going in search of Captain Frisbie, he found him on one knee in the sand locked in combat with Giuliano.

His eyes closed and an expression of enormous incredulity on his face, the captain clung to the waist of the big baritone, who had already knocked him down three times. "You little son of a bitch," said the captain, to whom the whole world was irrefutably little.

"Let go of him," said Nick.

"I can't," replied Giuliano calmly. "He wants to bite me."

Before Nick could intervene further he was attacked from the rear by Mr. Prentiss, still wielding the blunderbuss, but Prentiss's heart was no longer in the fight and he soon wandered away. All over the beach the signs of conflict were beginning to wane. Here and there men sat in the sand, studying their injuries or merely giving consideration to the fact that their hearts beat tocsins in their chests. The sand was filled with feathers and mangled ruffs; in a neat pile beside the Treaty Table, never to be delivered now, were the trade goods Sir Henry had brought for the purchase of Secost.

While the police advanced cautiously onto the strand, their chief began to broadcast over the public-address system. "Disperse. Disperse to your homes. I warn you, disperse. The fire department is on the way with hoses."

Sy Puckett, both eyes black and a long scratch running down his naked belly, stopped to enumerate his wounds. "Bastards," he said amiably and, dragging his war bonnet behind him, followed the recommendation of the chief of police.

Now men who a moment before had been the bitterest of enemies ignored each other completely; Indians and colonists, bemused by the events of the afternoon, limped away side by side from mutual disaster. Inside of five minutes the beach was clear of contestants and the ocean began to wash away the debris of battle.

The police arrested a photographer for trying to take a picture of Sir Henry as he came out from under the Treaty Table.

The mayor had disappeared from the bunting-draped box, followed a moment later by Frederic York, who, grown politely efficient, stopped only to say to Eddie Mack, "I'll give you until Friday to get out of here."

Eddie Mack didn't answer; instead he inspected the sea with a thoughtful persistence which it seemed pointless to interrupt. The sun sliding off the waves filled his head. Quiet. All quiet. In a minute, he thought, in a minute, submitting his mind to the movement of the water and the brilliance of its light.

At his side Elfrida, knowing that he would awaken soon enough, watched the police search the sand for malefactors.

Elfrida, all eye. Detached. Ironic. About to be divorced. Serene. Elfrida, who had signed a separate peace and would be the author of no more summers or winters either. Elfrida in perfect balance, exquisite harmony, nothing. She turned her head and saw Miss Felicity. The perfect balance, now only twenty-four hours old, began to waver. Miss Felicity. After the beach had been emptied, the tall woman had taken to her seat, but she gave no other sign of relaxation from the military calm with which she had viewed the events of the afternoon. "I'm sorry," said Elfrida, leaning toward her.

"Thank you," replied Miss Felicity automatically, and Elfrida was not sure that she had understood the apology.

"I know what this meant to you," said Elfrida. "I wouldn't have had it happen for the world."

Miss Felicity finally looked up. "It's not your fault. When I saw Henry down there, afraid he might get his feet wet, I finally understood what a mistake I had made. I should have let it all stay in my head where it belonged." Her long crusader's face softened under its helmet. "I'm sorry, too," she said, shaking hands with Elfrida. "I guess this hasn't done either of us much good."

And that was the last she said about the matter to anybody.

CHAPTER TWENTY-SEVEN

NOW THERE WAS NO TIME AT ALL.

The troupe, its hundreds of loves, friendships and aversions abruptly threatened, clung together briefly, then fell apart with the speed of a disintegrating comet. All at once, unbearably, everyone was in a hurry to leave, as though the smell of disaster might stick to them forever if they stayed a moment longer.

Frederic York packed his bags the same night, although he didn't go until the following morning. To Danielle he gave a lifetime supply of Lovalee cosmetics. To Eddie Mack he gave his hand—firmly and without rancor. "Good-by," he said. "You'll hear from my accountants this afternoon."

At this point Eddie Mack retained only one item of the

previous day's riches and that was Andrea, who had not yet succeeded in making her defection clear to him. Surrounded by bills and the importunities of his fleeing staff, he sat at his desk, smoking Romeo y Julieta cigars end to end while he examined his clouds for silver linings. He had been poor before, but then prosperity had always lurked around every corner; now poverty surrounded him like a prison wall. He had a thousand dollars, a withered wardrobe and no prospects. He looked at his watch as though it might tell him something; all it told him was that he was getting older by the minute. If he got up from the desk and started to walk, he would not know where to go. Confidence had been his capital, plans his currency, but now he had neither confidence in the future nor plans for it. A lifetime of debts had come due at once. He opened his desk. Inside there were three paper clips, a book of matches and a letter from a down-and-out actor whom he had helped in the past. It struck him with the force of ultimate revelation that hardly anybody tried to borrow money from him any more. He sat and watched the motes stirring in the sun.

There was Andrea. Yes. Looking at his watch again, he was surprised to discover that only two minutes had passed since he looked at it the last time. There was Andrea. A renunciation scene came into his mind, played in deep shadow. Go, fly, save yourself. As for him, he would do what must be done. No tears. Perhaps someday when she was old she would remember him; that was all he asked, a few seconds of remembrance spared from an otherwise happy life.

But you don't throw away your last hope quite that easily— at least not if you're Eddie Mack.

He stood up and the very act seemed to make him stronger. He threw away a half-smoked cigar as though considerations of economy were alien to him. He loved her. She loved him. Why shouldn't he continue his plans for her career? He saw her on a stage. Cheers. Applause. Bravo. And all this I owe to my manager and beloved husband, Eddie Mack. He would get a new suit of tails, for the old one had started to show bright spots under lights.

Opening the office door, he started down the ramp that led to the boardwalk, walking so swiftly that he scarcely noticed the signs of disintegration and departure around him. When he reached Andrea's room, she was packing her bags. "Where are you going?" he asked.

She continued to pack, irritated by the note of grievance in his voice. Although normally quite neat, she threw in her dresses without any regard to how they fell; Andrea was convinced that somehow she had been twice defrauded. She had already reached a decision that she wanted neither Eddie Mack nor a career, but she had felt that they were both hers to reject; she had not anticipated having them blown out of her hands while she contemplated their disposition. "I'm going home," she said when it became clear that he would wait indefinitely for an answer. "Back to Kansas City, where I belong."

"You don't belong in Kansas City."

Although she privately agreed with him, Andrea had no desire to give Eddie Mack anything but pain. She had been a fool to believe him for a minute. As she looked at him standing there in the doorway, worn and anxious and slightly shabby, she felt that some dubious sleight-of-hand had been practiced on her; she could not believe that this was the man she had considered marrying. "Where else can I go?" she demanded bitterly.

"Stay here. I'll be here a little longer and then we'll go to New York."

She pulled the orange leather bags from her bed and put them side by side on the floor. "What would I do in New York?" she asked, although that was no longer the question in her mind.

"There's your career," he said. "I thought it was all agreed on."

Andrea looked in the mirror and saw that she was young and beautiful. Talk merely obscured that fact; Eddie Mack's very presence in her room was a diminishment of what she was, a reminder of how she had nearly thrown herself away. "I don't need a career," she said. "Careers are for people who don't have anything else. If I want people to look at me, all I have to do is walk in the street. If I want to be loved, I can have my choice." His solemn, uncomprehending, badly shaven face drove her to a specific cruelty as though only that might penetrate this obstinate refusal of comprehension. "I don't need you," she said. "I don't want you. What do I have to say to make you understand?"

And finally understanding, Eddie Mack paused to search for words, realized that there were none, closed the door. Automatically he looked at his watch again. It was now only three-quarters of an hour since he had looked at it the first time in the office. Tic, toc, tic, toc, Eddie mock. He repeated the rhyme to himself all of the way back along the boardwalk, until he sat once more in the solitude of his four walls. What was happening to him? Tic, toc, tic, toc, Eddie mock.

Taking out the letter from the actor again, he decided to send the man twenty-five dollars. He had always prided himself on being an easy touch.

He thought of what had happened the previous afternoon and his whole body started to tremble with anger. If his plans had been wrecked by a tornado, he would not have minded. If his life had been laid waste by lightning, he could have accepted it. If war or depression or pestilence had put their hands on him, he could have found a way to reconcile himself to the very majesty of these disasters, but instead his plans had been overturned by a sequence of events so trivial, so ridiculous, that in another age, another town, he might have laughed at them. Time mocked Eddie Mack, people mocked Eddie Mack, even some hiding place in his own brain mocked Eddie Mack.

He stood up, still trembling. He didn't know where to go or what to do, but his body itself moved him forward down the ramp, through the dark secret regions of the theater, into corners he had never seen before. He wandered until he came to the dressing rooms and there he found Fisty Fuller packing.

"Hiya," said Fisty, who had just finished cleaning and oiling the two Colt .38's that were his constant companions. "Tough luck yesterday."

Eddie Mack grunted and started to turn aside.

"There are people like that," said Fisty Fuller softly. "You got to watch yourself with them every minute."

"People like what?"

"Nick West."

The name came to Eddie Mack slowly through his sea of troubles. He had not yet tried to sort out the blame among the principal actors in the Secost pageant. As a matter of fact, there had been so many people involved so quickly and the conclusion had been so swiftly disastrous that he had never understood the exact sequence of events which led to his downfall. "Nick West?" he said.

"I was watching him every minute," said Fisty Fuller. "I been watching him for some time now. He was the one who started with the fat captain. If it hadn't been for that, nothing would have happened at all."

Eddie Mack pondered this statement with great difficulty. His thoughts were occurring on so many different levels at once that they were scarcely thoughts at all but merely fragments, flashes, shreds of what was, tatters of what might have been. For a moment he noticed how the light glistened on the top of Fisty Fuller's head and that was as important as anything else. Andrea, he thought, tic, toc, Eddie mock. "Nick West?" he said.

Fisty Fuller shrugged away this confusion impatiently. "Kid Anything-for-a-Laugh himself."

Fisty Fuller's bald head, Andrea's orange suitcase, Elfrida's emerald ring, the face of a watch, the *Sea Sprite* coming into the harbor, the sound of darkness, the scratch of a pen writing "past due," a prophecy of doom made by his mother thirty-five years before—these things spun like a pinwheel in Eddie Mack's brain. Round and round they went, color on color, visible sound, and as they whirled, Nick's face appeared at their center, growing sharper and sharper, mockery in a war bonnet, a tomahawk in flesh, destruction in feathers. Suddenly everything disappeared but Nick West, Nick West once, Nick West twice, three four five Nick Wests, a ravaging army of them, Nick West cavorting on the beach, grinning on the stage, inviting Andrea to dance, Nick West Andrea's age and in love with her, Nick West tutored and touted by Elfrida. Even Elfrida.

All at once Eddie Mack, who had not been able to keep one direction all day, had a destination, a target, a point on which he could focus the trembling energy of his legs and arms, the wild despair, the pointless anger, the mockery that had turned inward. He had Nick West to hate and he hated him.

"He's out there on the stage right now making faces at himself," said Fisty Fuller, his eyes staring, his nostrils twitching slightly as though they might pick up the final nuance, the ultimate subtlety of what was passing through Eddie Mack's head. "Somebody ought to throw a scare into that bastard he'll never forget." And Fisty Fuller held one of his guns caressingly in his hand, held it until he was sure Eddie Mack had seen and absorbed it; then he disappeared discreetly from the dressing room.

Eddie Mack, who had not fired a gun since Belleau Wood, looked at this one now as though it were the solution he had been waiting for through all those years, obvious as steel, final as death. When he picked it up, it fit his hand like a second palm. One hundred steps and then down a staircase, fifty steps and there was Nick West walking the banks of the blue Danube, dawdling in the home of the Strauss waltz. *Blossom Time*. Eddie Mack was going down to defeat in blossom time. "Rahhhh," said Eddie Mack, startling himself with the sound; his voice seemed to have gone beyond the use of words into a language of unadulterated hate.

Nick looked up. The sudden dissolution of the summer had afflicted him with a loneliness sharpened by a sense of guilt. He had come to the stage because he could think of no place else where he would be welcome. He meditated on apologies; he contemplated magic combinations of words that would set everything right for everybody. Now somebody was coming through the darkness, a shadow among shadows advancing into the path of a single bulb. "Hello," said Nick uncertainly. Then he saw it was Eddie Mack. "Hello, Mr. Mack. Mr. Mack, I want to apologize for everything that happened."

Nick bent a little to search the shadows for Eddie Mack's face. There was solicitude in his bent back, in his outstretched hand, in the slight sag of his knees; he was prepared to apologize for anything and everything, including offenses that had not even occurred to him yet, but Eddie Mack never gave him a chance.

"Nyahhh," said Eddie Mack, his tongue still unable to capture the incredible fluency of his brain, which tumbled with a mighty agenda, spun with an array of indictments in which Nick stood not merely for himself but for a whole generation of the unknowing and the unknowable, for a joking fate, for malign chance. "Enough," he said. "How much?" he asked, for in all that flurry of charges, this was the closest he could come to the arraignment that swept through him like a wave. He struggled, he clenched his empty fist, strained his right hand against the gun butt; he shouted incoherently and then, since speech still would not come to him, in a final flurry of frustration, he raised the gun and let it speak for him.

221

Nick, who saw the gun for the first time when Eddie Mack raised it, ducked away from its flash, lifted an arm against its roar. To his surprise he felt no fear that he could recognize as such but instead a kind of mounting irritation, a vast and cranky sorrow at this infection of madness which had spread from colonist to Indian to colonist again and now had reached out to touch Eddie Mack.

"Oh, shit," he said, noting in the splendor of his calm that he did not even stutter. Later he was to remember that these might have been his last words.

Instead it turned out they were merely a period to the event, for Eddie Mack, shooting blindly, had hit and shattered a white plaster bust of Beethoven and thereby awakened himself from a dream that had lasted a lifetime. Listening to the echo of the gun's roar and confronted by the splintered reality of the broken head, all of a sudden he found himself outside the world in which the dead arise when the curtain falls, and throwing away the gun, he left the theater.

CHAPTER TWENTY-EIGHT

UNDER THE MARQUEE of the Secost Theater Eddie Mack turned without question toward the Hotel Florian; he told himself that he was going to salvage the remnants of his wardrobe from Elfrida's cottage. His hair was disheveled. His tie had slid around under his collar and hung like a hangman's noose. The thirst in his throat was so great that it was a kind of paralysis. His legs were stiff and uncertain with fatigue, and the sweat pouring torrentially from his body left it surprisingly cold. For the first time since his arrival he enjoyed the warmth of the Secost sun.

Possessed by an exhaustion close to walking slumber, he drifted along on aching legs, a peaceful wreck of a man, seeing with an appreciative calm the blue of the ocean, the glitter of

223

the sky, the whirl of the shining custard machines, the rows of frankfurters sizzling like small, brown torpedoes. He came to the Florian, recognized it slowly and walked down a ramp that led to the garden. In front of the cottage he stopped again, not thinking, not hesitating from any consideration of what would follow, merely halted by an unfamiliar obstacle in the form of steps. One foot went up, the other joined it and the problem was solved. He knocked on the door. Elfrida opened it.

"I shot Nick West," he said, since that was what he had intended to do, but, seeing the look of horror on her face, he corrected the statement. "No, I didn't hit him."

Elfrida reached out to straighten his tie. She saw that his clothes were as drenched as though he had been bathing in them. "Are you hurt?" she asked.

He shook his head.

"Are you sure Nick is all right?"

"Nobody was hurt but Beethoven." He leaned against the inside of the door, his body limp, his face in the grip of a silly peace which made Elfrida think for a moment that he might have been drinking. "I threw the gun away," he said.

Elfrida led him to a chair and with a slight pressure of her hand against his chest she sat him down in a cradle of wicker. For a moment his eyes closed; then they opened again and he reached into a pocket for a cigar. Like everything else about him, the cigar had been twisted, malformed, curiously damaged. With an air of complete absorption he set himself to the project of straightening it, his fingers shaking on the bent Havana leaf, his eyes blinking nearsightedly. When he was done he tried to light it, but Elfrida had to help him. Finally he puffed giant fumes into the room.

Reassured by this evidence of revival, Elfrida went to boil some water for tea. Why, she didn't know. In all the crises of life, she thought, women boil water.

224

"I don't shoot people," said Eddie Mack from the middle of the smoke. "That's not like me at all." He was too weary now to have more than one emotion at a time and it seemed that amazement at himself had replaced everything else.

While she waited for the water to boil, Elfrida sat down beside him. He was like the victim of an explosion, stripped of all disguises, skinned, bared to her view, Eddie Mack infinitely vulnerable and undefiled. "I thought it was all Nick's fault," he said. "You don't shoot people for things like that."

He meditated on this point or another with the same intense, somehow childlike concentration, completely self-absorbed until the tea was ready and she brought a cup to his chair. Like smoking the cigar, drinking the tea was a project to which he could devote the utmost of his attention. He raised the cup, tilted it, sipped the hot liquid with an almost fond concern for the details of what he was doing. When he was done he had evidently accomplished yet another step in his revival; he seemed to be reassembling himself out of a series of familiar acts. "That was good tea, Elfrida," he said, "strong. I don't know why so many people make weak tea."

"Do you remember when we went skating in Central Park?" he said. "It was tea we drank afterward." He sipped the tea, gulped it, asked for another cup. The parched burning in his throat reminded him of where he had been only a short while before, but he quickly put aside any further consideration of the matter, for it set his hands trembling again and started a shadow of the familiar pinwheel in his head. Glancing down the length of his legs, he saw that a shoelace trailed around his right ankle; he made a note to fix it later. He remembered that he had come for his clothing; that could wait until later, too. Putting his head against the flaring chair back, he felt the pattern of the wicker bones close against his skull, felt the skinny pillow hanging on his shoulders like a knapsack. "That year we went skating we had the apartment on Fifth Avenue," he said. "You have to admit it was a good year. Even the air smelled good."

"Yes," said Elfrida. It had been good until Arthur died; then it hadn't been good any more. As she looked at his newly transparent face, she realized that that was what he was thinking too.

The telephone rang in the bedroom. She went in and closed the door. It was Nick. "Did you hear from Mr. Mack?" he asked guardedly.

"Yes. He's here now. He told me what happened. Are you all right?"

Nick laughed in embarrassment. "Oh, I'm fine."

He probably was at that, she thought with a smile.

"I was worried about you," he said. "He seemed half crazy."

"He's over that now. He's ashamed, Nick."

"Tell him to forget it."

"I'll tell him."

"Look," he said, "are you positive you're okay?"

"Yes."

"Well." His voice wavered. "Everybody's leaving. Will I see you again?"

She thought of Eddie Mack in the next room and shook her head. "Not right now, Nick."

Disturbed by the abruptness of this farewell, she sought in her mind for something to say, a torch to pass on, but torches were getting harder and harder to come by. He was young enough to last out the century, but God alone knew what kind of a promise that was. Two thousand, enigmatic year of the three zeros. If the past didn't get you, the future might. "Oh, Nick," she said, "struggle."

"What?" he said.

"The world is full of invitations to nothing. Death is

everywhere. Respect life. Honor the present. And, for God's sake, don't mumble. *Coraggio*."

"Yes," he said.

The phone clicked.

Hesitating for a moment in the silent bedroom, Elfrida looked at the door that separated her from her husband. It was wood, it was white, there were fingerprints on it, and when she opened it, she would find Eddie Mack in his chair, awaiting the medicinal word, the curative act, the thing she was going to do to make everything better. You couldn't go on boiling water forever. Twisting the emerald ring on her finger, she remembered the deliberately drab and inconsequential ceremony that had united her to Eddie Mack. Night, rain, wind and a plump J.P. with a gravelly voice. I do. I do. Hurry, hurry, hurry. Get it over with. On the narrow porch stiff-jointed rocking chairs creaked back and forth in the wind like old ladies mourning their dead. Somewhere in the darkness stood the invisible members of her wedding party, her father, her mother, the child she had been. They had lived with her ever since.

They were what she was. What she was. For a single terrifying minute she looked at the door and that was what she was. A door, a window, a piece of furniture, a stranger passing in a crowd. She was Eddie Mack on the other side of the door. She stopped herself. No. She was Elfrida Mitchell, who was once that child. She was Elfrida Mitchell, who, if necessary, would re-create herself every morning.

When she opened the bedroom door, she found that Eddie Mack had fallen asleep, and knowing that this was more than anything else she could offer him at the moment, she let him sleep. His head hung toward his shoulder at a painfully broken angle, but his face was quiet, his breathing regular. While the disheveled hair made him look young, all his years were

227

in his face. Eddie Mack. Her husband. A man with lungs and heart and variable pulse. Alive.

Around her stood her father, her mother, the child she had been; on her finger Arthur's ring glowed, a fiery talisman. Elfrida the Uncommitted and her guardian. Queen of Love. Wisewoman. What you destroy in advance will never hurt you; what you diminish daily will never cause pain.

Elfrida went to the front door of the cottage. Opening it, she flung the emerald ring far into the garden, watched it soar green and quick as a miraculous bird, then saw it drop into the heart of a flowering bush. She waited a moment longer. When she went back to Eddie Mack's side, they were alone.

CHAPTER TWENTY-NINE

AS NICK CAME UP THE HALL, Andrea came down it, followed by a taxi driver carrying the orange suitcases.

"Hello," said Nick.

"Not hello. Good-by." The sun filtering into the hall had set a golden crown upon her head, her eyes were cased in endless darkness. Her lips, barely parted, promised mysteries never yet put into words. "I'm going back to Kansas City," she said, continuing down the hall. At the very last minute she turned to give him a glance of oracular sadness, first penetrating, then surprised and finally indignant, as though she had just discovered one more item in the history of her deception; then she was gone.

Late that night Nick stood beside Claire on the beach where colonists and Indians had fought to such a strange conclusion.

The sand glowed softly in the moonlight. Farther down the beach a Japanese master of the art decorated the night with fireworks that spilled across the sky in blazing waterfalls and flowered in bright, ephemeral gardens. A cold breeze traveled from the sea like an omen of the long Secost winter. Nick shivered. In the kingdom of clowns, he thought, the Indians always won, the last were inevitably first. But not here, not here. "Where will you go?" he asked.

"It's not bad where I am," said Claire. "I'm a good worker. They'll keep me on through the winter."

Nick watched her face with a curious feeling that it might vanish if he turned around. Her skin was clear. Her features were neat and made with a certain pleasant accuracy. Her eyes were the blue of the quietest of sapphires.

"Your dress is very pretty," he said.

She smiled. In the weeks since their first meeting she had confined her conversation to Nick, and now, as they prepared to separate, he was disturbed by the anonymity which surrounded her.

"Don't you ever hear from your brothers and sisters?" he asked.

She shook her head.

"I never asked you about your family," he said regretfully.

Staring into the darkness, she tried to discover something to tell him. She came from people who had flourished in the old days when there had always been green forests ahead in which they could repair their mistakes. When the frontier ran out, their luck ran out with it. She remembered dim tales of grandfathers and great-grandfathers who had never been cramped into cities. She remembered her father's red hair and loud voice. In the orphanage she had owned a plaster-headed doll with a single brown eye which winked up and down and sometimes got stuck; they had taught her to sew, but she had never cared for sewing. She enjoyed hot baths. She liked to ride on trains.

She looked at him and smiled. "Do you remember the time you came into my room in the middle of the night with your feathers and paint and did the rain dance? That was so wonderful."

She started to laugh. It was an unusually hearty laugh for such a little girl and it rang out boldly in the night, momentarily stronger than the whimper of the wind and the splash of the sea, stronger even than the red and white ghosts who still lurked murderously in the shadows of the boardwalk.

When Nick finally reached his room, he found a telegram waiting for him under the door. Phrased with a precision that his father reserved for moments of high emotion, it announced Jake's marriage—not as Nick had half expected to the fat widow, Mrs. Little, but to the small, quiet one who admired Shakespeare. MARRIED MRS MARTIN TODAY 10:30 EASTERN STANDARD TIME LOVE PAPA.

Nick went to the window and looked out into the street where the waning night crouched like an elderly lion, too tired to move on. It was the time when life is rumored to be at its lowest ebb, when the whole universe seems to hesitate on the edge of an enormous question, and as he read the telegram for the second time, Nick remembered the wasted years of the old man's rage; he remembered how small his father had grown. There should have been bells and rice, flutes and flageolets. Instead the smell of brine rose, sharp and sour, from the sea; there was no sound anywhere except the crackling of the paper in Nick's hand.

Suddenly, as though they could bear the silence no longer, the birds of Secost defiantly proclaimed the dawn. They were funny, screaming birds—jays, sparrows, starlings, possibly a wayfaring crow—but the song they sang was made for belated bridegrooms and refugees from doom; impertinent, loud, unafraid, it drove away the night.

As light poured over the town, Nick felt the world turn,

heard the waters of its oceans rush by. He lit a cigarette and the continents were at his fingertips; he was the lord of land, sea and air—all methods of locomotion were his servants.

Taking his suitcase from the floor, he began to fill it quickly with the contents of the brown, unlovely bureau, which rocked and bowed to his touch like a friendly drunk.

In a storm of socks and shirts and underwear Bongo West was on his way to the year 2000. The enigmatic year of the three zeros.

ABOUT THE AUTHOR

Arnold E. Grisman was born in New York and spent his childhood in the city and its suburbia. In 1941 he received an A.B. in English literature *magna cum laude* from Harvard and the next year an M.A. from Columbia. Then came three years with the Signal Intelligence and OSS in England, Africa and Italy, after which he returned to Columbia for further graduate work.

Finding university life a "tight fit" he answered the call of the theater—as assistant director of a summer stock company. A series of business enterprises was his next venture, ending with his present job as a copywriter for the J. Walter Thompson advertising agency. Mr. Grisman lives in North Arlington, New Jersey, with his wife and two children. A first novel, *Early to Rise*, was published by Harper & Brothers in the spring of 1958.

Set in Linotype Janson
Format by Jean Krulis
Manufactured by American Book–Stratford Press, Inc.
Published by HARPER & BROTHERS, New York